HARD PURSUIT

PAMELA CLARE

HARD PURSUIT

PAMELA CLARE

USA TODAY BESTSELLING AUTHOR

Hard Pursuit
A Cobra Elite novel

Published by Pamela Clare, 2020

Cover Design by © Jaycee DeLorenzo/Sweet 'N Spicy Designs
Cover photo: curaphotography

Copyright © 2020 by Pamela Clare

This book is dedicated to nurses, doctors, and first responders around the world who travel to the places where their skills are most needed. Through their dedication and compassion, they represent the best of humanity, risking their safety to stop suffering and save lives. This includes nurses and doctors who continue to serve on the front lines in this prolonged and deadly battle against COVID-19.

May you be richly blessed for the service you so freely give to others.

ACKNLOWLEDGEMENTS

Many thanks to Michelle White, Benjamin Alexander, Jackie Turner, and Shell Ryan. Additional thanks to Jacque Michelle Golden-Raines and Pat Egan Fordyce for reading through early copies of the story and sharing their feedback.

Special thanks to Nicola Brooks for once again helping with Glaswegian slang and to my mother, Mary White, RN, for helping with the medical scenes in this story.

I also want to thank my romantic suspense readers, those fans of the I-Team series that have stayed with me and new readers who discovered me through the Cobra series. You are the best. Writing for you is a joy.

PROLOGUE

Amundsen-Scott Station
South Pole

Kristi Chang picked at her breakfast of reconstituted scrambled eggs, toast, and bacon, a lump in her throat. She'd been dreading this day for a couple of weeks now. Today, Malik was leaving. He and the rest of the Cobra team were flying back to Denver, while she would remain here for the next six months working as the station RN.

Would she ever see him again?

The question made her throat go tight because she already knew the answer.

On the first night she and Malik had slept together—the night they'd inadvertently kept the entire AI Berthing Area awake—they had agreed to sex with no strings. It had made sense at the time. They'd known each other for less than a week, and the only thing that had mattered to Kristi in that moment was getting him into bed.

They had both just joined the 300 Club by streaking to the South Pole marker through temperatures below minus one-hundred Fahrenheit, so she'd gotten a good look at his naked body with its muscles and scars. A former Army Ranger, he was a walking anatomy lesson wrapped in smooth, dark skin. Pecs. Abs. Biceps. Quadriceps. Glutes. He even had obliques, for God's sake—to say nothing of his big, beautiful cock. She hadn't thought beyond how it would feel to get her hands on him. But then, neither of them could have predicted the chain of events that had kept him here for more than a month.

Treason. Murder. Attempted murder. Spies on station.

Kristi had never imagined she'd treat gunshot wounds here.

In the midst of the danger, Malik had ruined her for other men. He was sweet, caring, funny—and he knew how to use that body in bed. Not that they'd limited themselves to having sex in bed. To avoid keeping people awake, they'd found other places on station to have sex—the hydroponic greenhouse, the sauna, the weight room.

Now, the danger was past, and the Cobra team was going home.

She heard Malik's voice and felt the energy in the galley shift as he, Thor Isaksen, and Lev Segal walked in, women and men alike turning to look at the three Cobra operatives who had saved their lives.

"That bolt-action relic might be good against polar bears, but it's not so great against an enemy shooting back." Malik moved through the food line, his gaze gliding over the room, his lips curving in a smile when he found Kristi.

Her pulse skipped.

Thor, who'd served with Danish special forces, seemed confident. "When we get home, I'll take you on—my bolt-action rifle against the modern military rifle of your choice."

Kristi was gratified to see Thor doing so well. Two weeks

ago, he'd been shot trying to save Samantha's life and almost died of blood loss and hypothermia. Kristi had fought hard with Dr. Decker to keep him alive.

Lev, a former Israeli operative, laughed. "There's no way you can put as much lead downrange with your bolt-action as Jones can with a semi-auto."

Thor grinned. "Firepower is about hits on target, not just spraying bullets."

Samantha Park, who was now Kristi's closest friend on station, walked in and got into the food line behind the men, her gaze meeting Kristi's for a moment. Kristi could tell that Samantha was fighting despair, too. She and Thor had hooked up at some point in the past few weeks. Everyone could tell they were crazy about each other, even if they didn't know it.

Did Malik feel anything for Kristi?

Thor and Samantha went to sit at a table, just the two of them. Malik made his way to Kristi, while Lev sat with Ryan McClain, firefighter and acting station manager.

Malik's gaze searched her face, his brow furrowed as if there was something he wanted to say. He seemed to change his mind. "Hey, beautiful. How are you doing?"

"It won't be the same here without you Cobra guys." She'd meant to say that life wouldn't be the same for her without *him* here, but she'd stopped herself.

She had agreed to no strings. She couldn't ruin the fun they'd had by getting clingy and making demands now. Besides, what good would it do?

Their futures didn't overlap. He flew around the world doing security work, while she had nursing commitments stretching out over the next eighteen months. When she finished her contract here, she would visit her parents and brother in San Francisco and then fly to Nigeria to work for an international aid organization for a year. It was part of her crazy goal to work as a nurse on all seven continents and see the world while her parents, both doctors, were still in good health and didn't need her help.

He grinned, his dark eyes looking straight into hers. "You'll get a lot more sleep."

No man had eyes as penetrating or as intense as Malik's.

"You say that like it's a good thing." She willed herself to smile. "Are you excited to see sunlight again?"

If she kept the conversation light, maybe she wouldn't cry.

"MAKE sure you've got all your shit," Isaksen called from the hallway. "Anything that's left behind stays behind. We won't be coming this way again."

"Copy that." Malik shouldered his duffel, glanced around the tiny room that had been his home for the past month.

When he'd arrived at the South Pole, he'd wanted to finish their mission and get home as quickly as possible, away from twenty-four-hour darkness and the bone-chilling cold. Now, he found himself wishing for another week, a few days, even an hour.

Kristi.

The thought of saying goodbye to her put a hitch in his chest. Yeah, he was going to miss her. He wouldn't lie. She was beautiful, smart, funny, sexy as hell—and fucking incredible in bed. He'd gotten laid more in the past month than in the previous six months combined, and still he burned for her.

Get a grip, man.

They had agreed from the start that this was sex with no strings. She'd wanted that arrangement as much as he had. He couldn't go back on his word now. Besides, there was no way for them to be together.

He had his life, and she had hers. She would spend the next six months here, take a short vacation, and then head to Nigeria—not a good idea, in his professional opinion—while he flew back and forth from Denver to the company's next job site.

Still, he wished he and Kristi had spent a little less time screwing and a little more time talking. There was still so much he didn't know about her, so much he'd love to discover. Would she miss him, too?

He'd thought they might get time to talk this morning, but he'd gotten word during breakfast that the plane was arriving ahead of schedule. That had cut short what little time he'd had left with her. He and the guys had to be ready to board when the C-130 Hercules Globemaster landed. Any delay might result in the fuel or propellers freezing, and that would have fatal consequences.

Malik stepped into the hallway, closed the door to his room.

Segal did the same. "I can't wait to feel the sun on my face again."

Isaksen chuckled. "So, cold is your kryptonite, huh, Segal? I didn't think you had any weaknesses."

"I don't."

"Keep telling yourself that."

The three of them left the berthing area and walked toward Destination Alpha—the station's main entrance. Kristi stood near the door, wearing blue scrubs, Samantha beside her, the two of them waiting to say goodbye, neither of them looking happy.

"There's your collateral damage from this mission," Segal muttered. "I hope you're both satisfied."

Isaksen ignored him with his usual Viking detachment, but Malik's temper flared. "Sounds to me like you're jealous, brother."

Segal hadn't hooked up with anyone on this mission, not even when the work was done and they were just waiting for a flight home. "Is that what you think?"

Segal rolled his eyes and walked outside into the cold. The man must really want to get out of this place.

While Isaksen walked over to Samantha, Malik headed straight for Kristi, doing his best to seem casual and upbeat. He lowered his duffel to the floor. "Hey."

"Hey." She slipped easily into his arms, her cheek resting against his chest. "I wish you could stay a little longer. I'm not tired of you yet."

He chuckled, kissed her silky, dark hair. "I'm not tired of you, either."

For a moment, they stood there, neither of them speaking, Malik inhaling her scent, doing his best to memorize the feel of her.

She was trembling.

He caught her chin, lifted her gaze to his, saw tears on her cheeks, the sight striking a tender place inside him. "Hey, what's wrong?"

She sniffed. "Sorry. I'm just having an emo moment. I hate goodbyes."

He could understand that. "Don't apologize."

Malik drew her against him once more and held her while she wept, her sadness cutting at him, making it harder for him to keep his own emotions in check.

Then from outside the station came the sound of the approaching plane.

Segal stuck his head through the door. "He's landing. Let's move out."

"They have to refuel," Malik shouted back. "Chill, man!"

But the clock was ticking. After a month of spending every night together, he and Kristi now had only seconds left.

He stepped back, cupped her cheeks in his palms. "I wish you'd cancel your contract and go to Botswana or Zambia or Tanzania instead. Nigeria is an amazing place, but with Boko Haram, the drug trade, bandits, and human trafficking, it just isn't safe. I've been there. I know what I'm talking about."

She nodded. "I'm not sure I can change it, but I'll try."

Segal stuck his head inside again. "They're refueling. Time to roll."

Kristi jumped into Malik's arms, pressed her lips to his.

He kissed her hard and deep and long—then lowered her gently to the floor, searching for the right words. "Take care of yourself, Kristi. You're amazing. You know that, right?"

She took one of his hands, held it. "Promise me you'll stay safe. No getting shot or blown up."

"I'll do my best." He put on his mask, picked up his duffel, and followed Isaksen out into the frigid cold of austral winter.

KRISTI WATCHED MALIK GO, determined not to shed another tear. She was a big girl. She'd walked into this willingly, knowing he wouldn't stay. She couldn't fall apart now.

Beside her, Samantha sniffed, wiped her eyes—and then turned and disappeared into the coatroom. Kristi knew what she intended to do and followed. Quickly, they put on their snow pants, hats, gloves, masks, and parkas, and hurried outside and down two flights of stairs to the ice below to watch the plane take off.

They stood in silence, watching as the men walked to the skiway, where the plane waited, the Aurora Australis blazing in the dark sky above them. Fuelies rushed to get the C-130 refueled and in the air again as quickly as possible. Even from a distance and in the dark, Kristi could tell which of the three men was Malik from those long, sure strides, each one taking him farther away from her.

One at a time, they boarded—Lev first, then Malik, who glanced back over his shoulder and waved to her, then Thor, who turned and waved to Samantha just before the doors closed. Then the fuelies stepped away, and the plane was ready to depart.

Samantha gave a little sob, and Kristi could hear her whispering, "Don't crash. Don't crash. Don't crash."

Flying in Antarctica in the winter was extremely dangerous.

Kristi took Samantha's gloved hand in hers, neither of them speaking as the plane headed down the skiway, slowly gaining momentum. Then the rockets fired in a burst of orange, and the plane left the ground.

Kristi sniffed. "Well, I just said goodbye to the best sex of my life—and the nicest man I've ever known. I'm going to miss Malik so much."

The two of them stood there, watching until the plane's lights had vanished. Then, together, they walked back up the stairs and into the warmth of the station.

1

Kinu Village
Kaduna State, Nigeria
Eighteen months later

K risti Chang opened the plastic vial with gloved hands and squeezed the cholera vaccine into the mouth of a sweet little girl who couldn't have been more than five. "What a great job you're doing. You're standing so still."

When every precious drop was in the child's mouth, Kristi tossed the vial into the trash, watching to make sure the girl swallowed. "All done."

She was lucky that most people in Nigeria spoke at least some English, the country's official language. She spoke fluent Mandarin and decent Spanish—two languages that were useless here. In rural areas like this, people were more likely to speak Hausa, Igbo, Yoruba—or any one of the more than five hundred languages and dialects native to the country.

The little girl gave her a shy smile.

"Now, it's your mama's turn." Kristi opened another vial and stood to administer it to the little girl's mother, who was visibly pregnant. "You're all done."

Normally, they might hesitate to administer cholera vaccines to pregnant women, but these weren't normal times. The risks to a woman's fetus or her pregnancy from cholera far outweighed any risk from the vaccine.

It had been a long, wet rainy season, and Nigeria was in the midst of a cholera epidemic that had already left hundreds of people dead of dehydration and electrolyte imbalance. Rural areas in Kaduna State had been hit especially hard. Kristi was here with four others from her mobile medical unit and a group of Nigerian public health volunteers to vaccinate as many villagers as they could and to provide whatever medical care might be needed.

Rural parts of the country often lacked access to basic medical care, so their team came prepared for everything, complete with a van equipped as a mobile operating room. Kristi, as one of only two registered nurses, spent most of her time assisting Dr. Adamu. So far today, she had treated several people for malaria, tuberculosis, and HIV, and assisted the surgeon in removing a teenager's inflamed appendix.

Still in her blue surgical scrubs, Kristi was filling in for Chinara, one of the Nigerian volunteers, who was taking a very late lunch break. The long line snaked out of the tent, proof that the village health coordinator had done an excellent job getting out the word. They'd brought eight hundred doses of the vaccine, but now Kristi worried that it might not be enough.

"Hey, there." Kristi smiled at a young boy, who opened his mouth for her like a baby bird. She emptied the vial onto his tongue. "Well done."

She worked as quickly and efficiently as she could, keeping the line moving while still doing her best to make each person feel seen. Every vaccine she delivered meant another person who wouldn't become a victim of this epidemic. She loved being a nurse, loved knowing that her work made a real difference in people's lives. Though she fell into bed exhausted every night, the nine months she'd spent in Nigeria had been the most rewarding of her nursing career.

Antarctica was a close second but for reasons that had nothing to do with nursing and everything to do with a certain sexy operative. She hadn't heard from Malik since the day he and his team had flown off, but then they had agreed to no strings. Kristi had wanted to ask Samantha for his email address—her fiancé, Thor, worked with Malik—but each time, Kristi had stopped herself.

If Malik wanted to get in touch with you, he would have done it already.

It was then she noticed him—a tall wiry man in a red T-shirt, a green vest, and tattered jeans. He watched her as she worked, his gaze never leaving her. Maybe she was the first person of East Asian descent he'd seen, though Nigeria *did* have a small Chinese minority. Focused on her work, she put him out of her mind until he stood before her.

He was much taller than she was, so she handed him the vaccine and told him what to do, letting him squeeze it into his mouth. He dropped the empty vial into the trash bin. "Are you a doctor?"

"No, I'm a registered nurse." She twisted off the top of the next dose, expecting him to step aside.

He remained where he was, something in his gaze making her uncomfortable. "You take care of the sick?"

"I care for patients and help the doctors." She stepped

back, glanced over at the entrance toward the security guard. "If you need medical help, you can find that in the next tent. This tent is for vaccines only. Excuse me."

He raised two fingers to his mouth and gave a sharp whistle that made her jump.

Rat-at-at-at-at! Rat-at-at-at-at!

Gunfire exploded outside the tent, women and children screaming and dropping to the ground. Adrenaline hit Kristi's bloodstream in a rush. She would have gotten down like the others, but a strong arm encircled her neck, cutting off her breath.

He spoke directly into her ear. "Where are your tools and supplies?"

They were being robbed.

She'd been told not to resist in case of an attack, so she pointed, choking out the words, "Next ... tent."

The bastard shouted something in a language she didn't know and dragged her toward the door, arm still around her throat.

Was he abducting her?

Oh, hell, no.

Enraged and terrified, Kristi clawed at his arm, tried to bite him, tried to twist away, her pulse pounding in her ears.

"Come with us, or we will kill all these people!"

She fought to answer him. "I ... can't ... breathe!"

He loosened his grip but didn't release her, muffled sobs following them outside.

Bodies. Blood.

The security guards lay dead in the dirt, men whose faces were hidden behind balaclavas and bandanas pointing large rifles at the terrified crowd.

Were they Boko Haram?

No! Shit. Shit. Shit.

"In that tent?" he asked.

"Yes." She swallowed her fear. "I'll get you whatever you need, but don't kill anyone else. You didn't need to kill anyone."

"Shut your mouth, woman." He drew her into the medical tent, stopped, looked around, two of his buddies following them inside, rifles raised.

Patients huddled together. Those in beds stared, wide-eyed.

"Wh-what do you need?" Was this really happening? "You won't find it without my help."

He let her go. "We need to treat a bullet wound that has gone bad."

Kristi fought back her fear, let her training carry her. "Where is the wound? Is the bullet still there?"

He hesitated, as if this were secret information. "The bullet is in his leg."

Infection. Blood loss. Tissue damage.

"You could have just brought him here. We would have treated him without asking questions." She picked up a bag and opened one plastic supply crate after the next, packing things into an empty duffel bag.

Gunshot wound kit with hemostatic bandages. Drain kit. Trauma kit. Sterile gloves. Oral antibiotics. Oxycodone. Suture kit. Lidocaine gel. IV kits. IV fluids and broad-spectrum IV antibiotics. A pre-op scrub kit with extra sponges. Ibuprofen and Tylenol for fever. A vial of Versed. Syringes.

There was O-neg blood and plasma in the surgical van, but she wasn't about to lead the bastard to where Dr. Adamu was working.

She held out the bag. "That's everything you need."

He grinned, grabbed her by her hair. "You're coming with us."

"No!" Kristi fought to hold her ground, her mouth dry, her heart flailing in her chest. "Let ... me... go!"

If they took her away, she would likely never see home again.

But he was stronger than she was. Fist in her hair, he pulled her along with him to a battered white SUV, rough hands pushing her into the back seat. Men with rifles climbed in beside her, one firing his weapon into the air and laughing at people's terrified responses. Then someone put a hood over her head—and the vehicle began to move.

MALIK JONES PARKED in the garage at Cobra HQ, jogged to the elevator, and punched the call button with the side of his closed fist, rage thrumming in his chest.

Kristi had been abducted. Assailants had attacked her mobile medical unit, killing the security guards and taking her by force. Witnesses said one of the attackers had threatened to kill her patients and had dragged her away by her hair.

Fuck! Son of a bitch! Damn it!

Malik wanted to find him—and rip him to pieces.

He had gotten the news twenty minutes ago from Samantha, who'd heard it from Kristi's parents, who'd just gotten word from the State Department. They'd said it had happened at about three in the afternoon Nigerian time— five hours ago—but they had no idea who had taken her.

If it was Boko Haram...

Malik had gone up against those fuckers in a few covert ops in his Army Ranger days. They had no respect for human life and treated women like chattel, kidnapping young girls, raping them, forcing children into sham marriages, and killing those who refused. They abducted boys, too, using them as child soldiers and unwilling suicide bombers. If they had Kristi, they would hurt her, and, eventually, they would kill her.

He punched the call button again. What the fuck was taking so long?

Malik wanted to find Kristi—and kill every bastard who'd been part of her abduction. If he had anything to say about it, he and the rest of the Cobra crew would be wheels up in a few hours, bound for Lagos.

Goddamn it!

He should have stayed in touch with her. Not a day had gone by since leaving Antarctica when he hadn't thought of her. So many times, he'd come close to sending her an email. Every time, he'd stopped himself. They had agreed to no strings, and there was no chance that they could be together. He'd figured his feelings for her would fade with time and distance, but they hadn't. And now...

He'd warned Kristi. He'd told her to go somewhere else —Botswana or Tanzania. As beautiful and vibrant as Nigeria was, it wasn't safe. Boko Haram was to blame for most of the brutality Malik had witnessed, but not all of it. Corrupt special police, so-called bandits, and drug rings committed their share of atrocities, too. That's why Cobra had been tasked so many times with protecting US government representatives and business executives who traveled there.

The elevator car arrived with a *ding*, the doors opening to reveal Elizabeth Shields, Cobra's head intel analyst, who was perusing something on a tablet.

She looked up. "Hey, Malik."

Malik didn't wait for her to exit the elevator but stepped in and punched the button for the top floor. "Come with me. I'm going to speak with Tower. You should be in on this."

If she was surprised, she didn't show it. "What's wrong?"

The elevator began to move.

"Do you remember Kristi Chang?"

"The name is familiar." Shields' brow furrowed. "The op in Antarctica, right?"

"Yeah." Malik did his best to seem calm. No one but Thor Isaksen, Lev Segal, and, of course, Samantha knew that he and Kristi had hooked up during that assignment. "She's been working as a nurse in Nigeria for the past nine months. She was abducted from a mobile medical unit by armed assailants about five hours ago."

"Oh, shit. Do they know who did it?"

Malik shook his head. "No, not yet."

"How did you find out?"

"Samantha. She and Kristi are pretty close."

Shields nodded. "Oh. Right."

"I want Cobra to get tasked with this job."

Shields didn't seem surprised. "I suppose that could happen."

She didn't understand.

"I want Cobra to *make* it happen. We came to Glasgow to help you and McManus when you were knee deep in shit, remember?"

"Yes, but we're Cobra operatives, and there was a terrorist connection. The Brits invited Cobra to join in. Kristi isn't an employee of the company or someone's spouse."

"She's a friend. She helped save Isaksen's life—or have you forgotten?"

"I remember."

The elevator doors opened, and Shields followed Malik

to Derek Tower's office. One of Cobra International Security's two owners, Tower was a former Green Beret and a hard-as-nails badass. Malik respected the hell out of him—even if he could be an asshole.

Shields paused at the door. "I think he's in a meeting."

Malik didn't give a damn. "Kristi's life is on the line."

He knocked.

Tower called out to them. "Come back in five—"

Malik opened the door and stepped into Tower's office.

"*Malik!*" Shields whispered.

Hell.

Malik had interrupted his boss in the middle of a video chat with his little girl, Layla. The three-year-old looked down at her father from the large flat-screen monitor, dressed in some kind of dinosaur costume, a sparkly blue tiara on her blond head.

"This must be important." Tower glared at Malik then looked up at his daughter, his voice going sweet and gooey. "Okay, Princess T-Rex, Daddy has to go now. I'll see you tonight. Be good for your mommy, okay?"

Malik and Shields shared a glance, Shields biting back a smile.

Seeing Tower in daddy mode was new to Malik and ... strange.

Then Jenna, Tower's wife, appeared. "See you later, honey. Say goodbye, Layla."

Layla waved, her tiara tottering. "Bye-bye, Daddy."

The screen went dark.

Tower turned his chair to face them, irritation on his face. "What's so important that you two had to barge in here?"

Malik met Tower's gaze, fought to rein in his emotions. "Samantha, Isaksen's fiancée—"

"I know who Samantha is."

"She called me at home a half hour ago. A good friend of hers, Kristi Chang, was just abducted by unknown armed assailants in Nigeria, where she was working as a nurse with some international aid organization. The bastards killed the security guards and dragged her away. She was the only one taken."

"Shit." Tower nodded, then arched a brow. "Why did Samantha call *you*? Where's Isaksen? Shouldn't *he* be the one pounding down my door?"

And just like that, Tower had him.

Malik stammered out an answer. "He's, uh, on his way, sir."

Shields took over. "Kristi Chang was the nurse who helped save Isaksen's life when he was shot at Amundsen-Scott Station last year. She gave him round-the-clock medical care. The team on that op all got to know her pretty well."

Tower nodded, understanding on his face. "She's important to this company and its staff. That's what you're telling me?"

Malik and Shields answered, almost in unison. "Yes, sir."

"We're leaving in three days for a week in Burkina Faso. I'll connect with Corbray and have him check with the State Department. If they've got some idea where she's being held, maybe they'd be willing to bankroll a rescue before we head home."

Malik shook his head. "She'll be alone with those bastards for at least ten days."

And every hour would be a living hell.

"Most hostage rescues take weeks or even months. You know that." Tower picked up his smartphone. "Shields, start working on an intel package. Give us something to wave at the Pentagon. If you find a terrorism angle, so much the better. They like that."

"Yes, sir." Shields took Malik's arm, drew him out of the office with her, closing the door behind them and following him to the elevator. "Did you think he was going to put us all on the plane today?"

"Yeah." Malik pushed the button, stepped inside the elevator, helplessness welling up inside him at the thought of what Kristi might be going through. "Maybe."

Shields waited until the doors closed. "So, you and Kristi, huh?"

She had figured it out. Of course, she had. Damn CIA types.

"It wasn't like that. It was just ..."

"Just sex?" Shields didn't look like she believed him. "You almost kicked down Tower's door over a woman you had *just sex* with? I don't buy it. Tower will figure it out, too, if you don't dial back the rage."

"Right." Malik drew a breath, his mind made up before he exhaled.

If Cobra didn't get tasked with this rescue, he'd take leave and go after Kristi himself.

2

It seemed to Kristi that they drove forever over bone-jarring roads. Even with the windows open, the heat was stifling, the reek of unwashed bodies overwhelming. Her captors spoke to one another in a language she didn't know or sang along in English to the radio. She tried to count turns—left, left, right, left—but after a time, it was impossible to remember. She hadn't heard traffic or honking horns, so wherever they were taking her must be far from any village or city.

Her poor parents! When they got the news, it would shatter their day. They would call relatives in Beijing. The whole family would worry.

Malik had warned her not to come to Nigeria. She'd looked into changing her contract, but the need in Nigeria was so great that she hadn't been able to turn her back on the country. In truth, she hadn't believed this could happen to her. And now she would suffer—and her family would suffer—as a result.

Who were these bastards? Were they Boko Haram,

bandits, Fulani herdsmen? What were they going to do with her?

Kristi had heard stories of captivity, rape, and murder, stories of women and girls being sold as prostitutes abroad or forced into marriage. Those stories rushed through her mind in sickening detail, her stomach threatening to revolt.

But she was a US citizen and on the staff of a global aid organization. Surely, they wouldn't think they could get away with this. The US government would send someone.

A hostage negotiator? A SEAL Team? A private security team like Cobra?

And what if help doesn't come fast enough?

The thought made her adrenaline spike again.

Don't panic. Don't panic.

Then something Malik had said came back to her. She had asked him how he could face combat, how he managed his fear with bullets flying.

I don't let fear control me. A long time ago, I accepted that there was a bullet or an IED with my name on it out there somewhere, and my job was to keep fighting until it found me. It's incredibly freeing to embrace your mortality. You surrender hope and gain clarity and peace. You learn to live and act in the moment.

She closed her eyes, drew deep breaths, exhaling slowly.

She'd never given much thought to how she might die. She had always assumed she'd be a grandmother by then, a respected elder in her family. She'd never imagined dying at the age of thirty-two.

The vehicle turned, slowed, stopped.

Shouts. Men's voices. Laughter.

Her pulse raced.

The vehicle's doors opened, and rough hands dragged her from the backseat, forcing her to her feet. The duffel bag was ripped away from her, fingers biting into her arms, pulling her along. From the closeness of the men's voices, she knew a crowd had gathered around her. Then a hand reached between her legs, another grasping her butt.

She twisted, tried to smack the hands away.

Don't let them see your fear. Embrace your mortality.

Shit! What the hell did that even mean?

She tripped up a step or two, and suddenly it was a little cooler.

Someone ripped the hood off her head.

She found herself standing inside a one-room mud-brick house with a dirt floor. Rodent droppings were scattered in the dirt, spider webs on the ceiling. Two open windows covered with mosquito netting let in daylight. Against the far wall, a man lay on a mat, a bloody bandage wrapped around his left thigh.

The man with the gunshot wound.

A hand in the middle of her back sent her stumbling forward.

The man who'd abducted her dropped the duffel bag at her feet, took hold of her arm. "Take care of him. Promise you will save him."

She couldn't promise that. If he was septic or if gangrene had set in, there would be little she could do for him out here. She jerked her arm away, looked the bastard straight in the eyes, doing her best to hide her fear. "I don't know how bad it is, but I will do everything I can for him. If you want my help, keep your hands off me."

The jerk drew his hand back as if to strike her, but a shout from the wounded man stopped him. He lowered his hand, backed away.

Startled, Kristi looked down, found her patient watching her.

"He will not harm you." The man's face was lined with pain. He, too, was thin, but older than the men who'd abducted her, his short dark hair and trimmed beard shot through with gray. "Help me."

Kristi knelt beside him, pressed her hand to his forehead, doing her best to collect herself. She was a nurse. He was a patient in need of her help.

You can do this.

"You've got a fever. I need to check your wound. May I?"

"Yes."

Kristi removed the bloody bandage, relieved to find neither gangrene nor red streaks on his thigh. "You've got an infection. The bullet is still inside the wound. I will need to take it out. It will be painful."

"Do it."

She summoned her courage, met his gaze. "If I help you, do you promise to let me go, untouched and unharmed?"

She had never played hardball as a nurse, never made a patient's treatment contingent on how that person treated her. But this was about survival. She didn't have a lot of options here.

"Yes. Yes!"

"Okay, then I will help you." Kristi glanced around. "I need light. It's too dark in here. It would be easier for me to work if we could raise you up off the ground."

The man shouted at the others behind her. They lifted and carried him outside to a rough-hewn table roughly the size of a picnic bench, Kristi following behind with the duffel bag.

She glanced around, her stomach knotting. They were deep in the forest. Worse, there were no other women in sight.

Focus.

She set the duffel bag near his feet, took out some gloves and the IV kit. "Do you have a name you'd like to be called?"

"Jidda."

"Jidda, I'm going to hook you up to some intravenous fluids and antibiotics. I'll need someone to hold the IV bags high above you so the liquid can run into your veins. The fluids will make you feel better, and the antibiotics will kill the infection."

She wasn't sure any of this made sense to him.

Jidda spoke to the men, and one stepped forward.

Kristi went to work setting up the IV, checking Jidda's hand and arm for veins. "You'll feel a stick."

Jidda didn't so much as blink.

She set up the IV with lactated Ringer's, piggy-backing the antibiotics onto the fluids. Then she took out the Versed and a syringe, measuring out just enough to knock him out for about thirty minutes. "It's going to be very painful when I take out the bullet. This medicine will make you sleep so you don't feel it."

She injected the medication into his IV and watched his eyes drift shut.

THE NEXT MORNING, Malik stood with Isaksen and Segal in the hallway outside Conference Room 2 at Cobra HQ, the three of them speaking so as not to be overheard. "If Cobra doesn't get the assignment, I'm flying to Lagos myself."

"Alone?" Segal glared at him. "Brother, that's crazy."

Isaksen shook his head. "You think you can walk into a Boko Haram camp or a den of Fulani bandits and take them on yourself?"

"What would you do if it was Samantha?"

"Samantha and I are getting married. You and Kristi haven't talked for a year."

Shields came around the corner, leaned close, lowered her voice. "Good news. It wasn't Boko Haram."

Relief washed through Malik, almost knocking him on his ass.

Not Boko Haram.

He started to ask how Shields knew that, but she stopped him.

"Tower is right behind me," she whispered.

The conversation over for now, Malik and the others followed Shields into the conference room, where Dylan Cruz, Nick and Holly Andris, and Quinn McManus were already waiting. Cruz had served with DEVGRU—Seal Team Six—and was Malik's closest buddy in the company. Andris had joined Cobra after a career with Delta Force. Holly, Andris' drop-dead gorgeous wife, had done secret work for the CIA. Quinn McManus, a redheaded Scot who'd fought with the British Special Air Service, was Shields' husband.

Cruz gave Malik a fist bump. "I heard, brother. I'm sorry."

"Thanks." Malik took a seat.

Tower walked in, followed by Gabriela Marquez Cruz, another defector from the CIA and now Cruz's wife. "It looks like we're all here. Let's get started."

He sat at the head of the table, while Gabriela, with her big brown eyes and long dark hair, went to sit by her husband. Somehow Cruz had talked her into marrying him after the two had escaped a drug cartel in Venezuela, where Gabriela had been working undercover as a nun.

Yeah, that mission had been a clusterfuck.

Tower punched a button and Javier Corbray's face appeared on the wall-mounted flat-screen. "Good morning."

"Morning? It's almost noon." Corbray, also a former SEAL, grinned. "This assignment to Burkina Faso is pretty basic."

Malik willed himself to focus. Cobra would act as security for a delegation of executives from a US mining corporation that was hoping to develop Burkina Faso's vast manganese deposits. The trip would include two scheduled visits to the proposed mining site. They would spend the remainder of the week in meetings with government ministers in Ouagadougou.

"Shields has a risk assessment prepared for us." Corbray handed the floor to her.

Shields went over the very real dangers this trip would pose due to the constant threat of terrorism. "The two trips to the mining site will be the most perilous. We have strongly encouraged the mining company to travel via helicopter, and they have agreed. Traveling via armored vehicle comes with too high a risk of ambush and abduction."

Abduction.

Just like that, Malik's concentration shattered, his mind ricocheting to Kristi. He fought to rein in his impatience while Shields finished the risk assessment and Nick Andris, who had just been promoted to operations manager, went over the security strategy in detail. But there was only one thing Malik wanted to hear.

What was Cobra doing to free Kristi?

Finally, after more than an hour, they moved on.

Tower's gaze met Malik's. "I'm sure by now most of you are aware that Kristi Chang, the RN who cared for Isaksen at Amundsen-Scott when he was shot, has been abducted. Corbray, Shields, and I have been on the phone with the

State Department, hoping to get our guns into this fight. At this time, the US officials are working through other channels to secure Ms. Chang's release."

"What does that mean?"

"They're hopeful Ms. Chang will be released without further bloodshed," Corbray said. "Boko Haram has denied involvement. Witnesses said the men who took Ms. Chang forced her to steal medical supplies. They think she was abducted by bandits for her nursing skills. They expect a ransom demand and want to see how this plays out."

Malik gritted his teeth to keep from shouting, helpless rage churning inside him. "So, that's it. We wait."

Tower nodded. "I'm afraid so. I know that's not what you and Isaksen wanted. We'll keep this on our radar. If there's a chance to get in on a rescue operation, we'll take it. You have my word on that."

Malik nodded. "I appreciate that."

But this meant that Kristi would be a captive for weeks, perhaps months, or even longer. Kristi with her sense of humor, sweet face, dark silky hair, and dangerous curves. He could see her smile, feel her soft skin, hear her voice.

The men who'd abducted her had killed the security guards. Though it would be in their interest to keep her safe, that didn't mean they wouldn't starve, torture, or rape her in the meantime. The last time Cobra had been in Nigeria, Malik had heard a radio report about four hostages taken from a seminary. Their ransom had been paid in full. Despite that, three had ended up in ICU, and one had been murdered.

"I request permission to take an immediate leave of absence, sir."

Tower glared at him. "You think you can go after her alone? Request denied."

Malik knew what he had to do.

He stood, cutting off whatever Tower had been about to say. "You'll have my resignation within the hour."

Ignoring the astonishment on everyone's faces, he left the conference room.

KRISTI SAT with her back against the mud brick wall of the little hut, Jidda sleeping on the mat beside her. She hadn't dared close her eyes last night, even with the scalpel hidden in the pocket of her scrubs. She'd been afraid that the men who shared this hut with Jidda might take advantage of his drugged state to assault her. She also hadn't relished the thought of lying amid rodent droppings, which in this part of the world, carried some terrible diseases, including Lassa Fever.

Six other men slept in here, their bed mats rolled up during the day. Jidda had told her that he was their leader, but he failed to say who *they* were. She had figured out that they weren't Boko Haram when several of his men had crossed themselves just as she'd begun to extract the bullet. They must be bandits. They roved the forests, stealing cattle, kidnapping people for ransom, robbing, raping, killing.

At least she had her IUD. No matter what they did, she wouldn't get pregnant.

She hugged her arms around herself, hollow with hunger and aching with thirst.

If she'd known she was being abducted, she would have tried to bring food and water for herself, not to mention doxycycline to prevent herself from contracting malaria.

The medication was probably out of her system by now, making her vulnerable.

Had she truly believed they would drive away with the stolen medical supplies and leave her behind? She ought to have known by the questions the asshole had asked her and the way he'd looked at her that he'd had plans for her.

Are you a doctor?

No, I'm a registered nurse.

You take care of the sick?

How stupid could she be? Fatally stupid it seemed.

If she came down with malaria out here, she would most likely die.

Yeah, if they don't kill you first.

Jidda had promised to let her go unharmed, but she had no idea whether he would keep his word. For him to have any chance at that, he had to survive.

She crawled over to him, pressed her palm to his forehead. His fever had gone down, but that could be from the ibuprofen and acetaminophen and not the antibiotics. She'd pulled a bullet and a piece of fabric out of his leg. There'd been a lot of pus, so she'd wet a four-by-four piece of sterile gauze and tucked it into the wound to keep it open so that it could drain. Then she had wrapped his thigh in sterile plastic wrap.

Jidda's eyes fluttered open. "It feels better today."

"That's the pain-killers. I need to check it again, and I'll need more boiled water." Her stomach growled loudly enough for Jidda to hear it.

"Have they brought you no food?"

She was glad he asked. "I haven't eaten since yesterday, and I'm so thirsty."

"I will have them bring you food and water from the river."

She shook her head. "I can't drink river water. It must be boiled for at least three minutes, or it will make me sick."

He frowned, then called out a name. "Peter!"

The man who'd abducted her appeared in the open doorway.

So that was the bastard's name.

Jidda spoke to him in angry tones, then switched to English. "Bring our guest something good to eat, and boil more water for my leg and some for her to drink."

"Fetch and boil water?" Peter glared at Kristi. "Am I a woman? Get Obi to do it. It is not my job to make her comfortable. She is our captive, nothing more."

"Your job is to do what I tell you to do." Then Jidda switched into his other language, a rush of angry words spilling out of him.

Looking sullen, Peter left to do as he'd been asked.

"What is your name?" Jidda asked.

"Kristi Chang."

He repeated her name. "You are Chinese?"

"My ancestors were from China." Her mother's family had been in the US for generations now, while her father had remained in the US after coming from Beijing for medical school. But Kristi wouldn't explain. "I was born in the United States."

"Ah."

She rose onto her knees to check IV bags, which now hung from a peg they had hammered into the crumbling mortar. She'd brought enough IV antibiotics for about forty-eight hours. After that, Jidda would be on oral meds only.

God, she hoped that would be enough.

If it wasn't, if this infection got out of control...

"I'm going to check your wound now." She peeled back the plastic, saw that the wound was draining well and less inflamed than it had been yesterday. *Thank God.* "I need to change the gauze again."

He nodded, familiar with the routine.

She put on sterile gloves, took out the old gauze, and replaced it, Jidda grimacing as she worked. "Sorry. I know it's painful."

She wrapped his thigh in plastic once again.

Peter returned, set an aluminum coffee pot of steaming hot water down beside Jidda and handed Kristi a wooden bowl of spiced rice and vegetables called *jollof*, fried strips of plantain on top. "Eat with your hands."

Kristi loved *jollof*, the scent making her mouth water. "Thank you."

Peter grunted, glared at her, and then left the hut.

"Eat," Jidda said.

Beyond manners or caring what anyone thought of her, Kristi scooped the hot rice with her fingers and shoveled it hungrily into her mouth.

3

Malik led Kristi to his room, the two of them wearing only towels from the sauna.

She took hold of his towel, yanked it off, dropped it to the floor, her gaze moving over him, appreciation on her face. She slid her hands up his bare chest. "Damn. I want to play with you."

"Sounds good to me." He returned the favor, tugging off her towel, letting it fall.

God, she was beautiful—full breasts, a slender waist, thick dark curls between her thighs. He'd already seen her naked body when they'd joined the 300 Club, but that had been in the dark and in freezing temperatures. Now, he was free to savor her.

An annoyed voice came over his radio, interrupting them. "Jones, this is Isaksen. Turn off your fucking camera."

Shit.

Kristi jumped, covered her breasts. "You've got a cam in here?"

"Yeah. Sorry." He walked over, turned it off. "It's for security."

She wasn't supposed to know that. He would have to move it —and avoid bringing her here in the future.

Kristi laughed. "I guess that was my porn debut."

Sexual need thrumming in his veins, Malik turned back to her.

But she was gone.

Malik's head snapped up, adrenaline bringing him awake.

He raised his seat to the upright position, looked out the window, and saw the dense green of Nigerian forests below. He was almost there.

Isaksen had insisted on paying for the ticket. "She saved my life. Let me do something."

"Thanks, man."

Isaksen had stitched together a string of one-way flights to get Malik here—Denver to D.C., D.C. to London, London to Cairo, Cairo to Lagos. Lagos to Abuja. Ten hours of layovers and twenty hours in the air. It wasn't as nice as traveling in Cobra's private jet. That much was for damned sure.

Malik had used the time to study the intel packet Shields had put together for him.

She'd caught him in the hallway on his way out, handed him a manila envelope. "This is everything I could work up on short notice. I hope it helps. I activated one of Cobra's assets on the ground there. You remember David Ayodele Olatunji?"

"Of course." Cobra had worked with him on all of their Nigerian ops. "Cool guy."

"He'll meet you at the airport in Abuja. He'll have weapons for you and transportation. He'll also take care of all the paperwork—credentials, firearms permits."

Malik had been touched and surprised. "Thanks, Elizabeth."

"Take these GPS tags. If you tuck one in your clothing, we'll be able to track you if you go missing."

Malik had taken the small plastic case from her. "Are

you going to get yourself in trouble by giving me these?"

"Let me worry about that. I want you to come home alive with Kristi. You know how to reach me. Call or email if you need anything. I'll send you any new intel that comes my way and assist however I can in my downtime." Then she had hugged him. "Good luck, Malik. Be careful."

But Tower had been another story.

Malik had gone to his office to turn in his resignation.

Tower had unleashed on him. "Do you have any idea how risky this is? You're a kickass operator, a true warrior, but you could end up dead on this one. You won't have backup or air support or even an eye in the sky. There will be no one to watch your six, no one to pull your ass out of the fire, no medic standing by."

"I know."

"Damn it, Jones! Just wait! Wait until we get back from Burkina Faso. I'll do everything I can to get Cobra into this fight, but I need more time."

"Kristi might not have time. What if the State Department still isn't interested then? I'm sorry, sir. Working for Cobra has meant more to me than you know, but I can't abandon her."

For a moment, Tower had said nothing, the tension thick between them.

Then he'd picked up Malik's letter of resignation. "I'm not accepting this—not now. If you cause an international incident or get arrested, I might have no choice."

"Understood."

"Make sure your vaccines are up to date. Come back in one piece, and we'll talk about your future with this company."

It was more than Malik had expected.

But the real surprise awaited him when he'd climbed

into his car.

In the backseat, he'd found a small, state-of-the-art infrared mini-drone, still in its box. It had probably cost the company tens of thousands of dollars. It would give him eyes in the sky, help him to see through the canopy of Nigeria's forests to know what lay in his path.

The drone was now packed into the biggest suitcase Malik owned and padded with bubble wrap. He'd also brought ten grand in cash in his carry-on and a second bag with his own gear—boots, clothes, a K-Bar knife and ankle rig, body armor, helmet, night vision goggles, a trauma kit, and enough MREs to feed two people for a week. He just hoped Nigerian Customs didn't search his bags.

All that money and military gear would lead to awkward questions like, "What the fuck are you planning to do while you're here?"

The flight attendants went through their pre-landing routine, Malik watching out the window as the glittering lights of Abuja, Nigeria's capital, came into view. Built in the 1980s to replace Lagos as the capital, it was a beautiful, modern city surrounded by a rural landscape. Kristi was out there somewhere in the darkness far to the north.

And Malik would find her.

KRISTI CHANGED the gauze in Jidda's wound again, hooked up the last bag of IV antibiotics, and gave him another dose of oral pain meds. Around them, several men were bedding down for the night, including Peter.

Jidda swallowed the pills with a gulp of water. "I feel better."

The antibiotics had kicked in, and the infection was

beginning to clear.

Kristi checked his forehead for fever. "I think you'll heal."

He caught her hand. "You are very kind."

"I'm a nurse." She pulled her hand away. "Taking care of people is my job."

She wouldn't explain that she'd cared for everyone from inmates convicted of murder to mentally ill patients off their meds to violent addicts strung-out on meth. A nurse never got to choose her patients, but all deserved the same standard of care whether they were Charles Manson or Mother Teresa.

"Do you have a husband?"

She didn't like the way he was looking at her, so she lied. "Yes. His name is Malik. He fights with the US Army Rangers. He is probably very angry that I was abducted and eager to find me. He will be very happy when you release me."

The hard look in Jidda's eyes made her stomach sink.

She fought back a wave of despair. "You *will* keep your word, won't you? Or are you a man who makes promises he doesn't keep?"

The chatter of the men around them fell silent.

Jidda's gaze went cold. "Watch what you say to me, woman. I am the only one keeping these men away from you. They are lions. You are prey."

Kristi bit back the words she truly wanted to say, his implied threat clear. If she angered him, he would withdraw his protection. And then...

Shit! Shit! Shit!

Once he felt better and the wound had truly begun to heal, he wouldn't need her any longer.

If he doesn't let you go, the Nigerian or US government will do something. They won't just forget about you. They'll come for you.

And in the meantime?

Don't think about it. Don't think about it.

Aware that the men were watching her, she did her best to hide her sudden rush of fear, drawing slow, steady breaths as she packed away the medications. Then she unrolled her bed mat, checked it for spiders, scorpions, and other creepy-crawlies. She laid it out near Jidda's feet, putting herself in the corner, out of reach of his hands and far from the other men. Then, exhausted, she lay down on her side, careful not to poke herself with the scalpel, which was still in her pocket.

God, please get me out of this. Please help Jidda keep his word.

Kristi wasn't a religious person, but she'd take any help she could get.

She must have fallen asleep because the next thing she knew, a hand was sliding up her thigh. Her eyes flew open, and she sat upright, smacking the hand away and coming face to face with Peter. She kicked at him, her words coming in an angry hiss. "*Get your hands off me!*"

He grabbed her wrists, tried to force her back, hatred and lust on his face.

This time she shouted. "Let go of me!"

"Peter!" Jidda sat up. "Let her be."

Peter glared at Jidda, then leaned close to Kristi. "He will not let you go, whore!"

"I'm not a whore!" she shouted back. "I'm a married woman and a nurse."

"Quiet!" That was Jidda again. "Peter! Sleep now."

Peter made his way back to his own bed, his gaze on Kristi as he stretched out on his mat, his rage at her palpable.

Kristi let out the breath she hadn't realized she was holding.

Jidda had stopped Peter this time, but what would happen when Jidda felt better and no longer needed her?

She lay down once again, back to the wall, her body starting to shake in the aftermath of what had just happened, her heart still thrumming in her chest.

She drew deep slow breaths, pretended to sleep.

Then she heard Malik's voice as if he were beside her.

It's incredibly freeing to embrace your mortality. You surrender hope and gain clarity and peace. You learn to live and act in the moment.

Is that what she needed to do? Accept that they were going to rape and kill her? Surrender hope of a rescue?

The thought almost made her throw up.

She wasn't Malik. She wasn't a soldier. She was a nurse.

All she wanted was to go home.

In the darkness, scalpel still in her pocket, she counted the minutes till dawn.

MALIK CLIMBED into the passenger seat of David's black Mercedes-Benz G-Class. "Nice wheels, man."

"What can I say? I like luxury." David's accent was rich and melodious.

Malik pointed to David's time piece. "Is that a Rollie, man?"

"Rolex. Gucci. Prada. Mercedes. You hungry? Let's get something to eat."

Malik watched out the window as David drove them down to where the food trucks congregated at night. They both ordered chicken shawarma and beers and sat at a metal table near the curb to eat, people walking past, some wearing brightly colored traditional Nigerian clothes, some dressed as if this were LA or New York City.

David pulled something out of his jacket and slid it across the table to Malik.

The breath left Malik's lungs.

Kristi.

It was a newspaper clipping about her abduction, complete with a photo.

He hadn't seen her face since the day he'd left Amundsen-Scott Station. His gaze moved over the image—her beautiful eyes, those high cheekbones, her sweet lips. The knot of tension in his chest grew tighter.

"That answers my question." David took a bite, chewed, then took a drink. "I wondered why you came alone and why Cobra isn't behind this operation. You care about this woman."

He cared for her more than she knew. "Yes."

God, he'd been an idiot. He should have stayed in touch with her. He should have pushed her to change her contract.

"We will talk more later. Eat, man!"

"Right." The food, which had smelled good, seemed tasteless to Malik now. But he needed fuel, so he ate, washing it all down with cold beer.

David kept up a cheerful monologue, giving him all the latest soccer news—which Nigerian footballers had left to play in the UK and Germany, details of the most recent match between the Nigerian Super Eagles and Algeria, why he thought they might win the World Cup this year.

Then he laughed. "But why am I telling you all this? You are tired from your journey. Let's get home. Did you sleep on the plane?"

"Yeah, but it wasn't like traveling on Cobra's private jet."

David laughed. "Luxury, my friend. It is everything."

Back in the vehicle, David grew serious. "How do you know this woman?"

"She and I are ... were ... lovers."

"Did it end badly?"

"No, it wasn't like that. I had my work, and she had hers. We just couldn't be in the same place."

David glanced over at him. "You've never stopped thinking about her."

"Yeah." It was the truth.

"My government sources believe she was taken by one of the bandit gangs that hide in the forests in Kaduna State. They sometimes attack motorists on the Abuja-Kaduna Expressway, rob them, and kidnap them for ransom."

"I read about the bandit gangs in Shields' briefing."

"What you don't know is that there was an attack on the Expressway the day before Kristi was taken. The fools attacked a family. They did not see the police on the highway. The police opened fire, killed two of them, and shot another."

Malik put the pieces together. "They took medical supplies when they abducted her. You think they abducted her to take care of the bastard who got shot."

"It is a possibility."

If that was the case, they would keep her alive—at least until they'd gotten what they wanted from her. After that...

"Tell me the truth, Malik. Is your government involved in this operation?"

"No. I'm on my own."

David frowned. "And Cobra?"

Malik wouldn't share details, even with David. "The rest of the crew is working another op."

"Then it is lucky you have me. This is not going to be

easy, my friend."

Malik had to ask. "Why did you agree to help?"

Cobra wasn't paying him. Neither was the CIA.

"You and the Agency are my best customers. If I help you now, who's to say what might be in it for me down the line? Besides, I like you, Malik. So does Tower. He doesn't want you to get your head shot off."

That made Malik smile. "Yeah, neither do I."

David drove through the city to what was clearly an upscale neighborhood. Ultramodern homes lined curving roads, all glass and light and landscaped gardens.

Malik gave a low whistle. "How much do we pay you?"

"You pay me very well." David pulled up to a gate, which slowly opened onto a short driveway to a three-story house of white concrete, steel, and glass. "This was just built last year. I don't stay here often—only when I'm in Abuja. I have a much nicer penthouse in Lagos. When we find Kristi, you must be my guest there."

God, Malik hoped that's how this would end. "Sounds good to me."

They climbed out of the vehicle and were met by two burly, armed men. David introduced them as Bruno and Idris, his bodyguards. He spoke to them in Yoruba, then turned to Malik. "They will bring your bags. Come inside."

Malik stepped through a heavy glass door and glanced around. Gray marble floors. Recessed lighting. A lighted swimming pool and hot tub in the back. Burnished stainless steel appliances in the kitchen.

Our taxpayer dollars at work.

"There is a gym and theater downstairs. There are four bedrooms upstairs. All have their own baths and toilets."

Malik met David's gaze. "Luxury, huh?"

David laughed. "Luxury."

4

K risti awoke from a dead sleep thanks to a sharp kick in the ribs.

Peter glared down at her. "Get up. Jidda needs you."

She sat up, looked toward the open door, saw that it was after dawn.

Jidda sat up on his bed mat, a grimace on his face. "It is getting worse again. You have done nothing to help me!"

He'd gotten the last of the IV antibiotics early this morning, so it was time to switch to oral meds. If the infection was getting worse, he would need to go to a hospital—and she might wind up dead.

Pulse tripping, she stood, pushed past Peter, and knelt beside Jidda. She checked his dressing, saw that the redness and inflammation were substantially reduced, though the wound was still draining. "This drainage is normal. The infection is—"

"But it hurts!"

The pain meds had worn off while he'd slept.

"Of course, it hurts. Getting shot hurts. Your pain meds

have worn off." She checked him for fever. "Do you want my medical advice?"

He waited, listening.

"Stop being a bandit. You're less likely to get shot." She ignored his shocked response. "You don't have a fever. Let's get you your next dose of pain meds and start your oral antibiotics."

"Why do you talk to me like that?"

"I speak honestly. Would you rather have me lie?" Kristi took two oxycodone tablets and an antibiotic capsule out of the duffel bag and gave them to Jidda, who swallowed them with the remaining water in his cup.

He set the cup aside. "Listen well. I hold your life in my hands, woman."

She glared at him. "I held *your* life in my hands, *man*, and I saved it."

For a moment, Kristi thought she'd gone too far, the anger on Jidda's face making her heart thrum.

Then his head fell back, and he laughed. "You are a lioness—and too fine."

Then Jidda called to his men, and a teenage boy appeared in the doorway. Jidda spoke with him and then looked over at Kristi. "This is my nephew, Obi. He will bring us breakfast and more boiled water for you to drink."

"Thank you." She gestured to Jidda's arm. "I need to remove your IV."

She carefully pulled off the medical tape and then drew out the catheter, pressing down with clean gauze to stop any bleeding. "Why did you become a bandit, Jidda?"

"My parents died of AIDS when I was a boy. I needed to eat."

"I'm sorry about your parents." AIDS still killed tens of thousands of Nigerians every year. "You know what it means to suffer, so why make others suffer? Those guards at the medical clinic had families, too. When your men shot them, I'm sure it was very painful. Now, their children have lost a father. Their sons and daughters are crying today. Do you ever think about that?"

He smacked her hand away. "Does the crocodile worry about its prey?"

"You're not a crocodile. You're not an animal. You're a human—"

From outside came a cry, followed by whimpers of pain.

A shout. Men running.

Jidda called out, and a man answered, leaning in through the open doorway and speaking words Kristi didn't understand.

A moment later, men entered supporting Obi, whose face was screwed up in pain.

Kristi saw that his hand was red and covered with blisters. "What happened?"

"My fool of a nephew fell into the fire. Can you help him?"

Obi whimpered in pain. "I didn't fall. Someone pushed me."

"Are you going to keep your word to let me go?" Kristi didn't wait for Jidda's answer. She grabbed the trauma kit and lidocaine ointment out of the duffel bag and motioned for Obi to sit down. "I'm going to clean the burn first and then treat it."

Obi nodded.

"You understand English?"

"Yes."

"This will hurt." She poured sterile saline over Obi's blistered palm and fingers then took one of the surgical scrub brushes and used the soft foam side to wash the skin before rinsing it again. The burns didn't go below the dermis, which was lucky. "You're going to be okay, Obi."

After patting Obi's hand dry with a piece of sterile gauze, she spread lidocaine ointment over his burns. "This will stop the pain for a while. It takes time to start working. You'll need to re-apply it every hour."

The relief on Obi's face told Kristi the medication was already taking effect.

"You need to keep this clean, okay?" She carefully bandaged his hand. "Who pushed you?"

How could anyone mistreat this child?

Now that the crisis was over, the men began to tease Obi. Kristi couldn't understand what they said, but she recognized their body language and the embarrassment and humiliation on Obi's face.

He turned to her, looked at her through eyes that held far too much grief and fear for a boy his age. "You do well."

That was Naija—Nigerian pidgin—for *thank you.*

She answered *no trouble*, Naija for *you're welcome.* "*No wahala.*"

That made him smile.

Peter slapped Obi on the back of the head. "Do not thank a captive."

Admonished, Obi stood, glancing at Kristi as he followed the men out of the hut.

She found Jidda watching her.

"I think you are too valuable for me to let you go."

MALIK WOKE AND SHOWERED, washing away the grime of travel. He skipped shaving, impatient to get to work. Kristi was out there somewhere, in the hands of killers.

He'd dreamed about her again. In the dream, he'd kissed her, undressed her, and she had vanished from his arms, disappearing like a ghost. He'd run through Amundsen-Scott Station in a panic, searching for her, calling her name. But he hadn't found her.

To hell with these bullshit nightmares. It was time to gear up and go after her.

He dressed in tactical pants and a black T-shirt, then made his way downstairs, the scent of food making his mouth water. He found an older woman at work in the kitchen, a white apron over a bright blue dress, a blue and gold head wrap covering her hair.

When she saw him, she curtsied. "Mr. Jones, please sit. Mr. Olatunji will join you for breakfast shortly. Would you like coffee, tea, or cocoa?"

Malik wasn't used to having staff wait on him and would have been fine making his own breakfast, but he didn't say that. "Coffee, please. Thank you."

The rear sliding glass door opened, and David stepped inside wearing swim trunks and drying his hair with a towel. "Good morning! Did you sleep well?"

Malik wanted to get to work, but he forced a smile onto his face. "Yes. Thank you. My room is very comfortable."

David grinned. "Good. We have much to discuss, but I should dress first."

By the time David returned, breakfast was on the table —fried yams scrambled with eggs and tomatoes, fried plantains, beans, and bread. The food tasted as good as it smelled, but every bite reminded Malik that Kristi might well be going hungry.

He thanked his host for the meal, but David saw through him.

"You worry about her." He drew out his smartphone,

tapped in his password, and slid it across the table to Malik. "There is some good news. One of the aid workers got good photographs of the abduction, including the faces of some of the kidnappers. Here is the vehicle that took her away."

Malik looked through the images, his body tensing at the photo of some bastard with his hand fisted in Kristi's hair. He couldn't see her face, but he could see the faces of three of the assailants. The vehicle—an older Toyota High-lander—had no license plate. It did, however, have some features they could use to identify it, including dents and a triangle of three bullet holes near the left taillight.

"The NPF—the Nigeria Police Force—is running their faces through their database. In the meantime, you will be searching for that vehicle."

Malik slid the phone back over to David. "We should get these photos to Shields, too. She has a way of noticing things that everyone else misses."

David drank his juice. "Let's go upstairs to my office."

His office was on the top floor. Ceremonial Yoruba masks adorned the walls, a putting green with artificial turf on the balcony outside.

David walked to his desk, picked up several documents, handed them to Malik. "These are your firearms permits and a letter from the government giving you permission to operate in the country. They are forgeries, of course, but they are flawless. If you are pulled over by police and someone calls in to verify them, you will be exposed. There was no way to get authentic permits so quickly."

Malik looked them over. "I understand. Thanks."

"Now for the fun part." David walked over to what looked like a cupboard, pressed his thumb against a biometric scanner, and opened the doors to reveal an arsenal.

Malik crossed the room, took in the sight. "*That's* what I'm talking about."

"Take whatever you need. After all, I got most of them from Cobra."

There were rifles, handguns, shotguns, submachine guns, machine guns, bayonets, and combat knives, most of them current US military issue. There were cases of M18 smoke grenades and fragmentation grenades, as well.

"Sweet." Malik would need a good combat rifle with a bayonet, a sniper rifle with a night vision scope, a couple of pistols, lots of spare magazines, and a shit ton of ammo. He chose an M4 carbine, a scoped MK11 Mod 0 sniper rifle, and two SIG P320s.

While David sent the images of the attackers to Shields, Malik sat down at David's desk to study a map of the area around Kinu Village. His stomach sank. "Shit."

The area was a vast, rural landscape that was a mix of forest and savanna cleaved by rivers. Kristi could be anywhere out there.

For the first time, Malik's hope waivered.

"It isn't going to be easy, my friend." David finished uploading the images and joined Malik. "You are searching for one precious needle in a hundred haystacks. But I know this country. If they are encamped in the forest, they are going to need one thing above all else—water."

"Rivers." Malik's gaze snapped to the map. "We'll search stretches of forest along the rivers."

"*You* search along the rivers. I'm not getting paid, so I won't risk my neck. I'll take you to Kaduna to rent a car, and then you're on your own."

It was about damned time.

Malik folded the map, stood. "When do we leave?"

KRISTI WATCHED as Jidda walked through the encampment, supported by Peter and Obi. She had persuaded him to go for a small walk, afraid that lying on his mat for days would lead to blood clots. He grimaced with each step but kept going.

What he'd said this morning about her being too valuable to let go had stayed with her all day, fear gnawing at her until she felt almost sick. She couldn't stay here. She couldn't stay with Jidda. She sure as hell couldn't sleep with him.

She glanced up at the sky—or what she could see of it through the canopy. The air was alive with the songs of birds. Sunlight gleamed on the muddy water of the river maybe a hundred yards away. And yet she felt as cold as ice.

How long had she been here? Three days? Four? Now she understood why prisoners scratched marks into walls to keep track of time. It was easy to grow confused when you were surviving moment to moment.

She did her best to remember.

Three days.

It felt like an eternity.

God, how she wanted a hot shower, a change of clothes, and a chance to brush her teeth. A real meal would be nice, too. Or a cup of tea. Or a real bed, one that was raised off the ground and not in the dirt with rodent droppings.

You wanted to travel and see the world.

Being held hostage in rural Nigeria by killers wasn't what she'd had in mind.

If she made it out of this alive...

Malik had warned her. Sweet Malik. Malik who'd made her laugh and scream. He would hear about this eventually.

Samantha would find out sooner or later, and then Thor would tell Malik. Would he worry about her?

She should have kept in touch. She should have emailed him just to say hello and ask how he was doing. Surely, that wouldn't have been out of line. Now, she might never get the chance to talk with him again.

The thought made her throat go tight.

Stop!

She couldn't let them see her cry. They were predators. Any sign of weakness or vulnerability would make Peter bolder. The bastard would have raped her last night if Jidda hadn't told him to stop. And though she had the scalpel, she knew she could only use it once. The moment she turned it against one of them, they would kill her.

She ran her fingers through her tangled hair, wondered if she could talk Jidda into letting her boil water for a sponge bath. She had no intention of undressing in this camp, but since her arrival in Nigeria, she had gotten good at taking a bath out of a bucket.

Jidda was making his way back toward the hut now, wincing with each step.

She'd just started toward him when a small group of Jidda's men appeared, laughing and dragging something between them. Whatever it was, it struggled and cried out, sounding so much like a baby that chills skittered down her spine.

A little duiker.

Two men held it by its horns, dragging it, kicking and wailing, into the center of the camp. Another hurried toward them with a machete.

Kristi turned away, the little creature's distress tugging at her, its desire to live matching her own. Then its cries ended suddenly.

She fought back her disgust, pity for the animal putting another lump in her throat. She reminded herself that she wasn't in a position to judge these men. She'd never had to kill to eat or worry about starving to death. Her meat came neatly packaged from a grocery store. She couldn't begrudge them a meal—even if they were robbing, murdering assholes.

Still, there was no way in hell she would eat it. Undercooked or contaminated bushmeat was associated with a host of zoonoses—diseases that passed from animals to humans—including Ebola. She would stick with rice.

Not eager to return to the darkness of the hut, she found a tree stump, checked it for scorpions and spiders, and sat. She watched as the men built up the fire, singed the fur off the poor duiker, then cut it into sections to roast.

Obi ran over to her, an excited smile on his face. "You wan chop?"

Do you want to eat?

She shook her head. "No, thank you."

Peter yelled for Obi, and the boy turned and ran back to Jidda, who limped toward the hut once more with their support.

Knowing Peter would yell for her next, Kristi followed, dread settling in her chest at the thought of the night ahead.

5

Malik and David arrived in Kinu just as the sun was setting, David's bodyguards following behind in a black SUV. The drive from Abuja to Kaduna ought to have taken only three hours. Thanks to a collision between a dumper hauling rock and a truck carrying farm produce, it had taken twice that long.

"We should have stayed in Kaduna and waited until tomorrow to drive out here." David sat in the passenger seat of Malik's rental—a bronze-colored Ford Explorer—firearms and other gear in the back. "The drive back will be risky."

Malik hadn't been able to wait, not when Kristi's life was on the line. "If you're worried about running into trouble, we could use the drone to make sure the road ahead is clear."

"Drone?" David stared at him. "What drone?"

"The one in my bag in the back."

"You brought a drone?" The worry on David's face was replaced with glee.

"Yes." Malik fought to keep a straight face at the abrupt

change in David's mood. The man loved tech. "Infrared. Two-hour flight time. Roughly a ten-mile range."

David grinned from behind his Fendi sunglasses. "Excellent."

Malik parked across from the mosque and near the village market, where vendors had begun to pack up their wares. "Do you want me to do the talking?"

"Let me."

They climbed out, David's bodyguards behind them.

People ignored them or cast wary glances their way, women in hijabs hurrying to bring small children indoors, older men bending their heads together. Malik couldn't blame them for being cautious. Only a few days ago, bandits had attacked their village.

While the bodyguards stayed with the vehicles, Malik followed David toward a vendor who was packing up plantains, dried beans, and *tinko*—dried mystery meat.

David slipped off his sunglasses and spoke to the man in Naija, the words moving too fast for Malik to understand most of what was said. The vendor pointed with a nod of his head toward a bearded man with a red-and-white checked turban on his head who stood nearby, watching.

"You do well, friend." David bid the vendor farewell with a bow of his head, then turned to Malik. "He says we should talk to the village imam. Don't make direct eye contact, and bow your head in respect when you meet him."

But talking to the imam turned out to be much more than a simple conversation. After an exchange of greetings, the imam invited them inside for tea, most of the conversation beyond Malik's understanding. Tea became supper. It was only after bowls of goat stew and rice that the conversation turned to Kristi's abduction.

David explained that Malik had come from the US to

find her and showed the imam the photographs, including the newspaper photo of Kristi.

The imam studied the photos, a thoughtful frown on his face. He met Malik's gaze. "Your woman?"

Malik assumed that's what David had told him. "Yes. I must get her back."

The imam handed the photographs back to David, speaking in rapid Naija once more, gesturing with his hands. Then the conversation moved on to crops and families, the imam dandling one of his grandchildren on his lap.

Malik fought to conceal his impatience. He didn't want to offend David or the imam. But every moment they spent fucking around was another moment Kristi would have to suffer. By the time they got out of here, it would be too late to explore the forested area around the village.

This was taking too long. Every moment that passed left Kristi at risk.

Malik strode back to the vehicle, feeling as if his skin was on too tight. "What did the imam say? He talked forever."

David looked over at him, a concerned frown on his face. "You need to relax, brother. This woman—she has you turned inside out. You won't be able to save her if you rush in and get yourself killed."

"Right." Malik knew that. "It's hard to think of her alone with killers."

He didn't have to explain.

"If she is remarkable enough to win your heart, she will be strong enough to get through this." David answered his question. "The bandits who kidnapped your Kristi drove west after leaving the village. The imam thinks they cannot be too far from here because they come into Kinu to buy food from the market every few days."

Malik stared at him. "They come *here*?"

He would have to get this information to Shields when they got back to the hotel.

"Even bandits have to eat. Now, let's look at this drone."

Malik unpacked it, checked to make sure it was fully charged, and handed the controller with its view screen to David. "Do you know how to fly one of these things? I can't have you breaking Tower's expensive new toy."

David grinned. "Oh, yes. I have several of my own, but they're nothing like this."

Not wanting to attract too much attention, Malik drove a short distance from the village before they stopped, climbed out of the vehicle, and launched it, the device whirring as it took to the night sky.

David's gaze was on the view screen, a big grin on his face. "There we are—green shapes."

They got into the vehicle again, David keeping the drone airborne and about one klick ahead of them, watching the sides of the road for anyone lying in wait.

But Malik's mind was on Kristi. "We need to move quickly now. It's possible that someone in the village will warn the assholes about us next time they're around."

"This is true. Look!" He pointed at the drone's view screen. "There are patas monkeys running through that field."

By the time they got back to Kaduna, it was almost midnight, the drone sitting in the back, still in one piece, its battery spent.

"Thanks for your help today, David." Malik would give credit where it was due. "I'll put together a strategy in the morning and get out of your way."

"*We* will make a plan." He motioned to the backseat.

"Leave this drone with me when you leave Nigeria with Kristi, and I will consider it payment."

"I've got cash if you want cash."

David didn't look impressed. "How much?"

"Ten grand."

David laughed. "That's chicken change. Give me the drone, and we have a deal."

Tower wouldn't like this.

"Done."

KRISTI WOKE from a dreamless sleep early the next morning. Jidda and the others were still asleep, dawn's first light coming through the open doorway. She combed her hair with her fingers, men's voices and the scent of wood smoke telling her the camp was waking. At least no one had touched her last night. She'd gotten a little sleep.

Thirsty and hungry, she sat quietly, waiting for Jidda to wake so she could check his wound. She hoped to be able to suture it today or tomorrow. And then...

What would happen to her?

I think you are too valuable for me to let you go.

He hadn't brought it up again. They'd spent last night gorging on roasted duiker and had barely noticed her, full stomachs leaving them relaxed and sleepy.

She'd thought about trying to escape, but where would she go? She had no idea which direction to go to reach help. They had the vehicle and could easily catch up. In her blue scrubs, she wouldn't exactly blend into the landscape. If she ran and they caught her, they would make her pay.

What should she say if Jidda brought it up again? What

would she do if he tried to get physical with her? Would she rebuff him and risk losing his protection?

It came down to how much she was prepared to endure to survive.

She had a clinical understanding of her situation. She'd taken care of Nigerian women and girls who'd survived captivity, most of them enduring rape and other kinds of brutality. She'd listened to them tell their stories, reassured them that their lives still had value, taken care of their bruised and battered bodies.

But, God, she'd never imagined she'd find herself in their shoes.

How hollow her words sounded now—and how incredibly brave those women were. They had endured the unspeakable, some of them for years, in the hope that they would survive long enough to escape or be rescued. As long as there was hope that she would be rescued and return to her own world, that's what Kristi would have to do, too.

But that didn't mean she couldn't use what little power she had to her advantage.

It wasn't long before the men awoke, one by one rolling up their bed mats and heading out of the hut.

"How do you feel this morning, Jidda?" She sat near his feet to check his wound, careful to stay out of reach of his hands.

"Better." He watched as she removed the bandage. "It is healing."

"Yes, it is. I think I can suture it tomorrow. But now it's time for your antibiotics." She reached into the duffel, took out the medications.

"We spoke about you last night."

She feigned a calm she didn't feel, her pulse racing. "Is that so?"

"Every person has a fate, and it is time to accept yours. We cannot let you go because you know our faces. You will stay with us as our nurse and my concubine."

She placed the medications in his palm, almost shaking with rage and fear. "I don't believe in fate. People get to decide how they will live. I am fine staying with you as a nurse for a while, but I will be no man's concubine. I am married and will stay faithful to my husband."

Jidda took the pills, swallowed them. "You will never see him again, so he is no longer your husband."

"He *is* looking for me." If only that were true... "The US government will try to find me, too. It would be best for you all if you drove me back to Kinu and let me go or asked for a ransom. My employer has insurance and will pay. You can make money."

"It has already been decided." He was clearly a man used to being obeyed.

Kristi scooted farther out of reach, pushed a smile onto her face. "My husband *will* find me, Jidda. When he does, he will *kill* any man who has touched me. That will become *your* fate."

Jidda's face screwed up with anger. "With one word, I could turn you over to my men. By the time they are finished, there would be as little of you left as there is of that duiker."

"Who would help you then?" She stood, towering over him. "No, Jidda, I will be your nurse. I will take care of you and your men. But no man here will touch me—not even you."

She turned her back on him and walked out into the daylight, heart hammering behind her breastbone.

How long would she be able to keep up this verbal game of chess?

Right now, Jidda still needed her, but in another week, he'd be on his feet and almost done with the antibiotics. She would no longer be able to walk away from him or put herself beyond his reach. Her hold over him would be gone.

If only she knew SEAL Team Six was on its way...

Jidda shouted something from inside the hut, his voice angry. Obi ran to answer him, ducking inside the door, then turning to Kristi.

"He wants you, miss."

Kristi drew another deep breath, steeled herself. "I'm coming."

MALIK AND DAVID pored over a map after breakfast and discussed strategy. "We'll take this dirt road west from Kinu and head toward the Mariga River here. We can use the drone to do a systematic search of the forest near the river. With the drone's two spare batteries, we'll have about six hours of search time."

That enabled them to cover an area of about sixty miles each day. If the bastards who'd taken her were anywhere near Kinu, they would find them—unless something spooked them into moving.

"What if we acquired a portable solar generator? You have cash. We could recharge in the field and camp in the vehicle."

Malik grinned. "Is car camping luxurious enough for you?"

David chuckled. "I like roughing it from time to time."

"Sounds good to me." Malik got out the cash, while David gave instructions to one of his bodyguards, who left in search of the generator.

Malik studied the map once more. "If we find them, we'll get their location to the NPF and to Shields, so she can get the intel to the State Department."

"We should also notify my contacts at the army's First Division headquarters here in Kaduna. They can mobilize faster than anyone else."

"I'm going prepared for a long-term recon mission. Once we find her, I don't want to give them the chance to slip away."

David frowned. "Are you certain you can handle that? Can you stay there, watching while they beat her, torture her, maybe even rape her without charging in and getting yourself killed?"

Malik's chest constricted at the thought. "You know I can't."

"You see, my friend? It is better to keep an eye on them using the drone than to put yourself in that situation. If you die, she dies."

They packed up their gear once again and were ready to go by the time the bodyguard returned with the solar generator.

David knelt down beside it. "A nice bit of kit, don't you agree?"

Before Malik could answer, his phone buzzed. "It's Shields."

"Hey, I've got something for you."

"I'm listening."

"I sent the photos to my connections at the Agency, along with the intel you sent last night. I just heard back. They rerouted a drone that's been following Boko Haram and found the vehicle."

"What?" Malik ran to his laptop, explaining to David. "They found the vehicle."

Shields went on. "I'm certain it's the same one. I blew up the images and analyzed them myself. There's even someone standing there in what looks like blue scrubs. I'm sending you the images and the GPS coordinates now."

Malik booted up his laptop, set his phone on the table, put it on speaker. "Thanks, Elizabeth. I owe you—big time."

This was the break he'd been hoping for.

"I counted twenty-seven fighting-age males in the image, not including the figure in blue. Lots of AKs. I don't see any machine guns. My guess is that they holed up here with their injured guy, the one they wanted Kristi to treat. Once he's mobile again, they're likely to move on and either elimi-nate her or take her with them."

"The photos just arrived." With David leaning over his shoulder, Malik opened the files—seven pixilated images. "That's definitely the Highlander. See the three bullet holes near the taillight?"

David pointed. "And those dents. It's definitely their vehicle."

And there, standing at a distance from a group of men gathered around a campfire, was someone with dark hair and blue clothes.

His heart gave a hard knock.

Kristi.

"When were these taken?"

"This morning, so they're about three hours old."

"Have you sent this up the flagpole?"

"Yes, of course. I expect the State Department will pass it on to the Nigerian government, and they'll start working out plans for a rescue. It won't happen overnight. You should know that Corbray and Tower are pushing hard to get this assignment. They haven't forgotten, Malik. Don't do anything stupid."

"Me? Do something stupid?"

"Says the guy who quit his job and flew to the other side of the world to rescue a woman he hasn't seen or spoken with in more than a year."

David shrugged. "She has a point, man."

Shields appealed directly to David. "Don't let him do anything stupid, David."

David leaned closer to Malik's phone, grin on his face. "I'll do my best."

"I've got to go. It's our first day on the ground here in Ouagadougou."

"Good luck. And thanks again, Elizabeth. You might well have saved her life."

"I know." She ended the call.

"I like her. Why did she marry that orange-haired beast, McManus?"

"I think she loves him." Malik punched the GPS coordinates Shields had sent into his phone and closed his laptop. "We'll head to Kinu, make our way toward their position, and do some recon. We wait for your army friends or NPF to come in—unless her life is in danger."

"And then what?"

"Then I'll take them out, one at a time."

K risti put the last suture in Jidda's thigh, tied it off, and cut the thread.

She'd given Jidda a small amount of Versed, enough to knock him out for the short time she'd need to close his wound. By the time she had cleaned up, he was already coming around.

"You're all stitched up." She sat on her bed mat, well out of his reach.

He raised his head, blinked groggily, looked down at his thigh. "Will it be well?"

"It should be mostly healed in about six weeks. The muscle will probably be stiff for a long time. You'll need to keep taking the antibiotics."

He sat up. "You kept your word."

She leaned back against the cool brick wall. "Honorable people do that."

He looked troubled but said nothing.

After yesterday's argument, they seemed to have reached a kind of truce. He hadn't brought up her staying with him as his concubine, and she hadn't said anything about being released. But how long would this last? She'd heard stories of women who were held captive for months or even years before they were rescued.

Was anyone searching for her—the US military, the Nigerian police, anyone? Had Malik gotten the news yet? Was he worried about her?

Never had she felt more alone.

Still, she knew she had reasons to be grateful. This was her fourth day with these bastards, and she was alive and untouched apart from being groped when she'd arrived. She was certain most women they'd abducted hadn't been as fortunate.

After a breakfast of rice and tea, Jidda asked Obi for help walking outside. He sat on a log near the fire, which had burned low, and talked to his men, showing them his thigh. A group of the younger men walked out of the forest, arms full of firewood, and joined them.

Kristi couldn't tell what they were saying, but their laughter and smiles put her at ease. One of the younger men seemed to be telling a story about a monkey, given his gestures and the sounds he was making. She couldn't help but wonder what had led each of them to live as outlaws, stealing, kidnapping people, raping, killing.

She knew that the Fulani tribesmen of the north had resorted to violence when climate change had altered their traditional grazing grounds, turning them to desert. She knew, too, that the riches and modern conveniences of Nigeria hadn't reached everyone. About forty percent of its people still lived in poverty.

But why choose this life when it was likely to get them killed?

Unable to understand the conversation, she let her gaze drift, taking in the forest around the camp. She couldn't identify the trees, and she didn't know what wildlife lived here. She knew Nigeria had lions, leopards, elephants, and other megafauna, but she didn't know where they could be found. She had hoped to travel the country a bit before heading back to—

Someone shouted.

Peter.

He stood, his face twisted with anger, yelling at Jidda. Some of the other men nodded their agreement, their gazes turning to Kristi.

Her pulse raced. They were arguing about *her*.

Jidda stood, this time without anyone's help. When he spoke, his voice was low and menacing. Then he switched to English. "Listen well, Peter. She is *my* concubine. She saved my life, and I will reward her as I choose. Or do you wish I had died?"

An ominous silence hung over the camp.

Breath frozen in her lungs, Kristi watched as Peter, fury on his face, stalked off into the forest.

She exhaled, her pulse tripping.

Jidda resumed his seat on the log, and slowly the conversation returned to normal.

Obi left Jidda's side and walked over to her. He held out his burned hand. "My uncle wishes you to go inside the hut and check my hand, miss."

Kristi wanted to ask Obi a few questions and gladly returned to the relative safety of the hut. She took out the first aid kit, slipped on gloves, and took the dressing off Obi's hand. "What were they saying about me?"

While she spread lidocaine on his burns, Obi explained. "Peter is angry. He thinks you belong to all the men. But Jidda told them no other man will touch you besides him. He has taken you as his concubine as your reward for saving his life. Peter told Jidda this is not our way. Women captives are shared and sold, not kept for one man. Then Jidda reminded Peter who is the leader here. He alone answers to the Sky Kings and—"

Obi stopped, his gaze jerking to Kristi's as if he'd just said too much, his pupils dilated with fear.

Who or what were the Sky Kings?

Kristi pretended not to notice. "Jidda was kind to protect me. You are kind to me, too. How old are you, Obi?"

"I am twelve."

"How did you come to live with these men?"

"My uncle took me in after my parents were killed."

"You're a good young man, Obi." She took out fresh gauze to bandage his hand once more. "Don't let them turn you into a criminal."

His face crumpled. "Don't tell anyone what I told you."

"Don't worry." She gave him a warm nurse's smile. "I won't."

"You should stay in here for now." Obi turned and left her alone.

She took off the gloves, stuck them in the duffel bag, and sat on her bed mat.

Women captives are shared and sold.

Now she knew what kind of bandits these were. They were human traffickers who sold women into prostitution. And Jidda was the only person keeping her from that fate.

She hugged her knees to her chest and tried not to cry.

"THE DRONE STAYS PACKED up unless we need it." Malik stood his ground. "If we fly it over the encampment, there's too great a risk that they'll see it or hear it."

It wasn't a high-altitude military drone that could fly undetected.

"If they break camp and try to move her?" David wasn't giving up.

"Then we use the drone to trail them." Malik shook his head. "You just want to play with your new toy."

David chuckled. "I'm a patient man. I can wait."

Malik and David had hit the road an hour after speaking with Shields, the two bodyguards following in one of David's SUVs. David had passed the intel on to both the NPF and Nigerian Army HQ in Kaduna, and both organizations were waiting for confirmation from David that Kristi truly was at those coordinates.

They passed Kinu Village, Malik taking rutted dirt roads north and then northwest, circling the location of the bandit camp. He parked off the road when the camp was due south of them.

"It's a five-kilometer hike. Are you sure you can handle it?"

"Keep talking, brother. You will eat my dust."

Malik grinned. "If you say so."

Malik took out his face paint, and they began to paint their faces in non-glare greens, grays, and blacks, colors that matched their jungle camo. Then it was time to gear up. They shouldered their packs, checked their weapons, and moved south, leaving the vehicles with the bodyguards, David carrying the drone in a bag.

It was an easy hike, but they moved carefully, weapons at the ready. Malik had no idea whether sentries guarded the camp, and he didn't want to find out by getting a bullet to the brain. It took almost an hour, but they reached the position without being seen. They set up their recon on a densely forested rise about a half kilometer north of the camp, both settling in with scoped sniper rifles to watch the action below.

An hour went by. Two hours. Three.

Sweat trickled down Malik's temples, insects buzzing around his face.

There was no sign of Kristi. She was probably inside one of the huts. Then again, those drone images Shields had sent were now a good six hours old. These bastards could have moved her, sold her, shot her.

Focus.

All they needed was one glimpse of Kristi, and David would call it in. Then the two of them would wait for reinforcements to arrive and take these fuckers down.

It was getting close to evening when some of the men started making a meal. Then an older man limped out of the hut that stood closest to the fire, supported by a boy. And behind them...

Malik's heart gave a thud.

Kristi.

Malik nodded to David, who pulled out his satellite phone and sent a message.

She seemed unhurt. She watched the men, keeping her distance, a wary expression on her face. She had no obvious injuries apart from bruising on her cheek—or was that dirt? Her scrubs were filthy, her hair tangled.

The man with the limp—probably the man she'd been abducted to save—sat on a log, while the young man who'd helped him filled a bowl from the cookpot. Most of the bastards gathered around the fire. But not everyone.

One fucker sat at a table off to one side, talking with a few others, their heads bowed together. Malik got a look at his face and recognized him as the son of a bitch who'd abducted Kristi and pulled her hair. Then Malik noticed the firearms.

All of the men had weapons.

"*Wahala*," David whispered.

Malik knew that word.

Trouble.

"We don't let anyone harm her," Malik whispered back.

"Agreed."

The small group of men broke up, moving toward the fire, casually surrounding the others, their weapons concealed behind their backs or tucked into their trousers. The one who'd abducted Kristi walked up behind the older man with the limp, drew his pistol—and shot him at point-blank range.

BAM!

The older man fell into the dirt, probably dead.

The bastard who'd shot him put his pistol in the waistband of his trousers and strode over to Kristi, who tried to back away. He struck her so hard she fell into the dirt. He reached down, grabbed her by her hair once more, and dragged her to her feet, shouting words Malik couldn't understand.

Malik sighted on the bastard's head, finger on the trigger. "What is he saying?"

"I can't understand it all. Something about how she should be shared like all women and how the other man had kept her to himself. He says he is their leader now."

Well, he wouldn't be for long.

Malik willed himself to relax, to focus on his breathing and his sight picture. If he wanted to hit his target, he couldn't let anger or adrenaline get the better of him. An elevated pulse or erratic breathing would throw off his aim.

But, God, it wasn't easy.

The fucker dragged a struggling Kristi toward the hut, while the other men laughed and cheered, some of them following to watch.

Malik couldn't sit here, waiting, while they took turns brutalizing her. "I need a diversion."

"I'm already working on it."

Malik glanced over, saw that David had taken the drone out of the bag and was about to launch it. "You're going to give us away, man."

"Get ready to fire."

Malik looked through the scope and lined up his shot.

OH, God! Oh, God! Oh, God!

Jidda was dead.

Kristi clutched at Peter's hand, his grip on her hair painful as he pulled her toward the hut, her cheek throbbing where he'd struck her, fear making her pulse pound. "No matter what you do to me, Peter, I will think only of Malik. It's his face I'll see. You are *nothing* compared to him! You're just a bandit, a criminal!"

"Shut up, whore!"

This was it.

Peter would rape her. He would hurt her. Then he would let every man in this encampment do the same.

The scalpel.

She could cut him, stab him in the groin, try to cut an artery.

But he would most likely get the blade away from her and use it against her. Even if she disabled or killed him, there were at least two dozen armed men here. No, she couldn't use the scalpel on Peter. It would only make her suffering worse.

That meant she had no way to stop this.

Despair washed through her, dark and heavy.

They had just reached the doorway to the hut when she heard a buzzing sound, like a giant swarm of bees.

Men shouted.

Peter turned, and Kristi saw astonishment on his face. He shoved her toward the hut—hard.

She fell, pain exploding in her skull as she struck the side of her head on the brick wall. Darkness dragged at her, but she fought against it.

She blinked, saw something flying above the camp.

Not a bird. Not bees.

A drone.

It hovered near the center of the camp just beyond the men's reach, then flew off when they tried to shoot it down.

Had someone come to rescue her?

Then Peter hovered above her, anger on his face. He pointed a pistol at her head. "I will not let them take you back."

She managed a feeble protest. "No!"

Her parents' and grandparents' faces flashed through her mind. This would be so hard for them.

I'm sorry.

Peter fell in a spray of red.

Blood?

Had someone shot him?

It was so hard to think, her head throbbing.

You have a concussion.

She fought to sit up, saw Peter dead in the dirt beside her. A group of men chased the drone in circles, then followed it south toward the river. It felt surreal, like a dream, like something that was happening far away, something that wasn't even real.

So many gunshots. Men falling dead.

Instinct took hold, her scattered thoughts coalescing into a single word.

Run.

If she could get to her feet, if she could get to the forest and escape...

She tried to stand, but her head seemed to shatter, the world spinning. She sank to the dirt again, landing on her side, the pain inside her skull almost blinding.

"Kristi, stay down!"

Now she was hearing voices.

Great.

Then a man in camo ran out of the forest, heading straight toward her, rifle in his hand, his face painted. "Stay down!"

Was he talking to her?

Of course, he's talking to you!

That must mean he was here for her.

Thank God!

She rolled onto her back, watching as he dropped to one knee, aimed, fired.

Rat-at-at! Rat-at-at! Rat-at-at!

Then he rushed forward, clipped his rifle to a rig on his chest, and helped her sit. "It's going to be okay, Kristi."

She looked into his painted face, saw his eyes through his safety glasses. The breath left her lungs in a rush, relief washing through her, as sweet and pure as sunlight. She would recognize those eyes anywhere. "*Malik!*"

Cobra had come for her. Malik had come.

"I'm getting you out of here." Malik spoke to someone

through his mic. "Quit fucking with the drone and cover us!"

The drone flew over the camp, heading north.

Malik helped her to her feet, steadied her. "I need you to move as fast as you can. We've got a three-mile hike back to the vehicles."

"My head... It hurts. I hit it. Concussion, I think. I'm so dizzy."

"Can you walk?"

"I ... I think so." Then she spotted Obi.

He lay in the dirt beside Jidda, terror on his face.

She held out her hand. "Obi! Come with us! Hurry!"

"Kristi, I don't think—"

"He's just a boy." Kristi struggled to stay on her feet, dizziness dragging her down, black spots in front of her eyes. "He isn't one of them."

Malik spoke into his mic. "Don't shoot the kid. He's coming with us."

Obi looked over at the bodies near the river, then he clambered to his feet and ran to her, fear in his young eyes, tears on his cheeks. "Peter killed Jidda."

"I know. I'm sorry."

"Let's move!" Malik led the way.

7

M alik knew right away that Kristi was in trouble. She
must have hit her head hard. He wrapped an arm
around her, half leading and half carrying her toward
David's position. "Stay on your feet, Kristi. Come on, kid!"

To his surprise, the boy wrapped a skinny arm around
Kristi's shoulders, helping to support her.

Malik was reluctant to trust anyone with Kristi, but he
needed his hands to work his rifle. "Have you got her? Let's
go. Hurry."

As long as they stood in this clearing, they were sitting
ducks for any asshole with the balls to shoot back. Most had
fled into the forest or run downriver. But all it took was one
bullet.

From the rise ahead, David fired a three-round burst.

Someone behind them grunted, hit the dirt.

"Eyes forward! Keep moving!" Malik shouted to the kid,
who'd looked back over his shoulder.

Fuck.

Malik wished they'd been able to wait for the police or
the army to show up, but there was no way he could have sat

there while that bastard brutalized her. Now, they had a five-kilometer retreat back to the vehicles with no one to watch their six.

They reached the edge of camp.

"Keep going!" Malik turned and dropped to one knee to cover the kid and Kristi as they made their way into the cover of the forest.

He watched for movement, but the camp seemed deserted, bodies lying still in the dirt. The bastards had no idea they'd been attacked by a force of only two. When they figured that out...

The drone buzzed by above him, David's voice coming over his earpiece.

"They have all fled down the river. I see no movement around us. Let's go!"

Malik stood, caught up with Kristi and the boy in a few strides, and led them to David, who was ready to go, rifle over his shoulder, drone controller in his hand.

Kristi looked around them. "Where are the rest of the guys—Thor, Lev?"

She thought Malik was here with Cobra.

"It's just the two of us."

She gaped at him. "What?"

There wasn't time to explain or to introduce David.

With the drone giving them eyes in the sky, they made their way through the forest back to the waiting vehicles.

MALIK HELPED Kristi climb into the backseat of his rental, buckled her seatbelt, then got her and the boy bottled water and energy bars from the back. "We'll be in Kaduna in a few hours. You need to hang on until then."

She drank thirstily. "I'm fine now that you're here."

As good as that made Malik feel, he knew it wasn't true. He could see from her face that she was in pain. "Watch over her, kid."

Kristi closed her eyes, rubbed her temple. "His name is Obi."

"Good work, Obi." Malik gave the boy a smile.

What was his story?

With no time to ask, Malik took the wheel, rifle beside him, while David rode shotgun, his hands busy controlling the drone.

"The way ahead looks clear."

Malik started the vehicle, hit the gas, and they were off, bouncing over rutted roads. He glanced into the rearview mirror, saw Kristi pressing her fingers to her temple, the pain on her face putting a knot of worry in his chest. Head injuries were unpredictable. "When we reach Kinu, you're driving."

David looked over his shoulder, spoke to Obi. "Who are you?"

Obi spoke to David in rapid Naija, Malik catching some of it. He understood that Obi had lost his parents and someone named Jidda had taken him in. He understood, too, that Kristi had helped Obi. But the rest of the conversation escaped Malik.

By the time they reached Kinu, Kristi was asleep. Malik parked just outside of the village and climbed out to trade places with Obi, while David recalled the drone and updated his contacts about their situation via sat phone.

"You are Malik, her husband?" Obi asked as he passed.

That was ... interesting.

Malik didn't want to contradict anything Kristi might have told them. "Yes."

Obi smiled, the first smile Malik had seen on his young face. "She said you would come. She said you would kill any man who touched her."

She'd said that?

"She was right." Malik grabbed a combat first aid kit and another bottle of water for Kristi out of the back, then climbed into the backseat beside her and stowed his rifle, barrel facing downward, near his feet. He peeled off his gloves, reached over, and stroked her bruised cheek with his knuckles. "Kristi, sweetheart, wake up."

She whimpered, raised her head. "Worst headache ever."

"I've got some painkillers in this kit—oxy, acetaminophen, ibuprofen."

"Acetaminophen and ibuprofen, please."

He got out the pills, placed them in her palm, watched her swallow.

"Thanks."

To hell with this.

"Come here." Malik unbuckled her seatbelt, drew her toward him so that she rested in his lap now, her head pillowed by his arm. "Rest. I'll get you home."

"Malik." She said his name, smiled. "Will you be here when I open my eyes?"

"Damn straight I will be."

Malik watched her fall asleep. He told himself she was safe, that it was over, but the knot in his chest wouldn't go away, one thought running on loop through his mind.

What if he and David had waited?

What if they'd come tomorrow or a week from now?

Fuck.

∾

KRISTI WOKE WITH A START, found herself looking into Malik's beautiful brown eyes. "It wasn't a dream."

He grinned. "I'm real."

"Thank God for that." She sat up, her head still aching. "I've never been so happy to see anyone in my life."

"How do you feel?"

"A little better."

It was dark now, the streets busy with traffic, okadas and tuk-tuks—motorbike taxis and auto-rickshaws—competing with buses, cars, and vans for space.

She rubbed the ache in her temple. "Where are we?"

The Nigerian man at the wheel met her gaze in the rearview mirror. "Croc City."

She glanced around, recognizing it now. "Kaduna."

He grinned. "You know Nigeria. I'm David Ayodele Olatunji. I'm a friend."

That didn't explain why David was here rather than the rest of the Cobra team, but Kristi didn't have the energy to ask and wasn't sure she should.

Malik took her hand, his touch warm and reassuring. "We're driving you to a private hospital so someone can check you out."

"No, not a hospital. I'm fine, really. I just need a hot shower, food and water, and a real bed." She could barely stand to be in her own skin. "I'll need antimalarials, too, and, well, clothes."

Everything she owned was in her dorm room.

Malik frowned, concern on his painted face. "We can handle that, but I'd feel better if a doctor had a look at you."

"We can send for my doctor, have him come to our hotel. He can look her over and take care of Obi's burned hand, too. Does that work for you?"

"Yes," Kristi said.

Malik gave in. "She's the nurse."

Kristi saw that Obi was sleeping. "Thanks for letting him come with us."

David made a left turn into the downtown area. "He told us all about you—how you saved his Uncle Jidda, how you stayed faithful to your husband, how you told them Malik would kill any man who touched you, how you helped him with his burned hand. You've got courage, Miss Chang."

"He's right." Malik squeezed her hand. "What you did was incredibly brave."

David stopped at a red light, looked back at Kristi. "How did you know Malik would come for you?"

Kristi looked into Malik's eyes, a lump forming in her throat. "I didn't. I... I wasn't sure anyone would come."

A part of her still couldn't believe this was real, that she was free—and safe.

"We're almost to the hotel." Malik caressed the back of her hand with his thumb. "You can take a shower in my bathroom. We'll order you food and get some bottled water and whatever else you need."

"Thanks, Malik—for everything."

David pulled into the hotel's valet entrance, rested a hand on Obi's shoulder to wake him. "Get her and the boy inside, Jones. We'll take care of the gear."

"Copy that." Malik climbed out, helped Kristi down, steadied her as she found her feet. "Dizzy?"

"Yeah. A little."

Malik hadn't forgotten Obi. "You okay, buddy? Just follow me."

Kristi motioned for him to follow. "Come, Obi. It's okay. We're safe here."

Obi followed them up the stairs and inside, his mouth

falling open at the sight of the high ceiling, marble floors, and the uniformed staff.

The staff stared back, probably shocked by Obi's ragged, filthy clothing and Kristi's dirty scrubs. Or maybe a fighter in camo and face paint with a rifle in his hands made them nervous. Kristi couldn't blame them either way.

Malik led them to the elevator, punched the call button. "We've got a couple of suites upstairs—one for us and one for David's bodyguards."

It sounded like heaven to Kristi. "As long as there's modern plumbing and a bed."

How strange it was to stand beside Malik again after all this time. It had been more than a year since she'd seen him or spoken with him.

And still he came for you.

The elevator doors opened, making Obi smile.

Kristi stepped inside, Malik close beside her. "Have you ever ridden in an elevator, Obi?"

"No, miss." He followed, his grin widening when the doors closed and the car began to move.

The motion exacerbated Kristi's dizziness. She threw out a hand to steady herself, but a strong arm went around her shoulder.

"I've got you."

The elevator doors opened, and Malik led them to a door down the hall and to their left. He unlocked it and stepped aside to let Kristi and Obi enter first, then followed them inside.

Malik shut the door behind him and began to peel off his tactical gear—eye protection, chest rig, body armor. "My room is through there. There's a bathroom with a shower and lots of clean towels. I think there are some toiletries, but feel free to use my stuff. I'll get Obi settled."

"Thanks." Kristi walked into his room, closed the door, and made her way to the attached bathroom.

At the sight of the shower, she couldn't get out of her filthy clothes fast enough. She stripped, turned on the water, and stepped under the hot spray.

Oh, it felt good!

She shampooed and conditioned her hair, a big, tender goose egg on her scalp where she'd hit her head. Then she scrubbed her skin until it glowed, the water at her feet running muddy brown as she rinsed off. It was only when she wrapped herself in a fluffy white towel, stepped out of the shower, and saw her bruised face in the mirror that the weight of the past four days hit her, images running through her mind.

Peter dragging her past slain security guards to the SUV. An enraged Jidda telling her to accept her fate as his concubine. Peter shooting Jidda, striking her, dragging her toward the hut. Peter pointing a pistol at her head, then falling dead to the ground.

Four endless, awful, terrifying days.

And Kristi broke, sobbing, all of the tears she'd held back finally spilling down her cheeks.

MALIK SAT ON THE SOFA, elbows on his knees, chin resting on his hands, only half listening as officers from the NPF questioned Obi about his time with the bandits, David acting *in loco parentis* for the kid. The doctor had arrived with a nurse a half hour ago to check Kristi. Malik had wanted to stay with her, to support her. He'd heard her crying in the shower earlier, her sobs making his heart constrict, making him want to hold her. But they hadn't seen each other for eighteen months. So, he'd held back, uncertain where they stood. He didn't want to crowd her or invade her emotional space.

Instead, he'd washed the paint off his face in David's bathroom and had gone with Bruno to a nearby mall, where he'd bought clothes and toiletries for both Kristi and the boy, who owned nothing but the rags on his back. The kid had already taken his first shower and changed.

He'd emerged smiling ear to ear. "I make baff up."

David had translated the Naija. "He says he's all dressed up."

"You look good, man."

Malik was glad the boy hadn't gotten caught in the crossfire.

Malik's phone buzzed.

Shields.

"Jones here."

"You got her! Oh, my God, Malik, I'm so relieved. We all are. What happened?"

Malik went through it, pausing so that Shields could put him on speaker. "We set up a recon north of the camp and called in to David's contacts when we got confirmation she was there. But the situation went south fast. One of the assholes decided to kill their leader and take Kristi for himself. We had no choice but to move in early."

"Just the two of you—against at least twenty-seven combatants?" That was Segal.

"Yeah." An image of Peter aiming that pistol at Kristi's head flashed through Malik's mind. If Malik hadn't already had the bastard in his sights... "David used a drone to create a distraction, while I opened fire. I was able to reach Kristi and get her and a boy to safety. The surviving bandits fled, and we drove back to the city."

"How is she?" Shields asked.

"She's with a doctor now. She has some bruises and probably a concussion. The boy told us that she bartered her nursing skills for physical safety, making them promise not to hurt her if she helped their leader, who'd been shot."

He didn't tell Shields that Kristi had also told them she was married and that her husband would be coming to kick their asses. He didn't feel like being ribbed.

"Smart woman." Shields sounded impressed. "And brave."

That was an understatement.

"Good job, man." That was Isaksen. "Samantha is going to be so relieved."

"Tower here. We've notified the State Department that she's been freed. Well done, Jones. When do you expect to fly out—"

Then the door to Malik's room opened. The nurse stepped out in her crisp white uniform and motioned to him.

"I've got to go. Thanks, everyone, for your help and support on this. I couldn't have done this without you." He ended the call, slipped the phone into his pocket.

He found Kristi sitting on the side of his bed wearing a hotel bathrobe, arms hugged around her waist, her hair still damp. She smiled when she saw him. "I'm going to live— thanks to you."

The doctor chuckled. "She has a concussion, and she's probably still dehydrated. She needs food, water, and undisturbed sleep. But she is strong and healthy—and very lucky. I've given her a new supply of antimalarial drugs, as well as some pills for pain. She should rest now."

Malik walked the doctor and nurse to the door and paid in dollars. "Thanks for coming."

He grabbed the bag of clothes and other things he'd bought for her and carried them into the room. "I picked up some stuff at the mall. I hope it all fits."

"Thanks, Malik." She stood, walked into his arms. "Thank you for coming after me. I don't know how you did it, but I'll never forget it."

"What else could I do?" Malik held her, the feel of her precious in his arms.

She didn't pull away but looked up at him. "I need to call my parents. I don't want them to worry."

"The State Department will contact them, but they'll want to hear from you. You can use my phone."

From the doorway, David cleared his throat. "When you're dressed, the officers from the Nigeria Police Force would like to ask you some questions, Miss Chang."

Malik looked over at him. "Now?"

"I'll be fine."

Malik left her so she could dress in private, closing the door behind him. "The doctor says she needs food, clean water, and rest. He gave her some pain pills."

"We must all eat. I will place an order. Have you ever had room service, Obi?"

The boy shook his head. "Room ... service?"

Five minutes later, when Kristi hadn't emerged, Malik went to check on her, tapping on the closed door with his knuckles then cracking it open when she didn't answer. "Kristi?"

She lay asleep on the bed, still wearing the bathrobe, the clothes he'd bought her untouched in the shopping bag beside her.

He covered her with a blanket and left her to sleep.

8

K risti woke from an uneasy sleep, her dreams a commotion of images, shouts, gunshots. She glanced around, confused. She was in the hotel in Kaduna with Malik. It was over. She was safe.

Malik was in the room with her. Somehow, he'd managed to fall asleep in an armchair, his long legs propped up on another, smaller chair. He woke when she sat up, instantly alert. "Are you okay?"

"I just need to pee."

When she stepped out of the bathroom, she found him standing beside the bed, wearing a T-shirt and pair of sweats and waiting for her with a fresh bottle of water.

"Drink." He handed it to her. "How's your head?"

"Thanks. I still have a headache, but it's better." She took more acetaminophen, swallowed it with a few gulps of cool water, and set the bottle down on her bedside table. "You don't have to sleep in the chair. That can't be comfortable. We've shared a bed before—a much smaller bed."

The beds at Amundsen-Scott were notoriously narrow.

Then it dawned on her that there might be someone in his life now.

"Sorry. I didn't think. You could have a girlfriend or wife for all I know."

You're babbling.

"Is that your way of asking if I'm connected?" He chuckled, a soft, deep sound. "I'm not. No wife. No girlfriend."

She wouldn't deny that she felt relieved at his answer. "I just wanted to say that you can sleep in the bed—if you're comfortable with that."

"I didn't want to presume, especially after what you've been through."

God, he was sweet.

She held out her hand. "Come."

He pulled off his shirt, took her hand, and slid beneath the covers beside her.

She turned onto her side, facing him. "You shaved off your beard."

"You haven't changed. You're as beautiful as I remember —even with bruises."

She reached out, touched his cheek. "I still can't believe you're here."

He caught her hand, pressed his lips to her palm, laced his fingers through hers. "Where else would I be? I'm the dude who kicks the ass of any man who touches my wife, right?"

"Right." She kind of liked hearing him say that word—*wife*.

He seemed to study her, concern on his face, his gaze soft. "How are you doing, Kristi, really?"

"I ... I don't know. It's all so ... raw."

"Do you want to talk about it?"

She didn't, not really, but the words began to spill out of

her. She told Malik everything, starting with the moment she'd spotted Peter watching her in the vaccine line. She kept it together until she reached the point when Peter had come up behind Jidda and shot him. Then tears came, and her body started to tremble.

"I didn't like Jidda at all. He killed people to save his own life. I'm sure he trafficked women. But I thought he and I had reached a truce. I agreed to be a nurse for him and his men as long as they kept their hands off me. When Peter shot him..."

Malik wiped a tear from her cheek. "You must have been terrified."

"I knew it was over. I had the scalpel, but I was afraid to use it on him because I knew he'd turn it against me. I told him you would kill him. I told him that no matter what he did to me, I would think only of you."

"God, Kristi." Malik drew her against him, and for a time he just held her, his body warm and solid in a world that had come apart. "I'm so damned sorry."

She sniffed, fought to stop her tears. "I've never been so afraid."

"I was there the whole time. I saw him kill Jidda. I saw him hit you. At that point, I knew we couldn't wait for the police or the army. We had to move in to stop that son of a bitch from hurting you."

"When you shouted for me to stay down, I thought I was hearing things, that it was just the bump on my head."

"I didn't want you to get caught in the crossfire."

"I can't believe it was just you and David. When I saw you, I thought everyone was here—the whole Cobra team."

He shook his head, frowned. "They're on another mission, but they gave us some support. Corbray and Tower —Cobra's two owners—went to the State Department and asked to be assigned to your rescue mission, but State wasn't interested. They wanted to wait and see how things played out."

Chills skittered down her spine. "*What?* The US government wasn't going to send anyone? They were just going to leave me with those bastards?"

Malik nodded. "They were sure you'd be ransomed back."

"That wouldn't have happened. Jidda never mentioned ransom. I would have been their captive for months." The thought left her feeling sick. "They could have done whatever they wanted to me. Peter talked about selling me. He would have ra—"

"Don't think about it. That's not how it turned out."

"Only because of you—and David, whoever he is."

"He's a Cobra asset—and a friend. Elizabeth Shields, one of Cobra's intel experts, got in touch with him and asked him to hook me up with weapons and ammo. He offered to help if I let him keep that drone."

Then it hit her. "Cobra is somewhere else, and the US government wasn't planning a rescue. You came on your own—without authorization?"

"Tower wanted me to wait until the current mission was completed, but I couldn't. I couldn't abandon you, Kristi. I turned in my resignation and got on a plane."

"Oh, Malik." The extent of what he'd done for her left her stunned, warmth swelling inside her chest. "You quit your job and risked your life for *me*?"

He ran a thumb over her cheek. "I'd do it again in a heartbeat."

Kristi could see in his eyes that he meant it.

～

MALIK SAW the gratitude on Kristi's face, but he couldn't claim all of the glory. "I couldn't have done it without David and Cobra. David let me borrow weapons, watched my back. Tower sent me off with the drone. Shields asked the Pentagon to divert a high-altitude military surveillance drone to do a flyover of the forests west of Kinu. I'd sent her photos someone had taken of the bandits' SUV, and she spotted the vehicle in the drone footage. That's how we found you."

"But none of that would have happened if you hadn't gotten on that plane."

He supposed that was true. "You deserve some credit, too, you know. You held those bastards off for four days using your brain."

"It wasn't enough in the end. I've never felt so helpless."

Malik had never known what it was to be in her shoes. He was stronger and tougher than most men. He had better endurance and advanced military training. He could fight his way out of almost anything. She'd had only her wits and that fucking scalpel to protect herself.

But Malik shouldn't have dredged all this up for her in the middle of the night. "You should get some sleep."

She slid a hand up his bare chest, thumbed the hair on his sternum, her touch striking sparks off his skin. "Kiss me, Malik."

It was on the tip of his tongue to refuse her, to remind her that the doctor had said she needed rest, but then she closed her eyes, offered him her lips.

Ah, hell.

He had never been able to resist her.

He brushed his lips over hers, gratified by her little gasp, the contact electric. He did it again and again, until she whimpered, until his lips tingled. Then he took her mouth with his in a deep, slow kiss.

Geezus.

It was as if no time had passed at all, the heat that flared between them as potent as it had been eighteen months ago. It was like nothing he'd experienced with any other woman. He was gasoline, and she was the flame.

Knowing what she'd been through, he tried to hold back, but there was no holding back, not with Kristi. She answered every caress of his lips, every stroke of his tongue with her own, making him work for control of the kiss, taking as much as she gave.

Her hands slid from his chest over his bare shoulders as she arched against him, the terrycloth bathrobe falling open so that her bare breasts pressed against his ribcage.

"Mmm." Blood rushed to his groin, and he couldn't resist touching her.

He took a full, lush breast into his hand, palmed it, rubbed the already taut peak with this thumb, smiling when she broke the kiss and arched into his touch.

"*Malik.*"

They hadn't seen each other in a year and a half, but he hadn't forgotten anything. He remembered what turned her on. He remembered the light on her face when she came. He even remembered her taste.

He nudged her onto her back, lowered his mouth to one dark nipple, and sucked.

Her exhale became a moan, and she arched again, her fingers finding their way into his hair. "*Yes.*"

He feasted, suckling first one nipple and then the other, tugging her with his lips, nipping her with his teeth, flicking her with his tongue until her hips moved beneath him in instinctive imitation of sex.

She reached down between them, slid her hand inside his sweats, and took hold of his erection, heightening his lust with skillful strokes.

Hell, yeah.

She hadn't forgotten anything either.

She spread her legs. "I want you inside me—now."

"Do you still have the IUD?"

"Yes."

"Are you sure this is what you want?"

"God, yes. *Fuck me.*"

Lust thrumming in his veins, he raised himself up, settled his hips between her thighs, and let her guide his cock inside her. And—*oh, God*—it was like coming home.

They moaned in unison, Kristi's head going back, her eyes drifting shut, her hands sliding beneath his sweats to grasp his bare ass.

Malik willed himself to relax. It had been a long time since he'd been with a woman—eighteen months to be exact—and if he wasn't careful, he was going to disappoint her.

He willed himself to think only of her, moving slowly at first, watching bliss unfold on her face with each deep stroke. "God, you're beautiful."

"You are ... so *good.*" Her nails bit into his bare ass, urging him on.

Malik drove himself into her. He was lost in her... drunk on her ... so fucking strung out on her.

Body melting. Headboard slamming against the wall. Mattress squeaking.

Sweet curves. Musk. Slick heat.

Harder. Faster.

Ah, yeah, she was close now, her eyes squeezed shut, her every exhale a moan.

On a razor's edge, Malik fought to hold on, his mouth taking off without him. "Fuck, yes. *Kristi.* You're too sweet ... I want... *Geezus.* I've missed you."

"*Malik!*" She cried out and arched beneath him, a look of rapture on her beautiful face as she came.

Malik drove her orgasm home then let himself go, his hips pounding into her, his control lost, his body driving headlong toward release. Then he shattered, orgasm scorching through him, searing body and soul as he spilled himself inside her.

For a time, they stayed that way—Malik inside her, the two of them breathing hard, their hearts pounding. Then Malik shifted onto his side, drawing her with him, cradling her in his arms. "Sleep, angel."

KRISTI WOKE the next morning to find herself in Malik's arms, daylight peeking around the curtains. "Hey."

"Hey." He kissed her forehead. "How did you sleep?"

Last night had been incredible. She'd wondered if the spark between them would be as strong as it had been in Antarctica. If anything, it was stronger. They'd picked up where they'd left off without losing anything in the interim.

She stretched, smiled, her body languid. "Better than I have in a long time. You?"

"Same." His brow furrowed and he touched a finger to her bruised cheek. "How's your headache."

She rubbed her fingertips gingerly over the lump on her scalp. "It's still there, but it's not as bad. I think you fucked away my concussion."

He grinned, his face so damned handsome it made her chest ache. "I don't think that's how it works."

"I'm the RN, remember?" She ran her hands up the satin skin of his chest, her fingers caressing the gunshot scar he'd gotten in Afghanistan. "I've missed you. Not just sex, though the sex is still incredible. I've missed *you*."

She wouldn't make the same mistake twice. She wouldn't hold back this time. She would tell him how she felt.

He caught her hand, raised her fingers to his lips, and kissed them, his expression serious. "I've missed you, too. I should have called, kept in touch. I thought about it a million times. I know we agreed to no strings, but I care about you."

"I suspected you might—you know, given that you quit your job and flew to the other side of the world to kill bad guys and rescue me."

It didn't make him laugh.

"When I heard you'd been abducted, it gutted me. I knew there was a chance I'd never see you again. I kicked myself in the ass for not staying in touch."

"I did the same thing. I was angry at myself for not reaching out and for not listening to you about changing my contract." Tenderness for him swelled behind her breastbone. "I put you in danger. You risked your life for me."

He kissed her. "Danger is what I do. For you, I'd do it again."

It thrilled her to think he cared about her that much, made her hope.

For what?

Don't go there, not yet, not now.

"Let's hope I never need to be rescued again. I think my crazy traveling days might be over. I..." Kristi sat bolt upright. "My parents! Oh, my God! I fell asleep last night before I could call them. I am the *worst* daughter in the world."

She jumped out of bed, naked, and glanced around, looking for her cell phone. Then she remembered she didn't have it. She'd been abducted without it.

"Go easy on yourself." Malik picked up his phone from the bedside table, held it out for her. "You were exhausted."

"It's not right to let my parents worry." She slipped into the bathrobe and took his phone. "Thanks."

"You're welcome." He climbed out of bed, gloriously naked, his body looking like some sculptor's masterpiece. "I'll go take a quick shower."

It was midnight in San Francisco, but she was pretty certain her parents would still be awake.

She dialed their land line.

Her father answered on the first ring. "Chang residence."

"Daddy? It's me, Kristi."

"Meimei!" The emotion in her father's voice put a lump in her throat. "We heard you had been rescued. We have been waiting and hoping to hear from you. Let me tell your mother so she can get on the other phone."

"I'm here. Are you okay, Kristi?"

"I'm fine, Mom." She did her best to maintain her composure. "I meant to call you last night, but I hadn't really slept for days. I've got a concussion, and I was so exhausted I just fell asleep. I'm so sorry."

"What matters is that you are safe. But tell me about the concussion." Her father was a neurologist, so, of course, he would have questions.

She answered them, then told her parents what had happened from the beginning, once again breaking up when she got to the part where Peter shot Jidda, struggling for words. "He would have..."

A big hand came to rest on her shoulder.

She glanced up to find Malik standing beside her, a towel around his waist, his face shaven. "Peter would have hurt me, but that's when Malik and his friend started shooting. Peter pointed a gun at my head, and I thought it was over. Then he dropped to the dirt, dead. Malik shot and killed him before he could shoot me."

"Who is Malik?"

Oh. Right.

"I met him in Antarctica. We became ... close." She was pretty sure they would understand what that meant without her spelling it out. "Remember the crashed satellite and the murder on station? Malik was part of the security crew that came down, retrieved the satellite parts, and caught the murderer."

"I'm confused," her mother said. "The person from the State Department told us that the Nigerian military and police had rescued you."

Now it was Kristi's turn to be confused. "No, that's not true. It was just Malik and his friend. The Nigerian police and army were still a few hours away. If Malik hadn't moved in when he did... It would have been a lot worse."

"Malik," her mother said. "That's an unusual name."

Yeah, her mother was curious. Kristi knew she would be.

Kristi shared a little. "He's a former Army Ranger. He works as a security operative with Cobra—or he did. He gave up his job to come after me."

"You must thank him for us," her father said. "That is a great sacrifice for a man to make. We are in his debt. I hope to thank him one day in person."

"When are you coming home?"

"I don't know yet. I don't know what happens next." Kristi realized she'd been talking for almost twenty minutes.

"I should probably go. I'm using Malik's phone. I need to take a shower and have some breakfast."

Her mother urged her to come home as quickly as possible, and her father gave her some tips about recovering from a concussion. Kristi reminded her father that she was an RN and asked her parents to pass on her love to Michael, her older brother. Then she ended the call.

Malik sat on the armchair, now dressed in jeans and a T-shirt. "How'd that go?"

She walked over to him, gave him his phone. "My father said to thank you and to tell you that they are in your debt. My dad wants to meet you."

Men's voices came from the other side of the door.

Malik kissed her. "I think the Nigerian police are back."

"Oh, right." She grabbed some clothes from the bag of things Malik had bought for her—panties, jeans, a purple leopard-print blouse. "Can you hold them off while I take a quick shower?"

"You've got it."

9

Malik sat on the sofa, cup of coffee in hand, listening while a female officer with the Nigeria Police Force asked Kristi to recount what had happened and then followed with an endless stream of questions. Kristi answered as best she could. At least they'd waited until she'd showered and had breakfast before they'd started on her.

David, who sat beside him reading a newspaper, leaned closer. "Relax, my friend. They are not going to hurt her. You and I are here, as are Bruno and Idris. I can see why you thought she was worth leaving your job and risking your life. She is fine—and smart and very brave."

David had already explained to Malik in private that the Nigerian National Police and the army were taking credit for rescuing Kristi. "It would not look good to say that a foreigner came into the country without authorization and did what the NPF and army hadn't done. Also, if they take the credit, no one has to arrest us for your forged documents."

"That works for me." It didn't matter to Malik anyway. He hadn't come here for glory or to get his face on the TV news. He'd come here for Kristi.

Only Kristi.

What was it about her that drew him to her? Hell, yes, she was smart and funny. She was beautiful, too—silky light brown skin, those sweet brown eyes, full lips, lush breasts with large, dark nipples. And, yes, they fucked like they were made for each other, their physical connection combustible. But it was more than that. Even sitting across the room, he felt a pull, a physical need to be closer to her.

Don't let this end the way it ended in Antarctica.

He wouldn't make that mistake again. Yeah, their situation was still complicated. His job—if he had one—took him from home every couple of weeks. She technically had three months left on her contract here, though they would probably release her, given the circumstances. Then again, she was stubborn enough to choose to stay. For all he knew, she had another job lined up somewhere far away when she was done here.

But none of that seemed to matter now.

"Did anyone leave or enter the camp while you were there?" the officer asked.

"Not that I saw, but they rarely let me go out of the hut. Some of the younger men went into the forest from time to time for firewood. One day, they caught a little duiker and dragged it into camp to eat."

Malik had no idea what a duiker was, but he was impressed that she did.

"Did you ever see them speaking by mobile phone to anyone?" the officer asked.

Kristi shook her head. "No."

"Did they ever talk about their activities in front of you? It's rare for a random group of bandits to be involved in human trafficking on their own."

"They talked about robbing people. When they argued about me, they mentioned selling women. I thought they must be sex traffickers." She seemed calm and collected, but Malik knew her well enough to see that this was hard for her. "Peter said that they usually shared women ... before selling them."

Motherfucker.

Malik didn't enjoy killing, but he'd make an exception for that bastard.

"Did you overhear any of the bandits talking about the people they worked for?"

Nearby, Obi quit playing around on David's smartphone, his gaze on Kristi now.

Kristi's brow furrowed as she considered the question. "I only knew that Jidda was in charge."

Obi went back to his game.

"Thank you, Ms. Chang." The officer glanced at her watch. "We are taking you to our main headquarters here in Kaduna for a short press conference."

What the hell?

Kristi looked just as surprised by this as Malik.

"You don't have to say anything to the press. We want to let the country know that you are safe and that the bandits have been killed."

So, the NPF wanted a PR victory and needed Kristi and her bruised face as a prop.

Malik was about to object when David leaned in again. "It's part of the deal."

He stood. "Wherever Kristi goes, I go."

The officer got a bemused expression on her face. "She will be safe. We will have armed officers with her at all times."

David stood, set his paper aside. "Mr. Jones is her husband. It's ... uh... a secret, and they are in love. You know how it is. Newlyweds."

Malik met Kristi's gaze, expecting to see embarrassment or awkwardness. Instead, her eyes held only warmth.

His pulse skipped.

Kristi stood. "I would like to have my husband with me."

"Very well—but no firearms." The officer gathered up her digital recorder and notepad and spoke into her mic to let the officers downstairs know that she was finished and would be coming down. "Mr. Jones is coming with us."

It was settled.

Kristi sat in the back of a police SUV with Malik, another vehicle ahead of them and one following behind, lights flashing. She spoke to Malik in a whisper. "Why do they get credit for rescuing me? It was you and David, not the NPF."

He leaned close, whispered in her ear, the minty scent of his toothpaste and the spice of his shaving cream tickling her nose. "It's a deal David cut with them last night when you were sleeping. I wasn't operating legally in the country. My firearms permits were forged. This way, they get the PR boost, and David and I don't go to prison."

Her heart melted. "Oh, Malik! You broke the law to come after me?"

His lips quirked in a lopsided grin. "You make that sound like a big deal."

For her, it *was* a big deal. If not for him, she would be trapped in a living hell.

She took his hand, held it tight. "Thank you."

They approached a building that was surrounded by a low concrete wall painted sulfur yellow, dark blue, and green and displaying a sign that read *Nigeria Police Force*. The parking lot was full—television vans with satellite dishes on top, SUVs, reporters, photographers.

The sight of it put butterflies in her stomach. She wasn't used to being in front of cameras. But if this kept the Nigerian authorities from arresting Malik and David, she'd do whatever they asked of her.

Malik looked around them, a worried frown on his face. "Is there a rear entrance, a way to get inside where she won't have to face reporters?"

"Yes, Mr. Jones. That is where we are going."

They drove to a gated entrance in back and straight up to the covered rear door, where several uniformed officers awaited them.

From there, it was a whirlwind. An officer opened her door and escorted her and Malik inside and down a hallway, where she was introduced to the police commissioner for Kaduna. A serious man with a razor-thin mustache, he wore a black beret and a blue uniform with several medals pinned to his chest.

"Ms. Chang, I am Commissioner Ahmed Busari. I'm glad to see you safe and unhurt. From what I hear, you are an incredibly brave and clever young woman."

"Thank you." She held out her hand, and they shook. "And thanks for all the Nigeria Police Force has done for me. I'm very grateful."

Malik held out his hand. "Malik Jones, sir."

The commissioner shook Malik's hand, his expression going hard. "I know who you are. Next time you take up arms against Nigerians, you might not be so lucky."

"Yes, sir."

Then a white man in a black business suit and blue tie walked up to them, an American flag on his lapel. "Ms. Chang, I'm Richard Hartley, the US consul general. I am so relieved to see you safe and sound. Your safety has been the top priority of my office for several days now."

Kristi forced herself to smile. She'd love to tell him exactly what she thought of his priorities. They hadn't done a thing to help her. "Thank you for your concern."

He was somewhat less cordial to Malik but shook his hand. "I think the State Department wants to have a chat with your boss, Mr. Jones."

"I resigned from Cobra before I left the US. Cobra wasn't involved."

Hartley stared at him. "You came alone? You've got balls of steel."

Malik threw Hartley's language back in his face. "She truly *was* my top priority."

"Yes, well, I think we're about to start." Hartley ushered Kristi away from Malik to a large conference room with a long table and podium at one end. "You can sit here beside me."

Cameras clicked and whirred, at least a hundred reporters filling the seats, cameras and microphones at the ready. CNN. BBC. Al Jazeera.

Had her abduction made international news?

Kristi took her seat, looked out at the sea of faces and lenses.

Hartley patted her hand in a way that felt patronizing. "Don't let them get to you."

She gave him her sweetest smile. "I just spent four days in a camp with murderers and sex traffickers and watched them die in a hail of bullets. I don't think the press is going to scare me."

He laughed awkwardly. "Yes, well..."

But then Commissioner Busari took the microphone.

Busari described her rescue for the press and was accurate in every detail—except for who'd actually done the rescuing. He went on at length about the bandits and assured the public that the NPF wouldn't rest until all bandits were in prison.

Then Hartley took the microphone. He thanked the NPF for rescuing Kristi and talked about the warm relationship between the United States and Nigeria. "Ms. Chang, would you like to say a few words?"

That hadn't been part of the plan. They'd told her she wouldn't have to speak.

Nevertheless, Kristi stood, walked to the podium. "I want to thank the NPF for their bravery in rescuing me. Without their intervention, I might not be alive right now. I also want to thank the Nigerian people for their kindness and warmth. I've worked as a nurse here for nine months, and I've come to love this country and its people so much."

At least that last part was true.

When she stepped away from the microphone, the room exploded with questions.

"Ms. Chang, can you tell us what happened?"

"Do you know who was behind this group of bandits?"

"Ms. Chang, were you tortured or abused in any way?"

She smiled, waved, and followed Hartley out of the room.

Hartley gave her a patronizing smile. "Well done."

As they walked down the hallway toward the room

where Malik waited, she saw a notice on one wall. It was a warning of some kind, a wanted poster with several faces. On it were two words that were somehow familiar: Sky Kings.

MALIK WAS glad to get away from the bureaucrats and reporters. Now, he could focus on getting Kristi home— unless she wasn't planning on leaving yet. "When we get back to the hotel, we can look at flights back to the US."

The consulate was bringing her belongings to the hotel, including her passport.

She didn't seem to hear him, her mind elsewhere.

"Kristi?" He squeezed her hand.

She looked up, startled. "I'm sorry. What did you say?"

"Are you okay?"

"Yeah." She smiled. "I'm fine. I was just thinking."

He repeated what he'd said. "That's assuming you aren't going to be stubborn and insist on fulfilling all twelve months of your contract."

She got a look of feigned innocence on her face. "Moi? Stubborn?"

"Hell, yes, you." Oh, how he wanted to kiss that smile off her lips.

"I feel bad leaving the other nurses and volunteers in a lurch, but I also have an obligation to my parents. They've been through hell worrying about me. My mother just wants me to come home. It would be selfish to make them worry more by staying."

Malik wouldn't argue with that. "I think your coworkers would understand. Besides, it might not be safe for you to stay. The men David and I took out had families, buddies. Everyone in Nigeria knows who you are now."

Her brow bent in a worried frown. "I hadn't thought about that. Do you think I could be a target?"

"I don't know, but it's a possibility. I could ask Shields to do a threat assessment if you want."

Kristi shook her head. "No need for that. The best thing I can do for my parents is to go back to the US. I don't want to worry them any more than I already have."

Malik knew her well enough to understand this was hard for her. Kristi wasn't the kind of person who gave up when the going got rough. "For what it's worth, I think you're making the right decision."

She looked up at him, eyes narrowed with suspicion. "You're biased. You didn't think I should come here in the first place."

"That wasn't bias. That was experience talking." He'd seen shit here that would sicken her, shit he'd keep to himself—for her sake.

They arrived at the hotel, and NPF officers escorted them up to their suite, where they found David talking on the phone and Obi sulking on the sofa.

Kristi sat beside the boy. "What's wrong?"

"He is sending me away." Obi clearly wasn't happy.

"What do you mean, buddy?" Malik felt for the boy. He didn't know the kid's full story, but a life of suffering had given him the eyes of an old man.

David ended his call and answered Malik's question. "I am taking him to live with my sister. She is a schoolteacher and lives here in Kaduna with her husband and three children. She can teach you to read and write, Obi. You will have a home with a mother and a father. That's better than living in an orphanage. Wouldn't you like to go to school and spend your days playing with other boys?"

Obi didn't look convinced.

Kristi sat down beside him. "It's okay to be scared. New things are always scary. But you are brave, Obi. I know how brave you are. If you can survive in a bandit camp, you can go to school and meet a new family. This won't be nearly as scary as that."

While Kristi spoke with Obi, Malik turned to David. "You're doing a good thing in finding a home for him."

"He cannot live with me, but he is a good boy. I don't want him to end up on the streets or turning to banditry himself."

No, they didn't want that.

Malik glanced over at the sofa, where Kristi was checking the kid's burns.

Then her head snapped up, a look of realization on her face. "Obi, can you go get the ointment the doctor gave you?"

The boy stood and walked toward David's room.

Kristi stood and walked over to David. "Who are the Sky Kings?"

David frowned. "Where did you hear about them?"

"It was something Obi said when I first treated his burns in the camp. He said Jidda was the only one who answered to the Sky Kings—or something like that. I saw a poster in the police station with those words on it, but I couldn't remember where I'd heard it before. It just came back to me."

"Pack your things—*now*. We must get you out of Kaduna as soon as possible." David stood, strode to his room, calling someone on his phone, his voice drifting back to them. "Get the helicopter ready. We'll be there within the hour—two adults."

Kristi looked up at Malik through wide eyes. "What's happening? Who are the Sky Kings?"

"I don't know." Malik typed a quick message to Shields asking for every bit of intel she could gather on them. "But I'm going to find out."

10

K   risti followed Malik into his room. "What's happening?"

"I'm not sure, but if David says it's time to go, we go. He'll fill us in when he's able." Malik picked up his duffel bag, fished around inside, and pulled out a small box. He opened the box, took something out, and walked over to her. "This is a GPS tag. Keep it hidden on your body somewhere. If we are separated for any reason, this will enable Cobra to track you. Do *not* take it off."

His words scared her. "Do you think that will happen?"

"I'm just doing everything I can to protect you."

"Thanks." Kristi took the strange little patch. It looked like a computer chip with a sticky adhesive side. She peeled off the adhesive and stuck the chip inside her bra.

Malik zipped his duffel bag. "Carry your bags to the door. If you need to use the restroom or get some bottled water, do it now."

Unanswered questions rushing through her mind, Kristi packed up the clothing and toiletries Malik had bought for her, rolled her bags to the door, and checked the contents of the little backpack she'd used as a handbag here. Her phone was there, but it needed to be charged. Lip balm. A comb. Breath mints. She made a quick stop in the bathroom and then grabbed four bottles of water out of the suite's refrigerator.

In less than five minutes, she found herself sitting with Obi in the backseat of Malik's rental, David driving, Malik riding shotgun. Bruno and Idris followed in two SUVs— David's fancy Mercedes and a Toyota.

David looked over his shoulder at Obi, a broad smile on his face. "You will love my sister. Everybody does. I will come to see you as often as I can. I promise."

Obi looked miserable. The poor kid had been through so much already. He'd endured the deaths of his parents and months with killers in that camp. He was probably terrified at being shuttled off to a new life where he knew no one. He'd clearly come to idolize David since the rescue, and now he was going to have to say farewell—another loss in his short life.

Kristi tried to reassure him. "I know you're going to miss David, Obi, and I know it's scary to go to a new home, but you're getting a new mother and father. It will be safe, not like the bandit camp. You'll have food when you're hungry, people to care for you, and a real bed."

"My sister makes the world's greatest *jollof*."

Obi reached out, took Kristi's hand. "You are going away?"

"Yes. I have to go home now. My family is worried about me."

Obi leaned against her, a pleading look in his eyes. "I beg, don go."

She hugged him, a hitch in her chest. "I will miss you, Obi. Do you want me to write to you?"

"Yes."

David seemed pleased by this. "You must learn to read, Obi, so you can read the letters Miss Chang sends you."

The boy nodded. "I will learn."

Kristi gave him what she hoped was a reassuring smile. "I know you will. One day, you can write letters to me. I would like that."

Kristi knew Kaduna enough to realize they were heading for one of the city's more exclusive neighborhoods. They parked in front of a large three-story home, and a woman in a bright red and yellow dress and matching *gele*, or head wrap, stepped outside.

"You two stay in the car. Someone might recognize you. Obi, come." David walked with Obi up to the door.

His sister welcomed the boy like a long-lost son, arms outstretched. "Welcome to your new home, Obi. I hope you will be happy here."

Lump in her throat, Kristi watched as David said goodbye.

"I will visit. I promise. You listen to your new mother and do as she tells you. If you behave and are happy here, she and her husband will adopt you, and I will be your uncle forever. Would you like that?"

A big hand closed over Kristi's, Malik's voice soft. "He's going to be okay, angel. Because of you, he's got a chance now."

Kristi blinked back tears. "What did I do?"

"You're the one who said we should take him with us, remember?"

"Oh. Right."

Malik frowned. "How's your head?"

Now it was her turn to laugh. "I'm fine. So much has

happened this past week. I'm just having trouble keeping up."

His phone buzzed. He let go of her hand, drew the phone out of his pocket, and tapped it to read the message, his expression going dark. "Fuck."

Kristi's pulse picked up. "What's wrong?"

"Shields just got back to me. I asked her to send whatever she had on the Sky Kings." He read Shields' reply. "'The Sky Kings started as a confraternity on college campuses but morphed into a criminal organization with international reach. They run heroin from Asia to Europe and the US. They also run major sex-trafficking operations in cities throughout Europe and in Russia and possibly the US. They are known for brutality, torture, and murder. If they were behind Kristi's abduction...'"

His words trailed off.

"If they were behind my abduction... then what?"

Malik looked up from his phone. "Then we need to get the hell out of the country before they come looking for payback."

Oh, God.

Kristi's stomach knotted. She'd just been on TV. If any of those Sky Kings had seen her, they would have some idea how to find her.

David opened the driver's side door and climbed in. "Now we head to the airport. You asked about the Sky Kings. You have kicked the hornet's nest, my friend."

Malik held up his phone. "Shields just got back to me. They're some kind of college fraternity that functions like a cartel."

"Yes, very much like a cartel." David started the engine, made a U-turn, the three of them waving to Obi as they drove away. "The men who abducted you must have been one of their strike groups, men who do their dirty work—robbing, trafficking, killing. They live on very little, while the members live like royalty. With any luck, the bastards saw the press conference and believe that the NPF rescued you."

"If they don't?" Kristi was afraid she knew the answer.

David met Malik's gaze, something passing between the two men. "Let's not worry about that yet."

THIS SHIT WAS GETTING REAL. As much as he trusted David, Malik had questions. "How connected are these bastards?"

"Most of the members live in the southern part of the country in the bigger cities, but their strike groups are everywhere. Members join in college, and they help one another in the business world afterward. They have eyes and ears in the police force, the military, the corporate world, and the government."

"How do we evade them?"

David merged onto the highway. "The plan is for you to get on a helicopter and fly to Abuja, where you catch a flight out of the country. I will drop you off, return your rental, and drive back to Abuja with Bruno and Idris—and the lovely drone."

That was a start.

"Are these assholes going to be able to connect you and Obi with us?" Malik didn't want to put David or the boy in danger.

David turned onto the main expressway, heading north. "I doubt it. I wasn't at the police station. No one at the bandit camp saw me. The imam won't talk. The only people who know about my involvement are my contacts in the army and the NPF and the officers who came to the hotel. If they were dirty, we'd be dead already."

Malik supposed that was true.

David went on. "My name wasn't on the hotel registry or your rental vehicle. Even if they had my name, all of my property, including my vehicles and aircraft, is owned by a corporation registered in the Cayman Islands. All my family's property is owned by this corporation, so Obi is also safe."

"Can't they just look up who owns the corporation?" Kristi asked.

Malik explained. "Corporate records in the Caymans are private. No one can gain access to that information. The owners have anonymity."

"Oh. That's useful."

David grinned. "In my line of work, I must be cautious, Miss Chang."

"I believe that."

Malik looked back at Kristi, saw the worry on her pretty face. She'd been through enough already. "What about the airport? Could they be waiting for us there?"

"Anything is possible." David slowed the vehicle, stopped, the traffic coming to an abrupt standstill. "*Wahala.*" *Trouble.*

"What is it? What's happening?"

"I don't know." David called Idris, spoke to him in rapid Naija.

The black SUV ahead of them pulled off the road, and Idris climbed out and strode along the side of the highway toward the source of the traffic jam. "He will find out what is happening."

"What about the drone?" Kristi asked.

"It would draw too much attention. Besides, it's in my Mercedes."

Malik was going to catch hell from Tower about that.

David's phone buzzed. "Idris says it is a roadblock. Men without uniforms. It could be the Sky Kings, or it could be SARS—the Secret Anti-Robbery Squad. Either way, it's bad news."

"What are we going to do?" Kristi's voice was calm, but Malik sensed her fear.

David dialed a number on his phone. "If we cannot get to the airport, we will bring the airport to us."

Malik understood what he meant, but Kristi probably didn't. "The helicopter will pick us up somewhere else."

David spoke to someone in Yoruba, then sent a text message to Bruno and Idris. "They will escort us to the old, abandoned airfield. The chopper will meet us there. I will park the rental downtown and call the company to retrieve it."

He made a U-turn and drove back into Kaduna, heading southeast this time. They passed through downtown and reached a run-down industrial area on the outskirts of the city, the sound of a helo passing somewhere overhead. There, inside a broken gate, Malik could see crumbling asphalt—the remnants of old runways. Waiting for them on the tarmac was a bright red Bell 407, its rotors running.

"Do you trust this pilot?" Malik didn't like the idea of depending on someone he'd never met.

"He, Bruno, Idris and the other staff know that if they betray me, there will be nowhere in the world for them to hide. So, yes, I do." David parked, and they all climbed out. "This is where we say goodbye for now, friend."

Malik shook David's hand. "Thanks, man. I couldn't have done this without you."

David chuckled. "That is the truth."

Kristi gave David a hug. "Thank you, David. Please give Cobra an address where I can safely send letters to Obi. Let him know how much I care about him."

"You have a good heart. I can see why Malik is mad about you."

Wait. What?

Okay, so David wasn't wrong. Malik *was* mad about her. He was out of his fucking mind over her. How else could he explain the past week?

Kristi kissed David on the cheek. "Please stay safe."

"You, too. Take care of her, Jones."

"You know I will."

Bruno and Idris had already loaded their bags onto the helo, so there was nothing left to do but cross the tarmac and climb aboard.

"Have you ever flown on a helicopter?" Malik hurried with Kristi toward the bird, her hair flying in the rotors' downwash.

"No." She didn't sound excited.

Bent low, he helped her board, climbed in beside her, and buckled his belt. Then he showed her how to wear her earphones and adjust her mic. "Can you hear me?"

She nodded. "Can you hear me?"

He took her hand, held it. "Lima Charlie, angel. Loud and clear."

As the helo gained altitude, he saw David, Bruno, and Idris driving away. Getting Kristi to safety was entirely on Malik's shoulders now. They had a long journey ahead of them and a lot of unknowns.

He wouldn't fail her.

～

SAMUEL KUTI WALKED into the warehouse where the nine survivors from Jidda's strike group had been taken. He knew the basic story already, thanks to their informant with the NPF. What he didn't understand was how *one man* could attack the camp in broad daylight, kill sixteen armed men, and escape unharmed with a woman.

The Sky Kings would want answers. If word got out that one of their camps had been attacked and sixteen of their men killed by an angry husband, they would lose face. That would be bad for business—and bad for Samuel.

Though the Sky Kings could be generous, they weren't forgiving.

The men sat on the dirt floor, silent, heads bowed, not one of them daring to look him in the eyes. They had arrived last night, all nine of them crowded into Jidda's old white Toyota and telling the same story. A man had flown a drone into the camp before killing the rest of the men and taking their female captive with him.

Samuel walked down the line and back again. "The first person to tell me how one man got the better of you will live with no punishment. Who will it be?"

No one spoke, nervous sweat beading on the men's foreheads.

"Can none of you even look me in the eyes like men?" He motioned for Akunna to step forward with the ropes. "Last chance."

Cowards.

Each one was gambling that he wouldn't be chosen.

"Take Mobo."

Mobo's eyes went wide. "No, sir! No! There is nothing more to tell!"

Akunna and Joshua dragged Mobo to his feet, Joshua holding him while Akunna tied his elbows together behind his back, making sure the ropes were tight enough to cut off Mobo's circulation. Then Akunna threw the long end of the rope over a beam and hoisted a screaming Mobo off the ground, suspending him there. The technique, called *tabay*, was excruciating—and effective.

Mobo writhed. "There's nothing to tell!"

Samuel walked up to him, looked into Mobo's contorted face. "How could one man kill sixteen of you? Did you not have weapons?"

"Yes! At first, we could not see him, only the drone. It flew through the camp. I'm telling the truth! Please let me down!"

"A drone flew through the camp, and what did you all do?"

"I was surprised! We all stared at it. Some of us shot at it. Then this man started shooting. He shot from the forest. Automatic weapons. Men fell. Jidda. Peter. I ran. I hid. I beg you! Don't do this to me!"

"A drone came out of nowhere. You stood there like idiots, not realizing that an attack was coming. Then, when the bullets began to fly, you ran?"

"Yes. Yes! I was afraid!"

"Did Jidda not give you orders to follow? Did you disobey him?"

"He was the first to die. Then Peter."

That explained some of it. Men were like sheep without a leader.

"You said the drone came first and then the bullets. What did Jidda command you to do when he saw the drone?"

"I ... I didn't hear!"

That split second of hesitation gave Mobo away.

Samuel turned to Akunna and Joshua. "It's cold in here,

don't you think? Let's light a fire beneath Mobo to keep him warm."

"No!" Mobo screamed, kicked. "I'm telling you the truth!"

"I don't believe you." Samuel stood back, ignoring Mobo's pleas as Akunna piled up kindling and bits of wood beneath Mobo and ignited it with a lighter.

"Peter killed Jidda! Peter killed Jidda!" Mobo shouted the words, then lapsed into screaming.

Samuel had to laugh. The fire hadn't harmed Mobo yet, and still he carried on as if he were being butchered. "Why would Peter kill Jidda?"

"For the woman! Peter wanted her. Jidda would not share. I told you everything! Put the fire out!"

Samuel nodded to Akunna, who kicked dirt over the flames. "Jidda wanted to keep this woman for himself, and Peter shot him to take her."

"Yes. Yes!" Mobo's tongue had been loosened, and the entire story poured out. "She made Jidda promise to let her go if she healed him. Jidda wouldn't let her go, but he protected her. He would not share her. Peter and the others planned it. Peter shot him in the back and dragged the woman toward the hut to have his way. Then the drone came."

Samuel worked through Mobo's gibberish. Jidda had made a deal with the nurse—her help in exchange for freedom. Of course, Jidda couldn't let her go, but he'd done the best he could by claiming her and protecting her from the others. He'd kept his word as best he could. Peter, who had always been jealous of Jidda, had shot him in the back. The woman's husband had clearly taken advantage of the confusion to distract them with the drone—and then attack.

Then something hit Samuel. "You said 'others'? Did others help Peter?"

"Others planned it with him."

Samuel got right in Mobo's face. "Which others? Are any of them here?"

"Yes! Yes!" Mobo looked up. "Uvo. Chibunna. Everyone else was killed."

Leaders were chosen by the Sky Kings, not by Samuel or the men who served beneath him. Loyalty was an absolute. Betraying one's leader meant death.

"Were you one of these conspirators, Mobo?"

Mobo writhed. "No! I had just come back with firewood."

"Take him down." Samuel walked over to Uvo, who sat trembling in the dirt. "Is this true? Did you conspire with Peter to kill your leader over a *woman*?"

Uvo looked up at him, the truth mingled with terror on his face. Then Chibunna jumped to his feet and bolted for the door.

Joshua stopped him, threw him to the dirt.

"Peter got what he deserved, and now you will, too." Samuel turned to Akunna. "Kill them."

But what was Samuel going to do about this woman and her husband?

Oh, he didn't care about the woman, not really. Jidda had made her a promise, and Samuel could respect that. But her husband—that was another story. Samuel needed to find him and take him to Lagos, where the Sky Kings would make him pay in blood.

11

K risti walked with Malik across the tarmac toward the terminal, rolling her bags alongside her. "That was actually nicer than flying in a plane."

"It's not always that smooth." He glanced up from his phone, a lopsided grin on his face, duffel bag on his back like a backpack. "Helicopters like to crash."

"You tell me this now?"

"I didn't want to scare you."

She had to ask. "Have you ever been in a helicopter crash?"

"Twice."

"*Twice*?" *Good grief!* "And you're brave enough to climb aboard anyway?"

He seemed to find this funny. "Risk goes with the job."

He stopped walking, his attention back on his smartphone.

"Are you checking in with Shields?" Kristi hoped one day she got to meet this woman who had done so much to help her.

"Yeah. Also, I bought two plane tickets to Cairo with

Cobra's credit card. Tower can chew my ass off when we get home. I'll pay them back. I just want to keep my name off the transaction."

"Cairo." Kristi had always wanted to visit Egypt. "That's exciting."

Inside the terminal, Malik printed their boarding passes, and they went to stand in line at the ticket counter to check their bags.

"I can't believe I'm going home."

They reached the counter, and Malik showed the woman their tickets and passports. The woman thanked him. Then she lifted her gaze, looked at Kristi and Malik—and her eyes went wide. She tried to cover up her reaction with an uncertain smile, but Malik had seen it, too.

He leaned over the counter, looked down at something, then took Kristi by the arm. "Grab your bags. We're leaving."

"What?" Pulse pounding, Kristi grabbed her luggage and hurried after Malik, aware now that people were staring at her.

"She's got photos of the two of us. I bet everyone in the airport does. The bastards are here, and they're looking for us. Hurry." Malik opened the door. "Keep walking. Don't ask questions."

They left the terminal and crossed the street, where Malik flagged down a taxi. They climbed inside, and Malik asked the man to drive them to the Abuja Market, the dark monolith of Aso Rock visible on their right. While Kristi did her best not to let people see her face, Malik got back on his phone again. The taxi moved erratically through the traffic, dodging motorcycles, okadas, trucks, and tuk-tuks. When they arrived at the market, Malik hailed another cab and had the driver take them downtown.

"You can let us off here," Malik told the driver. "My cousin's business is just over there."

Malik paid, and Kristi found herself standing on the street with her bags and no idea what was happening. He pointed. "Over there."

Kristi looked and saw Praise the Lord Car Rental. "We're renting a car?"

"We need to disappear." He set off.

Kristi hurried just to keep up with his long strides. "But the roads aren't safe either. There are bandit gangs, terrorists, militant groups..."

He slowed his pace, letting her catch up. "Nothing is safe, Kristi. Public transportation isn't safe, and it's unreliable at best. We have to go with what gives us the best chance of evasion and escape. That's how we survive."

Dread settled in the pit of her stomach. "I thought it was over."

He stopped once more, took her face between his palms, his brown eyes looking deep into hers. "I know, angel, and I'm sorry. You've been incredibly strong through all of this. I need you to be strong just a while longer. Can you trust me?"

"Of course." There was no one on earth she trusted more than Malik, especially in these circumstances. "I'm ... I'm just not used to this."

"I know."

While Kristi waited out of sight on the side of the building, Malik went inside. Careful to keep her face averted from the busy road, she drew deep breaths, fighting to quell a rising sense of panic.

Don't lose it.

She couldn't lose it. She couldn't make Malik's job harder than it already was. The man had quit his job and broken the law to save her life. The least she could do was keep it together.

Cars drove by, hip hop and gospel music blaring from their speakers. A young man in jeans and a black T-shirt passed, earbuds in his ears, phone in hand. A Muslim woman in a white hijab walked by, three small children hurrying after her. It was an ordinary urban scene, something a person might see in any big city on earth. New York. London. Amsterdam. And yet Kristi couldn't shake her fear.

It's post-traumatic stress.

That's what she would have told a patient who'd gone through what she'd endured. And yet, her diagnosis as an RN didn't bring her any relief or comfort.

A black Toyota Rav4 with tinted windows drove around the corner and stopped right in front of her.

Kristi's pulse spiked, and she took a step backward, some thought about running half-formed in her mind.

The driver's side door opened.

Malik.

He climbed out, grabbed her bags. "Let's go."

She hurried around to the passenger side, hopped into the seat, and buckled up, relieved to be off the street. "Where are we going? Do you know?"

Malik turned onto the main road. "It's roughly a twelve-hour drive from Abuja to any of the borders or to the coast."

That was true. The capital city had been built in the center of the country to give people from all regions equal access.

"Cameroon to the east is a mess right now—war, terrorism, refugees. The population in Nigeria gets denser toward the south, and the coast and Gulf are plagued by pirates. Heading north leads us into Niger and the Sahara Desert—a bad plan unless you're a camel. That leaves Benin. There's an international airport in Parakou. That's a thirteen-hour drive west."

Thirteen hours.

To Kristi, that seemed like an eternity.

MALIK TURNED ONTO THE STREET, hoping he'd bought them some time. They had a long drive ahead of them, and so many things could go wrong along the way. All these Sky King assholes had to do was connect Kristi to this rental vehicle, which surely had anti-theft technology and was traceable. "Are you ready for a road trip?"

"I guess so. Do you know how to get to Parakou?"

"Yes." He knew Kristi was afraid, and he couldn't blame her. He reached over, took her hand, tried to reassure her. "We're loading up on supplies first—water, food, gas cans, and sunglasses for you if you don't have them."

"Good idea."

"If there's anything you need, you should make a list."

She answered without hesitation. "Chocolate. Lots of chocolate. A woman can only take so much bullshit before she needs chocolate."

She was so serious about it that Malik was tempted to laugh, but his survival instincts, honed through a decade of warfare and experience with two older sisters, warned him against that. "Chocolate. Got it. Anything else?"

"Hand sanitizer. Wipes. Soap. Do you have a first aid kit?"

"Yeah. It's in my bag." He drove them to Best Choice Supermarket, parked, and retrieved one of David's SIG P320s from his duffel in the backseat. He'd kept both pistols, along with the M4 carbine. "You stay in the car with the windows up and the doors locked."

But she'd seen the pistol. "I thought the guns belonged to David."

"They did. He donated this and the carbine to our cause, along with some spare ammo. He just doesn't know that yet."

Kristi gaped at him. "You *stole* them?"

"*Stole* is a strong word." He tucked the SIG in the rear waistband of his jeans, covered it with his T-shirt. "I *borrowed* them. There's a difference."

"How did you plan to get them onto the plane?"

"Airport security here is notoriously lax."

"Don't get me wrong. I'm *glad* you have them. I just don't want David coming after us, too, or you getting arrested."

"Don't worry about that. I'll square things with David when you're safe."

He climbed out, locked the vehicle behind him, and walked into the store. He worked his way down a mental shopping list that included everything Kristi had mentioned, as well as a pair of sunglasses for her, two cases of bottled water, and two five-gallon plastic gas cans that he would fill on their first refueling stop.

The cashier didn't bat her eye at the two dozen chocolate bars.

Malik bagged their supplies and paid with the Cobra card once again. He gave the cashier a nod, and left without speaking, rolling the cart out to the vehicle. He loaded everything up, returned the cart, then climbed into the driver's seat and handed Kristi her chocolate. "Is that enough?"

She glanced inside, a look of relief coming over her face.

"Oh, thank God! Snickers! Twix! Baby Ruth! Dairy Milk bars!"

Malik got them back on the road, working hard to keep the smile off his face as she ripped into a Snickers bar. "How long has it been since you've had chocolate?"

"Almost nine months." She moaned, a sound of pure female pleasure that hit him square in the groin. "Mmm."

It's the chocolate, dude.

His brain knew this. His dick didn't.

He ignored his dick and switched on the vehicle's navigation system, choosing English for the language and tapping in their destination. He excluded toll roads and asked it to reroute around heavy or stalled traffic. He hoped that would steer them clear of any surprise roadblocks.

He glanced over, saw that Kristi had devoured that Snickers and was now licking her fingers.

A memory of her going down on him in the greenhouse at Amundsen-Scott flashed into his mind, making his jeans uncomfortably tight. The woman knew how to use her tongue. That was for damned sure.

Eyes on the road, bro.

He turned on the sound system and synced it with his phone, while she tore into another Snickers. "Are you going to eat the whole bag?"

He'd never understood the mystical connection between women and chocolate.

She glared at him, chocolate on her lower lip, her mouth full. "Are you judging?"

"Hell, no. After what you've been through, eat all the chocolate you want."

"That's what I'm thinking."

He was glad she was recovering her smart mouth. That

was one of the things about her he'd enjoyed the most. "Is hip-hop okay?"

She nodded, licking the chocolate off her lip.

Fuck.

With Drake dropping beats, Malik headed west, making his way toward the A124, his cock half hard. He needed to get his mind off sex and stay sharp. He couldn't afford to be distracted with fraternity mafia assholes hunting for them.

You wanted to get to know her better. Now is your chance.

There were a lot of miles between here and Parakou.

"I want to hear what you've been doing these past nine months. How was life here before this shit happened?"

HER CHOCOLATE CRAVING TEMPORARILY SATISFIED, Kristi did her best to recap nine months of nursing without boring Malik to tears. Giving vaccines. Prenatal screenings. Setting and splinting broken bones. Assisting with emergency surgeries. STI screenings. Treating infections. Handing out mosquito nets. Catching babies.

"We had a laboring mom who tried to reach our mobile medical unit, but she started to deliver on a rutted dirt road that passed through the village. I grabbed some gloves and a towel and ran out there. She squatted down and pushed out the first baby, a little boy, and then I realized there was another."

"Wow. Twins?"

"I only had one towel, so I took off my lab jacket, caught the second baby, and wrapped him in that. By then, some men had come with a litter. They carried her and the babies, still attached to their umbilical cords, the rest of the way to the unit."

She couldn't help but smile at the memory. "It's funny, but I had to come all the way to Nigeria to do the kind of nursing I love."

"What do you mean?"

"At home, nursing is as much about hospital policy, insurance companies, and lawyers as it is patient care. This patient needs that test, but insurance won't cover it. That homeless woman has nowhere to go, but the hospital orders you to discharge her anyway. I'd be in the middle of setting up an IV on someone in serious pain, and the finance people would walk in and ask for money."

"Shit. Yeah, we've got problems."

"The bureaucracy wears nurses down. You can't necessarily give your patients the attention and care they deserve. But here, there's none of that. There are limited resources, and so many people live far from adequate healthcare. Few of the hospitals here are up to what I consider modern standards of care. But every day was about using my skills and the available resources to save lives and stop suffering. I made a difference every day. That's what I wanted to do when I became a nurse."

"That's amazing. I mean it, Kristi. Your parents must be so proud. They're doctors, right?"

She was impressed that he'd remembered. "My father is a neurologist, and my mother is a pediatrician. When I showed an interest in medicine, they expected me to become a physician. But I'd spent enough time in hospitals as their daughter to see that nurses, not doctors, do most of the patient care."

"And that's what you wanted to do."

"Yes." She remembered her parents' dismay when she'd applied to the nursing program instead of pre-med. "I think they were disappointed at first. They tried to talk me into med school, but when I gave them my reasons, they came around."

"You're a damned good nurse. I've seen you in action, remember?"

"When Thor was shot." She remembered. "Working here in Nigeria is the most rewarding thing I've ever done. I loved every moment of it, even on the hard days. I'm going to miss it so much."

They'd reached the outskirts of Abuja now, the city falling behind them, the setting sun low on the horizon ahead.

"Did you lose people?"

"Yes, sometimes. But it was hard in other ways, too."

"What do you mean?"

"I treated girls who'd been freed or escaped from Boko Haram. That was tough. To hear their stories... It broke my heart." It was some of the worst violence Kristi had ever seen on a human body. "One had been raped pregnant at age fifteen. She managed to escape and gave birth to a boy. Both had contracted AIDS from her attacker. When we found her, it was too late to save her baby, but we got her on good medications. Even after all of that, she was resilient enough to take in two little boys orphaned by Boko Haram. She's just a kid herself, but the three of them are a family now."

"Geezus." Malik took her hand. "You don't know how much I wish we could take those Boko Haram fuckers out for good."

"When I was abducted, I thought at first that they were to blame. I thought about that girl, about all of those girls and how brave they were. I couldn't help but think about what had happened to them and wonder if that's what was going to happen to me, too."

"Not as long as I'm alive." Malik looked over at her, sunglasses hiding his eyes, his grip on her hand tightening. "I know what they're capable of doing. That's why I couldn't wait. That's why I had to come, even if I came alone."

She raised his hand to her lips, kissed it. "I'll never be able to thank you enough."

Lips that had kissed her senseless curved in a soft smile. "You already have."

How could a man who'd spent his adult life at war be so sweet?

"Did I bore you to death with all the medical stuff?"

"No, you didn't bore me. I asked, remember?" He changed lanes, merged onto a highway, the traffic light. "I'll let you in on a secret. When you and I said goodbye at Amundsen-Scott, I wished that I'd taken the time to get to know you better."

"I felt the same way."

"Now we've got another chance."

12

Malik pulled over at the first filling station they saw, uncertain how many miles lay between them and the next one. "I think this place has restrooms. Take advantage of it while you can. There aren't many public restrooms here, and the ones that exist are pretty disgusting."

"I've lived here for the past nine months, remember? Do you have any Nigerian money? They might charge."

He reached into his wallet, drew out a ten. "That ought to be enough. I think I've got a baseball cap to help you hide your hair, too."

He grabbed it out of his duffel, handed it to her. "Try not to let anyone see your face, and pretend you don't know me if we run into each other inside."

She tied up her hair, hid it under the cap. "Got it."

SIG tucked in the waistband of his jeans, he watched as she made her way indoors. Then he topped off the fuel tank and filled both gas cans. He wanted some insurance that they wouldn't run out of fuel if they were forced to leave the highway and take backroads. When he was done refueling, he went inside to pay, entering the building just as Kristi was walking out.

She didn't so much as look at him.

He paid for the gas and the restroom, took a leak, and then walked back out to the vehicle. While Kristi sat inside with the windows up rubbing her hands furiously with hand sanitizer, he went to work, searching for the anti-theft GPS tracker. It would be small, not much bigger than a deck of cards. Based on experience, he checked beneath the engine and found it attached by magnets to one of the struts.

He ripped it off, tossed it into a trash bin, and got back into the driver's seat.

"What was that?"

"It was a GPS tracker—an anti-theft device. I wanted to get rid of it so they can't track us if they connect us to this vehicle."

"Shit. Do you think they know where we are?"

"No." He didn't want her to worry unnecessarily. "If they did, their trail ends here, near the intersection of two highways, one heading north and the other heading south to Lagos. Once they realize we didn't catch a plane, I'm sure they'll think we're on our way to Lagos."

They set off again, merging back onto the A124.

"What do your parents think of you flying off to Nigeria by yourself to risk your life rescuing some woman they haven't met?"

That was a question he hadn't expected.

"My parents don't know about my missions. They don't ask, and I don't tell. Operational security. I couldn't share information when I was with the Rangers, and I don't share it now."

"Don't they worry?"

"I'm sure they do, but they've learned to live with it. They didn't want me to enlist. They wanted me to go to law school."

"Law school?"

"My mom is a district court judge. My old man teaches law at Emory University. My older sisters both studied law, but only one practices. The other runs a restaurant in Marietta, outside Atlanta, with her husband, Dustin."

"God, that sounds like my family, only lawyers instead of doctors. They're proud of you, though, right? I mean... how could they not be?"

Malik was touched by her pride in him. "I think they've come around, but they did everything they could to talk me out of it. My dad told me he hadn't put eighteen years into me only to have me die in some godforsaken desert somewhere. He just didn't understand."

"Why did you choose the army over college and law school?"

"I couldn't stand the thought of spending more time in school or working behind a desk for the rest of my life. I didn't want to spend my days in an office—being cooped up indoors, talking on the phone, wearing a suit and tie. Hell, no. I wanted to do something physical. I wanted to be out in the world and a part of something bigger."

"Why not sports? Or becoming a firefighter? Or a park ranger?"

"I was sixteen when the Twin Towers fell. They turned on the TV in our classroom just after the second plane hit. I saw the first tower fall. It hit me that someone had to be willing to go after the bad guys so that everyone else could live in peace."

Kristi's heart melted to think of Malik as a boy, just four years older than Obi, deciding to put his life at risk for his country. "That's more noble than my response. I was twelve. I worried that terrorists were going to attack San Francisco next."

"It was a hell of a time to be a kid."

"So, you joined the army and said, 'Hey, I want to be a Ranger.'"

He laughed. "If only it were that easy. I enlisted, sailed through basic and airborne training, and then volunteered for RASP—the Ranger Assessment and Selection Program. After that, I had to complete Ranger School."

"Is it as grueling as they say?"

"It's pretty tough, but I was ready for it—physically fit, mentally prepared for the challenge, and hungry to prove myself." He'd made it through and had worn his beret and gold Ranger tab with pride. "I won't lie. Graduation was the proudest day of my life."

"I would love to see you in your uniform. I bet you look *hot*."

He liked where her mind was going. "Yeah? I've got it all at home."

"How about you put it on—and I'll take it off?"

"Angel, it's a deal."

His phone buzzed, made Kristi jump.

Shields.

Malik pushed a button on the console. "You're on speaker."

"I just wanted to let you know that one of David's contacts came across men who were showing your picture to businesses and cab drivers around Abuja. They weren't wearing uniforms, but they were armed. He guesses—and I concur—that they're associated with the Sky Kings."

Fuck.

That wasn't the news Malik wanted to hear, but it wasn't surprising. "Where'd they get my photo?"

"David says it was a clear shot of you at police head-quarters."

"Copy that."

"David also said to tell you you're a bastard for stealing the SIGs and the carbine, but under the circumstances, he's glad you did. He'll consider it a loan."

Malik chuckled. "Tell him I'm grateful."

"Your GPS trackers are working. Keep them on you. You two stay safe."

"You, too." He ended the call, glanced over to find Kristi watching him, her eyes shadowed by fear.

"There's no doubt then. These bastards are after us."

Malik took her hand. "Fuck them."

THE SUN HAD SET NOW, scattered headlights moving toward them in the dark, red taillights moving away, the savanna on either side of the highway cloaked in darkness.

Kristi had to focus on her breathing to keep her panic at bay, but Malik didn't seem worried. "How do you stay so calm?"

"When someone comes into your ER all shot up, what keeps you from panicking? I've watched you work, remember? Samantha was hypothermic. Isaksen was hypothermic and halfway to Valhalla from blood loss. You had two people on the brink of death, and you were calm and cool."

"It's training. I know what I'm doing. We quickly assess a patient and treat the most serious problems first."

"That's how it is for me, too. This is what I'm trained to

do. I triage our situation, work out the most likely scenarios, and try to reduce our risks before anything happens."

Kristi saw where he was going with this. "There's one important difference. If something goes wrong in the ER, I'm not the one who dies."

He grinned, his teeth flashing white. "You've got me there."

"When they abducted me, I remembered what you said about embracing your mortality and surrendering hope. I tried, but I couldn't. I don't know how to do that."

Malik took her hand again. "I'd be surprised if you did. It's not part of your job description. Your work is all about life, Kristi. You catch babies, treat sick people, help with surgeries. I take lives, but you save them. I respect the *hell* out of that."

The way he said it made her feel special, as if being an RN were a big deal. Still, she had to ask. "Does it get to you? Do the people you've had to kill stay with you?"

"I don't regret killing terrorists—or those men at the camp. They worked hard to earn a bullet." He looked over at her, his face illuminated by the faint light of the GPS screen. "Mostly, it's the buddies I lost that hurt, the men who died when I got back alive. But that's not happening this time. We're *both* going to make it home."

The steel in his voice helped soothe the anxiety that had gnawed at her since she'd learned who and what the Sky Kings were. "Thank you, Malik."

"For what?"

"Everything." Her stomach growled.

"You hungry? There are some snacks in the back—chips and such. I've got some MREs in my duffel bag."

"MREs?"

"Meals Ready-To-Eat. Pre-packaged army food."

"Ew." She could only imagine what those were like. "That sounds scary."

That made him laugh. "You have no idea."

She took off her seatbelt, and leaned between their two seats to dig around in the bags of supplies. "Oh, you got plantain chips. I love those."

There were also crackers, a jar of peanut butter, cashews, and rice cakes.

"Oh, man." Malik moaned. "Your sweet ass is *right there*, right next to my face, but I have to keep my eyes on the road."

She wiggled her butt to tease him. "Focus on your driving, soldier. When we get home, you can grope my ass all you want."

"Yes, ma'am."

Then everything changed.

"Kristi, get down!"

On a punch of adrenaline, she slipped into the backseat and got down on the floor, her cheek pressed against his duffel bag. "What's going on?"

"There are two white Toyota trucks full of armed men speeding up the highway behind us, gaining fast."

Kristi's pulse tripped. "Do you think it's them?"

"Hard to say. Whoever they are, they're not friendly."

She heard the roar of an engine coming up behind them, headlights illuminating the interior of their rental. The seconds ticked by like hours, at least one truck right on their tail. Had these bastards connected them to this vehicle? Were they trying to read the license plate?

Then the roar grew louder—and passed by.

She let out the breath she'd been holding. "Did they pass us?"

"Yes, but stay down until I know what's going on."

The minutes crept by, then the vehicle slowed.

"It looks like traffic is stopping up ahead. I think they put up a roadblock."

"Does that mean they traced us to that filling station?"

"I'm not going to hang around to find out. There's an exit just ahead."

She heard the turn signal click on, and the vehicle veered to the right, the noise of traffic falling behind them, the exit taking them slightly uphill.

"Yeah, they threw up a roadblock. I can see them about a half mile ahead. They used their trucks to block the road, and now men with guns are searching cars."

"What are we going to do?"

"It looks like we're taking the scenic route to Benin."

And Kristi knew they wouldn't be flying home tomorrow, either.

MALIK TURNED off the music and followed the exit into Gulu, a small town surrounded by farms. He saw a gas station and decided to risk a refueling stop. "Stay back there and keep out of sight. I'm going to top off the tank again."

"Okay."

He climbed out, refueled, and walked inside to pay. The young clerk was too focused on a small television to notice him. He walked back to the vehicle, thinking through their options—not a complicated process when there weren't many.

If they stayed on the highway, they'd travel faster, but they'd also face the very real threat of roadblocks and capture. If they left the highway, they'd have a much longer trip on roads plagued by bandits and might lose access to cell service and gas stations.

But the biggest obstacle was the river.

No matter which road they took, they had to cross the Niger River to get to Benin. He remembered Shields telling them in a briefing on one mission that there weren't many bridges crossing the river—at least not bridges capable of supporting vehicles. That was a problem.

If he were one of these fuckers, he'd use the bridges as chokepoints—a sure way to catch anyone traveling by car or bus.

He climbed behind the wheel. "Stay down for just another minute. I'm going to pull over on that side road ahead. I need to look at a map."

"Did we lose navigation?"

"No, not yet." He drove to a spot beneath some overhanging trees and parked. "Okay. You're good."

While Kristi crawled over the console into her seat, he sent a quick sitrep to Shields. Then he called up a map of Nigeria on his phone, blew it up until he found Gulu, and studied the surrounding area.

"If we bypass the roadblock and get back onto the highway, we'll eventually cross the Kaduna River at a little town called Wuya. Then we could either continue northward to cross the Niger at Kainji or veer southwest to cross it at Jebba."

"Which do you think is safer?"

"Neither." He scrolled around, looking for a solution. "Bridges are natural bottlenecks—places where it's easy to stop and screen traffic. If I were trying to catch someone, I'd use them as chokepoints."

"Do we know for sure those guys were Sky Kings?"

"No, but we can't take any chances."

"Then what do we do? We can't drive across the river. It's too deep and wide. The SUV won't fit in a boat, even if we had one. We can't swim across—not unless we want to be crocodile bait. I don't know about you, but I don't want to be eaten."

He couldn't help himself. "But you taste *so* good."

"Stop." But she smiled.

While she opened the peanut butter and crackers, he searched for a solution, looking for smaller bridges, railway bridges, even pedestrian bridges. "There. We'll take back roads toward the Okobi Wildlife Preserve. We'll try to cross on the old railway bridge there. That way we won't have to cross the Kaduna River at all."

He typed the coordinates into the vehicle's navigation system.

"What about trains?"

"According to the map, it's not an active rail line."

"Is the bridge safe?"

"It was built for freight trains, so I'm sure it can hold us —if it's still standing."

"Maybe we should ditch the SUV and hire a boat."

He'd thought about that. "We could do that and rent or steal another vehicle on the other side. But I see that ending in one of two ways. Either the boat owner or witnesses sell us out, or they and their families end up dead. The fewer people we drag into our situation, the less collateral damage we leave behind."

"Oh, God. I hadn't thought about that."

He started the engine, drove back through Gulu, and crossed over the highway, where traffic was backed up for a mile and the exit they'd taken was now blocked.

Kristi's jaw dropped when she saw. "We barely got away."

While she passed him a dinner of crackers covered in

peanut butter, Malik watched the rearview mirror, leaving Gulu behind them and muting the navigation system, which kept trying to get them to turn around. Farms quickly gave way to scrubland crisscrossed by dirt roads and deepening forest. He followed the roads, moving steadily southwest.

But out here, far from other sources of light, the vehicle's headlights were like beacons. Anyone hiding on the forested hillsides would see them.

He stopped, turned off the vehicle.

"What's wrong?"

"It's time to switch gears. I have no idea what we'll run into out here, so I want to be ready. I'm going to move a few things around, position my firearms, and grab my night vision goggles in case I need them."

He climbed out, got out the M4 carbine and the other SIG, along with spare magazines, which he arranged near his seat. Then he took his helmet out of his duffel bag and settled it on his head. He flipped down the NVGs and turned them on to check them.

"Whoa."

Staring straight at him from a nearby bush was a big, fat warthog.

13

"Malik? What is it?"

"*It* looks like a warthog." Malik didn't sound afraid, but she heard a *click* as he checked his pistol. He wasn't taking chances.

Kristi leaned forward and looked out the driver's side door, but it was so dark she couldn't see anything. "Be careful. They can be aggressive."

A sleepy grunt.

"Hey, dude. Don't make me turn you into bacon, okay? I'm just going to get back into the vehicle and drive away." Malik backed into the driver's seat, both hands gripping his pistol. "Good warthog."

He pivoted into his seat, closed the door, and let out a breath, grinning, goggles covering his eyes. "Good thing it wasn't a lion."

"I've only seen warthogs from a distance." She'd always thought the mothers looked cute, running through the grass with their tails sticking straight up, babies scrambling after them. "Now that we're on the outskirts of a game preserve, we need to watch for animals, too. I don't think there are any big cats here, though."

She took Malik's phone, googled. "I stand corrected. Lions. A small population of leopards. Hippos. Elephants. Remind me not to need to pee."

He chuckled. "Just stay close to the vehicle. I'll cover you."

He locked the doors, started the engine, then removed his helmet and the goggles, which seemed to be fastened together.

"You look like a cyborg when you wear those."

He handed them to her, a grin on his face. "Try them out if you want. Just don't drop them. They cost about thirty grand."

"Wow." She took the helmet, settled it on her head. "It's so heavy. I think my head is too small. It wobbles."

Malik reached over, tightened the strap beneath her chin. "How's that?"

"Better."

He flipped the goggles down and turned them on.

She laughed, a new world before her eyes. "You're green. Everything is green."

"Why don't you keep a watch on the sides of the road? If you see anything moving, let me know. Hitting an elephant would bring our escape to a sudden and dramatic end."

"Got it." Kristi found she needed to move her head back and forth, her vision limited to a circle right in front of the goggles. "This is so strange—and a little creepy."

Malik drove slowly over rutted roads, Kristi looking out at a world that would otherwise be hidden to her. As the miles crept by, they talked about everything and nothing. What it was like to be the youngest in the family. Past girlfriends and boyfriends. Their favorite holidays growing up.

"I loved Christmas," Malik said. "Waking up early in the morning, sneaking out to the Christmas tree, knowing I couldn't touch anything until my parents woke up. It was magical."

"We celebrated *so* many holidays. My mom was raised Presbyterian, but my father's influences were Buddhist and cultural more than religious. So, we celebrated Easter, Fourth of July, Thanksgiving, Christmas, but we also celebrated Chinese New Year, Ancestors' Day, Dragon Boat Festival, and Mid-Autumn—"

A green shape moved among the trees.

"Stop!"

Malik hit the brakes. "What do you see?"

Kristi pointed. "There's something big moving toward the... Oh, my God! Look!"

A male lion stepped out of the trees.

She flipped up the goggles to see him clearly. Huge and tawny-colored with a dark mane, he stopped to sniff and bite at a bush. Then he sprayed.

"He's marking his territory, leaving his scent. There must be a female around."

"Listen to you, Ms. National Geographic."

"He doesn't seem to care about us." Heart thrumming with excitement, she watched as the lion walked along the edge of the road, his movements powerful and fluid, his body all muscle. "He's coming this way."

"Why are you whispering?" Malik whispered.

She hadn't realized she was.

"I don't want to scare him," she whispered back.

Malik grinned. "Does he look scared to you?"

Only when the lion drew close to the SUV could she see how truly enormous he was, how big his head was, and those paws—like dinner plates.

"*Holy shit.*"

The lion glanced up at her, his amber eyes looking right into hers as he passed, the tip of one of his ears missing, a scar on his nose.

A thrill shivered through her, a primal and wild terror that made her come alive.

"Wow," she whispered, watching the big cat disappear into the darkness.

Malik spoke in his normal voice, startling her. "That was cool."

"He looked straight into my eyes."

"He was checking you out, wondering what you were doing on his turf."

"For a moment, I felt this primitive reaction. It was like my DNA recognized the lion as a threat, even though I'm safe in the car." She flipped down the goggles again. "God, that was exciting! Did you see how big he was?"

"You really are a thrill-seeker." He took his foot off the brake, and they moved down the road once more.

"The last time you called me that, we had just joined the Three Hundred Club, and all I could think about was getting my hands on you."

"I remember you holding your breasts to keep your nipples from getting frost bitten. I wanted them in my mouth."

The road curved to the left and went slightly downhill, the trees falling back to create a kind of clearing. Kristi glanced back and forth, watching for wildlife, but saw nothing. The vehicle came to a sudden stop—and then the front end began slowly to sink.

"What's happening?"

"I think we're stuck in mud." He tried reversing, but it didn't help.

If anything, it made things worse.

"Why are we still sinking?"

"Stay inside, and let me know if you see Simba creeping up on me."

"Right." She glanced around, but saw no movement among the ghostly green shapes of the trees.

Malik climbed out, walked toward the front, then staggered back. "Fuck!"

She'd heard that even with the windows up.

He opened the door. "You're not going to fucking believe this."

"What?"

He lifted his right leg, showed her his boot. "Quicksand."

"Quicksand?" Kristi stared at him, her mind taking a moment to catch up. "Is it going to swallow the SUV?"

She'd heard about people being rescued from quicksand during the rainy season, when sandy soil became saturated, especially around Lagos, but she hadn't worried about quicksand since she was about nine years old.

"I don't think so." He moved carefully toward the front again. "We're no longer sinking, but the front tires are almost buried."

"How do we get it out?" She glanced around, some image in her mind of thick banyan vines.

"We don't, not without a winch. We're not going anywhere—not tonight."

Kristi's stomach knotted. "We're just going to stay here?"

"For now." He walked to the driver's side passenger door and grabbed his duffel. "Climb out here. I'll set up a bivouac. You can get some sleep."

"You want to *camp*—with the lions?" She had one particular lion fresh in her mind, and that lion wasn't too far away. "There are snakes, too—poisonous ones—and spiders and scorpions."

He took out his body armor and strapped it on. "Where's your spirit of adventure?"

She sat on one of the back seats. "It's here in the vehicle where it can't be eaten."

He chuckled, reached for his helmet. "I promise I won't let you become dinner."

She took it off, handed it back to him, the world going dark. "Why can't we sleep in the SUV?"

He strapped on the helmet, flipped down the NVGs, and glanced around. "We don't want to be inside the vehicle if the bad guys find us. We'd be sitting ducks. We want to be watching from a distance so that we can conceal, evade, and escape."

"Okay. That makes sense." Still, she didn't move.

"In the morning, we'll take only what we need and start walking. I can try to rent another vehicle or hotwire something on the other side of the river."

"Steal a car? You know how to do that?"

"I learned all kinds of skills in special operations." He held out his hand, helped her climb out. "I'm going to put on my chest rig and holsters. Can you carry the water? Grab whatever you need, but leave the food. We don't want to draw in predators."

Kristi reached for the water, the darkness seeming to press in on her.

You can do this.

She'd just spent four days as a prisoner of traffickers. She could handle a night in the wild, especially with Malik beside her.

Looking like a soldier now, he walked to the rear of the vehicle, opened the lift gate, and rummaged around. "They should have an emergency kit. Here it is. There's a flashlight for you. They've got a plastic tarp, too. Cool."

She took the flashlight from him, turned it on, pointed the narrow beam of light at the wall of trees to the left of the poor SUV.

"Just don't shine it in my eyes."

"Right."

He slipped his duffel on like a backpack, then locked the vehicle, pocketed the keys, and led the way into the trees, testing the ground before each step, the soil wet and muddy. "I don't see anything here that might want to eat us."

Kristi used the flashlight to watch where she stepped, following closely behind Malik, her senses trained on the forest around her with all of its strange noises.

The chirping of insects. What sounded like a monkey. The breeze in the canopy.

The ground began to slope uphill.

"Don't look to your right."

Naturally, that's where she looked, the flashlight revealing an enormous spider in a web that stretched between two trees and was taller than she was. "Shit!"

"I told you not to look."

"I can't help it." She thought she heard him chuckle.

"I know."

They walked toward a rise, Malik picking a safe path.

"Stay here." Rifle raised, he hiked to the top of the rise, glanced around, then turned and pointed his rifle toward their vehicle, as if checking to see whether he had a clear shot. "Let's camp here."

She hiked up to where he stood, glanced around.

He spread the plastic tarp on a relatively level area. "I

know it's not a nice soft bed, but you can lie down here and get some sleep."

Kristi wasn't sure about that. "What are you going to do?"

"I'm going to keep watch. I don't want anyone or anything sneaking up on us."

"Won't you be exhausted tomorrow?"

He lowered his duffel to the tarp. "I've gone days without sleep. Don't worry about me."

Kristi set the water down beside his duffel bag and sat. "This is better than that awful hut with the rodent droppings."

"Hell, yeah, it is. Fresh air. You can see the stars. No bad guys." He knelt beside her, rifle pointed at the ground, and raised the NVGs. "I'm right here, Kristi. Just use my duffel bag as a pillow and get some sleep."

"I'm not sure I'll be able to sleep."

"Then just lie down, breathe, and close your eyes."

She lay down on her side, rested her head on the duffel.

"Turn over."

She did as he asked, her gaze fixed on the dark wall of the forest beyond.

He rubbed her back, one big hand sliding up and down the column of her spine. There was nothing sexual about it. He was trying to help her relax—and it was working. Slowly, the day's tension began to leave her.

"Just close your eyes, angel. You're safe here."

She must have been more tired than she realized because she began to drift. The last image in her mind before she fell asleep was of the lion's amber eyes.

～

MALIK STOOD OVER KRISTI, watching the forest around them while she slept. They faced a long damned hike through the forest tomorrow. She needed her rest.

He had no idea how many miles they'd covered before getting caught in the fucking quicksand or how close they were to the river. What he *did* know was that they had long, dangerous miles ahead of them.

The rental vehicle wasn't going anywhere, and when it was found, those Sky King fuckers would know exactly where to pick up their trail.

Malik didn't know what kind of tech they had at their disposal, but it would be hard to evade search helicopters, especially if the people onboard were equipped with thermal imaging. The trees offered some cover, but, unlike the jungles of Vietnam or the Amazon, the forest here wasn't impenetrable from the air.

He hadn't talked with Kristi about any of this yet. After what she'd been through, he knew it would scare her. He needed her to sleep tonight, not worry.

He kept his gaze moving over the forest around them, careful to look up at the canopy above them and to watch the ground, too. Bats. Some kind of bush baby thing. A big python snaking its way up a tree.

Yeah, he could do without the snakes.

He glanced down, the peace on Kristi's face putting a hitch in his chest, unleashing a rush of emotion. He'd had a year and a half to sort out his feelings for her, to figure out why he hadn't hooked up with other women after Antarctica. He'd almost succeeded in convincing himself that their connection was just great sexual chemistry and that he'd been too busy with missions to meet other women. But now, as he watched her sleep, he knew that was bullshit.

Was he in love with her?

Whoa! Don't get carried away, bruh.

Sure, he cared about her—a lot.

You cared enough to drop everything, fly around the world, and kill and maybe die to rescue her.

They were good in bed together. He just loved having sex with her.

Keep telling yourself that.

Okay, there was more. He loved her sense of humor, too. He loved her big heart, her compassion. He loved her courage, her hunger for adventure. And that sparkle in her eyes when she smiled.

You're in love with her.

The realization ought to have scared the shit out of him, but it didn't. Instead, he found himself smiling, a feeling like sunlight spreading in his chest.

Yeah, you love her.

He'd thought he was in love twice before, but this was different. Of course, he'd been a lot younger then. Neither relationship had lasted.

Whitney, his high school sweetheart, had wanted him to go to college. His decision to join the army had split them apart. Several years later, he'd met Veronica. They'd moved in together, and he'd thought that was it. He'd caught her poking holes in his condoms with a needle, trying to trick him into getting her pregnant. He'd broken up with her. After that, he'd kept things casual, focused on his job.

And then Kristi had come into his life.

They had agreed to a simple exchange of sexual pleasure, but it hadn't been simple at all. She'd been so much more than he'd expected. She'd gotten inside him. They'd spent a month together, only a month, but he'd never stopped thinking about her.

How does she feel about you?

He didn't want to think about that. Not here. Not yet.

He needed to focus.

He turned slowly, scanning the forest around them for movement or predators, his gaze drawn once again to her face.

She shifted in her sleep, reached for covers that weren't there.

She was cold.

He knelt and unzipped his duffel bag far enough to reach inside and pull out his jacket. Then he draped it over her. "Sleep, angel."

Tomorrow would bring a world of trouble their way.

14

K risti was awakened by a chorus of birds. She opened her eyes to see the sunlight streaming through the trees above her.

"Good morning, beautiful."

She stretched, sat up, and discovered that Malik had covered her with his jacket during the night. God, he was sweet. "Good morning. Did you sleep at all?"

"Nah, but I'm good." He tore open a small paperboard box and removed a green plastic bag.

"What's that?"

"Breakfast. I got these MREs out of the truck just before you woke." He drew items out one at a time. "Hash brown potatoes with bacon, peppers, and onions. Granola with milk and blueberries. Filled bakery item. Cheddar cheese spread. Crackers. Dry-roasted, salted peanuts. Orange beverage base, sugar-free. Accessory Packet A."

"Filled bakery item?" She laughed. "That's so ... appetizing. What's Accessory Packet A?"

"In this case, it's coffee." He opened a bottle of water and set it aside, a grin on his face. "This is the US military's idea of haute cuisine, so don't get excited."

While she watched, he stuck the plastic package of hash browns into the green bag, poured in a little water, and set it aside. "Does that rehydrate the food?"

"No, it heats it." He opened another box and repeated the same process. "This is how soldiers get warm meals when we're out in the field."

A delicious aroma wafted from the packet as it warmed, making her mouth water.

But what if animals smelled it, too? "I thought you didn't want to have food outside of the vehicle."

"We'll be leaving when we're done. Did you sleep well?"

"Thanks to you." She was a little stiff, but she *had* slept. "I had strange dreams. I kept seeing the lion, watching it walk by, looking into its eyes. Sometimes, I knew you were the lion. Its eyes were your eyes. Dreams are weird."

He handed her a plastic spoon. "I don't know what that means, but I like it."

"Did you see anything last night—lions, maybe?"

"No lions. I saw lots of bats, a big python that's still in that tree over there, a bush baby, and a family of pangolins that shuffled by not long ago."

"A python?" She decided not to look this time.

He took one of the green heater bags, pulled out the food packet, peeled it open, and handed it to her. "Bon appétit."

"Thanks." She took the packet, which was almost too hot to hold. "That smells so good. Mmm. It tastes good, too."

Malik tore open his food and began to eat. "I'm glad you think so. It's calories—fuel to get you through the day."

Kristi finished quickly and then ate her granola without the powdered milk. Uncertain when they'd be able to eat again, she saved the rest for later, tucking it inside her backpack and putting the trash inside the brown paper box.

"We'll clean up, pack up what we need, and use the compass on my phone to—"

The sound of an engine.

"Get behind that rock!"

Kristi did as he'd ordered, dragging the tarp with her.

Malik concealed himself beside her, stretched onto his belly, rifle raised.

Pulse pounding, Kristi lay still.

Now she understood why they hadn't stayed with the vehicle.

"Breathe, Kristi," Malik whispered.

She exhaled, watching the road as the sound of the engine grew closer.

A green pickup truck came into view, the words *Okobi Wildlife Preserve Ranger* painted on the door in white. The truck stopped behind their rental vehicle, and a man wearing a green uniform with a green beret stepped out. Hand on his weapon, he moved carefully toward the vehicle, looked inside the windows, then down at the ground.

He knelt, touched the sandy soil. When he stood upright again, he looked straight at them—and reached for his radio.

"He's tracking us, but doesn't see us," Malik whispered, quickly stripping out of his military gear and tucking a pistol in the back of his jeans. "I'm going to take a chance. I have to stop him from calling this in. You stay here until I call you, okay? And hide my gear in the duffel bag."

"No! What if he's one of them? What if he kills you?"

"I'll kill him back." He took off his helmet, set the rifle aside, then called out. "I'm a tourist, and my car got stuck! Don't shoot."

Slowly, Malik stood, hands raised.

The ranger shouted back. "Walk out slowly."

"Yes, sir." Malik disappeared from Kristi's view. "I was driving through last night, got lost, and then got stuck in that quicksand. I've been out here all night, hoping someone would come by to help."

Careful to stay out of sight, Kristi did as Malik asked, listening, her body tensing in anticipation of gunshots.

"We had a sign blocking this road, but poachers removed it," the ranger said. "Are you alone?"

A moment of silence.

"No, sir, my wife is with me, but I asked her to stay back."

"She need not be afraid of me. I am a ranger. Come out, ma'am!"

Kristi's pulse raced, but she stayed where she was.

Then Malik called to her. "It's okay, Kristi. I think he's one of the good guys."

"I am a ranger, not a bandit. See my truck and my uniform?" The man sounded insulted. "I will not hurt her."

"When you see my wife, you'll understand why I'm being so careful. Kristi, just stand up slowly, hands over your head, and walk toward me."

Kristi stood, hands raised.

MALIK WATCHED the ranger as Kristi slowly emerged from the shadows, ready to draw his pistol. He saw the moment the ranger recognized her.

The man's gaze moved from Kristi to Malik. "She's the woman who was abducted and rescued by the NPF."

"Yes, but now the Sky Kings are after her."

The ranger's eyebrows almost disappeared behind his beret, his pupils dilating. "How do you know this?"

The man was afraid of them.

"The bastards who'd abducted her were one of their strike groups. Many were killed. We tried to catch a flight out of the country, but they had men at the Abuja airport waiting for us. We were trying to drive across the border, but men with weapons put up a roadblock on the highway. So, we left the road and got stuck here."

The ranger lowered his rifle, gave Malik and Kristi a nod of his head. "I'm Chief Ranger Isaac Tinubu."

"I'm Malik Jones."

Tinubu met Kristi's gaze, sympathy on his face. "I'm very sorry about what happened to you here in Nigeria, ma'am."

"Thank you."

A burst of static from Tinubu's radio.

The ranger reached for his mic.

"Don't tell them about us." Malik didn't want to have to hurt this guy.

Tinubu nodded. "Tinubu here. It was just some tourists from Ghana stuck in the road. You know how they are. All is well. Tinubu out."

Malik exhaled. "I'm grateful."

"If those fools are after you, you must leave the country and get back to America as fast as you can."

Malik couldn't agree more. "Can you help us get the vehicle out?"

Ranger Tinubu pointed. "I have a winch on my truck. We can try to pull it out. Then I'll guide you to a safer road."

Malik helped Tinubu hook the truck to the rental, then took the driver's seat, started the engine, and put the SUV in reverse just as Tinubu activated the winch. The vehicle rocked, seemed to slide forward, and for a moment Malik thought it was hopeless. Then abruptly the front tires came free, the vehicle lurching backward. "That's what I'm talking about."

Malik hit the brakes, cut the engine, and climbed out. He met Tinubu at the back of the vehicle and shook his hand. "Thank you, sir."

This was going much better than he'd hoped it would.

"You are welcome. But now you must tell me the whole story. We Nigerians love stories, and yours sounds very interesting."

Under normal circumstances, Malik wouldn't share information with someone he didn't know, but his gut told him he could trust Ranger Tinubu. His gut was rarely wrong. Malik and Kristi took turns explaining what had really happened and why Malik hadn't been mentioned during the press conference.

Tinubu seemed impressed. "You went in *alone*?"

"I had no idea what the Sky Kings were or even that they were involved until afterward. Now we need to cross the border so we can catch a flight home."

Tinubu shook his head. "If you're trying to get to Benin, you must cross the Niger River. There are only a few bridges, and they are all on major highways. If you can't cross the bridges, you will have to take a small boat."

"Then we would have to leave the rental vehicle behind. What about the old railway bridge?"

Tinubu's eyes went wide. "You would be crazy to cross there."

"Is it still standing?"

"Oh, yes, it still stands. It is rarely used these days, but it is narrow and a hundred feet above the river."

Kristi didn't look happy to hear this. "A hundred feet?"

"Unless you have a better idea, that might be our only way to get across without being seen."

Tinubu seemed to consider it. "You need your rental car, so you can't take a boat. If they are blocking the roads and bridges... You have very few options, my friends."

Tinubu went to his truck, grabbed a map—the old-fashioned kind—and spread it on the hood of his truck. "You are here. To safely reach the park boundary, you need to turn back, and follow this road here."

Malik took a photo of the map with his phone.

"This route will take you the rest of the day. If you stop here, you can stay in our ranger cabin for the night. No one is using it now. There's a key hidden beneath a rock next to the door. It is not fancy, but it has clean well water, solar power, a latrine, a bed and a stove for cooking. It also has its own fuel pump. It is much safer than sleeping in the open. You must be careful, because there are both bandits and poachers in the park, not to mention predators."

"We saw a lion last night," Kristi blurted. "It walked right past our vehicle."

Tinubu's face lit up. "Can you describe him?"

Kristi looked confused for a moment. "Well, he was big and had a mane and..."

Tinubu grinned. "Was his mane dark or light?"

"It was dark—and the tip of one of his ears was missing. Oh! He had a scar on his nose, too."

Tinubu seemed delighted. "You met Oba. That is Yoruba for *King*. He is the oldest male in the park. Was it far from here?"

Kristi shook her head. "Maybe a few miles in the other direction. Malik stayed awake all night in case he came back this way."

"I'm afraid you would not have been much of a match

for dear Oba, Mr. Jones. But let us get on our way. You have far to travel."

KRISTI TOOK the wheel in the afternoon, while Malik rode shotgun, rifle in hand.

"There it is." He pointed.

The ranger cabin.

She turned off the rutted road and followed the tire tracks to the front door. "This is not what I was expecting."

The cabin turned out to be a cute little thatch-roofed cottage that looked like it belonged in a children's story. It stood back from the road in a clearing, its walls painted the same rust-red color of the soil, an old-fashioned water pump out front, the setting sun glinting off the glass panes of its single window. The only sign that this wasn't some idyllic retreat were the iron bars over the window.

She parked, turned off the engine.

"Stay here, keys in the ignition and lock the doors. I'm going to clear the place."

"Okay." She had no idea what he meant by that. Clear it of what?

She watched while he climbed out, rifle in hand, and moved around the house, body tensed for action, rifle raised, finger on the trigger.

Damn.

He moved with the grace of a predator—and it turned her on.

He disappeared behind the cabin for a time, emerging on the other side. Then he retrieved the key from its hiding place, unlocked the door, and walked inside. A moment later, he stepped out, rifle pointing at the ground now. "Clear."

She took the keys out of the ignition, hopped out, and got her backpack and one of her bags out of the back.

"You get inside. I'll bring whatever I think we need."

"Okay." She went inside.

The place smelled of wood smoke and was dimly lit, one bare lightbulb hanging from the ceiling, a simple wooden shelf holding spices near the stove. A table with two chairs stood against one wall, the bed against the other. The bed wasn't much bigger than the one they'd slept in at Amundsen-Scott, the mattress bare, no pillows to be seen.

Malik stepped inside with his duffel bag and a few bottles of water. "It's not the Hilton, but it's more secure than the forest."

"Are you kidding? After Jidda's hut and last night, this place is a palace." She set her backpack down on the table, then went into nurse mode, checking beneath the mattress for creepy-crawlies and bedbugs.

"What are you doing?" Malik stood there watching, a puzzled look on his handsome face.

She used his language. "I'm clearing it."

He watched, obviously still confused.

"Clear." She settled the mattress back into place. "No bedbugs."

"Good." He chuckled, dropped his duffel onto the floor, unzipped it. "The latrine and gas pump are out back. Let's get some grub, and then I need a few hours' sleep."

"Yes, you do." She knew he must be exhausted. She'd once gone forty-eight hours without sleep when a bus full of school kids had gone off the road and rolled. By the end, she'd been running on fumes. By her count, Malik had been awake for about thirty-six hours now.

Malik held up a couple of MREs. "Do you want the spaghetti in meat sauce or the meatballs in marinara sauce?"

"You choose." She sat at the table, set the hand wipes out for him to use. "You're the one who stayed awake all night."

"I've eaten both of these so many times..." He set them on the table, tore open the boxes, and went through the same process as this morning.

While they ate, they talked about what they'd seen along the way. Different kinds of monkeys. Another pangolin. A small herd of duikers. A mother warthog with her brood of three.

Kristi took her last bite of spaghetti, chewed. "I always wanted to go on safari. If we weren't running from killers, it would have been a really fun day."

He reached across the table, covered her hand with his. "We'll get through this."

She wanted to believe that. "I hope so."

He collected their trash, packed it into a plastic bag, and shoved it into his duffel.

She spotted a water bucket by the door. "I'm going to go out and get some water to take a bath."

"Let me do that." He grabbed his rifle and the bucket and opened the door, glancing outside. "You never know if one of Oba's cousins is hanging around."

He returned a few minutes later, bucket brimming. "It's cold."

"Good!" She unzipped her bag, took out a little wash-cloth and her bar of soap.

"I'm going to refuel the truck in case we need to leave in a hurry." He grabbed the keys, and left once more, rifle still slung over his shoulder.

A moment later, she heard the SUV's engine start.

Kristi undressed, set her clothes on the bed, then lifted the bucket of water onto the table. She dipped the washcloth to wet it, got it good and soapy, and then washed, starting with her face and moving down her body.

The cool water felt so good, sweat and dirt from the past two days washing away, leaving her skin clean.

She rinsed over the bucket with small handfuls of water, then bent over and washed her hair. She was in the middle of rinsing the shampoo out of her hair when the door opened and Malik walked in.

He shut the door, locked it, and stood there, watching. "*Damn.*"

She saw the lust on his face, felt the trill of desire. "Get a fresh bucket of water, and I'll give you a bath."

15

Malik set the bucket of clean water on the table, unable to take his eyes off the woman who stood naked before him, drying her hair with a towel, her breasts swaying, her brown skin damp. A few minutes ago, all he'd wanted was sleep.

Now, he wanted her.

He took the towel from her, dropped it on the table. "You're so beautiful."

Her black hair hung in thick ropes, her dark nipples peeking out from between the strands, already puckered. "Are you sure we should do this? I know you're tired."

"Oh, there's no going back now, angel." He caught her wrist, drew her to him, and bent down to kiss her, his body alive with anticipation, his cock already hard.

She kissed him back, her hands sliding beneath his T-shirt, cool fingers setting fire to his skin. She drew back, reached for his zipper. "Get naked, soldier."

"Yes, ma'am." He made short work of it, tossing his clothes and boots onto a chair, until they stood together in nothing but skin.

She took a clean washcloth, wet it, lathered it with soap, then rubbed it over his chest, abs, arms, and groin, cold water making him suck in a breath, his nipples drawing tight. She rinsed him and then knelt to wash his legs. "God, I love your body."

He let her indulge herself, checking his own impulses to let her have her way, sliding his fingers into her wet hair. "I fantasized about you every damned night, Kristi."

It was the truth.

She looked up at him through those beautiful dark eyes. "You ruined me for other men—not that there have been other men."

"Good." He felt a fierce wave of possessiveness, a question he hadn't asked her now answered.

She stood, move behind him, her hands moving methodically over him, lingering on his shoulders, his hips, his ass, her touch raising goosebumps on his skin.

But the torture wasn't over.

She rinsed him, pouring water over his skin, letting it pool on the wooden planks at his feet. She walked back to the table, set the washcloth aside, her sweet ass just beyond his reach.

At the end of his patience, he moved in on her, drew her back against him, one hand squeezing a breast, the other sliding between her thighs to cup her. "I want to fuck you so bad it hurts."

"*Yes.*"

But this wasn't going to be like the other night in the hotel.

He was going to make this last.

He closed his eyes, focused on the feel of her, the pebble-hardness of her nipple, the slick, sensitive nub of her clit, her silky skin.

She leaned against him, her hips moving in time to the motions of his hand, one of her hands holding onto his forearm for balance. "*Malik.*"

"I love how you say my name when you're turned on."

Her head fell back against his chest, her brow furrowed, her lips parted. "You're so *good* at that."

"At what? This?" He pinched her nipple, felt her tense. Then he ran his finger quickly back and forth over her clit. "Or this?"

All he got was a moan.

But he wanted more.

He pushed her up against the table, turned her to face him, kissed her hard and deep, breathing in the sweet scent of her skin, taking her breath into his lungs. She arched against him, her arms going around his neck, drawing him closer.

He lifted her off her feet, bore her back onto the table, then dropped to his knees, draping her knees over his shoulder. "I let you play. Now it's my turn."

He parted her, tasted her with a long, slow lick, her taste exploding on his tongue. Then he closed his mouth over her, suckling her clit, teasing it with his tongue, drawing it into his mouth.

She arched, moaned, her fingers sliding through his hair. "*Malik.*"

That sexy whisper again.

He found a rhythm, stayed with it, her clit swelling as he sucked, her breathing erratic, her body arching. He knew how to read her, knew she was close to coming. Oh, but he wasn't going to make it easy for her.

He stopped, brushed kisses over her inner thighs, grinning at her frustrated moan.

"*Maliiiik!*"

This time, he started with his fingers, sliding two deep inside her, stroking her, letting it build before taking her with his mouth again, her scent filling his head, her taste sliding down his throat until he was drunk on her.

Again, he brought her to the brink, and again, he stopped, letting her cool down, making her wait, his blood burning for her.

"You're torturing me."

He chuckled, went back to work on her, until she twisted and writhed, forcing him to pin her hips to the table with an arm. Still, he kept up the rhythm, her body tensing, her climax drawing near.

"Oh, yes! *Fuck!* Yes!"

For eighteen long months, he'd had to remember the sexy sound of those cries.

Now he was going to make her scream.

He sucked hard, thrust his fingers deep—and felt her shatter.

She bucked, cried out, arching off the table, her inner muscles clenching around his fingers.

He stayed with her, made it last, until she lay limp and breathless.

He stood, smiled to see that her eyes were still closed, the aftermath of bliss on her sweet face. Then he scooped her into his arms and carried her to the bed.

KRISTI FELT Malik lower her to the bed and stretch out beside her. She looked into those intense dark eyes of his, his dilated pupils turning them almost black. She spread her legs for him, slid her fingers into his short hair, drew him down. "Kiss me."

He settled his hips between her thighs and kissed her, soft and slow, his hard cock resting against her belly. Lord, he could kiss, the lips and tongue that had just made her scream teasing her, arousing her again, carrying her taste into her mouth.

He broke the kiss, looked down at her, one big hand moving over her, his gaze following his touch. "Kristi ... angel. I missed you so much."

He cupped one breast, lowered his head, and sucked her nipple into the heat of his mouth, the sweet tug of his lips sending jolts of arousal to her belly, rekindling the fire he'd just quenched.

Oh, she loved this, loved the way he made her feel desperate and needy, the way he made her ache as he feasted on first one breast and then the other, drawing her nipples to tight peaks. Then he reached between her thighs, careful with her, knowing she was hypersensitive now, the gentle probing of his fingers adding to her arousal, fanning the flames of lust.

She slid one hand along the curve of his back, drank in the feel of him, hard muscle shifting beneath soft skin. She was more than ready for him, but he wasn't the kind of man to rush her. He always took his sweet time with her, never once putting his pleasure ahead of hers, slowly unraveling her until she came completely apart.

Oh, she was so far gone already, her body taut with sexual need and longing for him. "I want you inside me."

He lifted his head, grinned. "Yeah?"

"*Now.*"

He shifted his hips, lifted himself up, holding his weight with both arms.

But when she reached down to guide him inside her, he

stopped her, drawing back, pulling his cock out of reach. "Not yet."

Anticipation shivered through her.

That was the thing about Malik. He was amazing with his mouth and his fingers. He was even more amazing with his cock.

He rested his erection against her clit, made little thrusting motions with his hips, rubbing her with the head of his cock, the friction enough to make her want him even more, but not enough to make her come.

"You're driving me crazy."

"I love to watch you squirm."

Soon, she was doing exactly that, her hips lifting, her body instinctively reaching for his. Then he reached down, rested the tip of his cock against the opening to her vagina —and she moaned. But he didn't enter her—not yet.

Instead, he teased her, rubbing himself over her entrance, his brow furrowed with concentration—or pleasure. "You are so wet."

When she couldn't take it any longer, he nudged himself into her with deliberate and agonizing slowness, inch by delicious inch.

Kristi's exhale became a long moan as he went deeper. She wanted all of him, wanted him to fill her completely. But he had other ideas.

He withdrew and then entered her slowly again... and again... until it was almost maddening. She reached down, took hold of his ass, tried to pull him into her. He chuckled, kept up his assault on her senses, not yielding to pressure.

Then without warning, he changed the pace, driving into her hard and fast a few times, making her cry out. Then he withdrew and entered her with another achingly slow thrust. He did this again and again, carrying her closer to the brink each time, only to leave her hanging.

"*Malik.*"

He chuckled again, but there was just a hint of a moan at the end, a tightness to his voice, proof that it was getting harder for him to hold on, too.

Two could play at this game.

When he next entered her, she tightened herself around him, clenching her inner muscles as hard as she could.

His response was an immediate, low moan. "Geezus."

She felt his control begin to fray, his body tensing, his breathing as ragged as hers.

He slipped into a regular rhythm with deep, gliding strokes, stretching her, satisfying that inner ache, pleasure drawing tight in her belly.

Oh, God, yes, that's what she needed... harder... faster ...

"*Ooh*, Malik. Fuck me."

It felt so good, each thrust a taste of heaven, carrying her higher and higher, until she hung, suspended, on the bright edge of another orgasm. She was burning up, burning up with him inside her. Then the heat in her belly drew tight... and exploded.

She cried out, bliss burned through her, scorching and sweet. But this time, Malik was just behind her. He drove her climax home then moaned her name, his body shaking apart in her arms as he came inside her.

Kristi opened her eyes, met his gaze, saw a tenderness there that made her pulse skip, warmth blossoming behind her breastbone.

He kissed her—her lips, her nose, her forehead—then rolled onto his side, drawing her with him, cradling her in his arms, their legs twined together.

Spent and sleepy, she spoke from the heart. "I want

strings, Malik. I don't want this to end when we're back in the US."

When he didn't answer, she looked up at his face.

He was sound asleep.

A NOISE WOKE Malik from a dreamless sleep early the next morning. He found Kristi curled against him, still asleep, peace on her face. He hated to wake her, but something was out there. "Hey, angel, wake up. We've got company."

Kristi opened her eyes, smiled at him.

The sound that had awakened him came again—a long, deep roar.

There was only one thing that could make that sound.

A lion.

Kristi sat bolt upright. "That's close."

Malik got up from the bed, walked to the window, and stared. "It's very close. Yo, check this out."

Kristi stood, walked over to him, still naked. "Oh, God! Look at them!"

A pride of lions had stopped to explore the SUV. One lioness sat on the roof, another on the hood, their cubs playing near the front tires. A male lion sat a short distance away, watching over his family, letting the other lions know this was his territory with deep, short roars.

"That sound—it gives me shivers." Kristi slipped her arm around Malik's waist.

He wrapped an arm around her shoulders, kissed the top of her head. "I think it's supposed to. That's your DNA saying, 'Run!'"

They stood there, Kristi watching and laughing at the antics of the cubs, some of whom climbed on the male, who endured it all with patience. "Those cubs are so cute."

But Malik's gaze was on Kristi—the happy smile on her face, the light in her eyes, her beautiful naked body.

Her smile faded into a look of concern. "If that's now the lions' SUV, how are we going to get out of here?"

"Let's hope they move on by the time we're ready to go. If not, I can try opening the door and firing a shot to scare them off." Malik took her into his arms. "Think of it this way. As long as a pride of lions is hanging on our front steps, no one is going to sneak up on us."

"That's true." She stood on her tiptoes, kissed him. "You're incredible, Malik. No man has ever made me feel the way you do.

"Good." He kissed her back.

Graceful brows drew together. "I tried to tell you something last night, but you were already asleep."

"Sorry about that." Sex had finished what was left of him. "Tell me now."

She hesitated. "I want strings."

"Good." He couldn't help the idiotic smile that spread across his face—or the way his pulse skipped. He cupped her face between his palms. "I'm not walking away this time, Kristi. Not this time."

Her face lit up with a smile that he felt in his bones. "You'd better not. Saying goodbye once was hard enough."

It *had* been hard.

"I won't be that stupid twice."

More roars from outside.

He kissed her again, reluctant to let her go. "I hate to say it, but we need to get moving."

They dressed, and he dug through the MREs. "Guess what? Same thing for breakfast today as yesterday."

"Sounds good to me."

They ate quickly, packed up their things, and straightened the cabin, wanting to leave the place the way they'd found it.

Kristi glanced outside, backpack on her shoulder. "Now what?"

The lions weren't gone, but they had moved a short distance away from the SUV.

"If I unlock the SUV's doors from here and you climb in on this side, I think we can make it. What do you think?"

They would have to move fast, but the SUV was now between them and the pride.

"I'm game if you are."

Malik put his duffel on his back, grabbed the rifle, checked it. Then he used the remote to unlock the doors. "I'll get in the driver's seat. You climb into the rear passenger seat."

"Got it."

"Ready?" He opened the door—and the lions fled, heading toward the trees. "Well, that made this easy."

But Kristi ran past him. "Not taking chances!"

She opened the door, threw the water inside along with her backpack and shut the door behind her.

Chuckling, Malik got into the driver's seat, settled the rifle, its barrel pointing down, and closed his door. "See? No problem."

While Kristi made her way into the front passenger seat, Malik entered the coordinates of the railway bridge into the navigation console and started the engine, sending silent thanks to Ranger Tinubu.

Because of him, they were rested and had a full tank of gas.

They stayed for a moment to watch as the lions disappeared into the forest.

"You don't realize how big they are until you see them up close like this." There was a note of awe in Kristi's voice.

But it was time to go.

The predators that were hunting them were far more dangerous than lions.

"Next stop, the Niger River." Malik could only hope that his crazy gambit would pay off and they'd be able to make it safely across the river.

16

The forest gave way to savanna as they drove toward the river, the sun well over the horizon now, a hip hop mix playing on the sound system. It was almost like being on a fantastic road trip—except, of course, that killers were after them.

Kristi listened to Malik as he told her about the first time he'd come to Nigeria back when he was an Army Ranger.

"The plan was to train a regiment of Nigerian soldiers to fight the way we fight so they would be better equipped to deal with Boko Haram. We got settled in at our new base and my staff sergeant asked me if I felt more at home here." Malik shook his head. "I didn't know what the hell he meant at first."

Kristi understood. "He thought that you would feel at home in Africa because you're Black."

"Yeah." Malik gave a snort. "What the hell was he thinking? I've got African ancestry, but I have no idea where my people come from. I was born and grew up in the States. The US is my home. I'm as American as he is."

Kristi could relate. "When I did a semester abroad in

China, my American friends in the dorm thought I knew everything about China just because I was Chinese-American. The train schedule, how to get to places I'd never been, where to get the best street noodles, how to clear up a visa dispute. I had to remind them that I was American just like they were and that, although I speak Mandarin, I'd never lived in China."

"I bet that got old real fast."

"It did. I felt responsible for everything, even though it was all new to me, too. I had my grandparents, of course, and they helped. But they expected me to understand parts of Chinese culture that I'd never experienced before. I felt lost in the middle."

"That must have been hard."

"Sometimes, but it was worth it. By the time I went home, I had learned so much. It helped me to understand my father and to appreciate how complicated it must have been for him to adapt to American culture when he married my mother."

Ahead of them, just off the road, a group of vultures crowded around roadkill, hopping from spot to spot, a confusion of dark wings, bald heads, and hungry beaks.

"I guess these guys found some breakfast," Malik said.

Interested in the enormous birds, Kristi looked as they passed—and her stomach fell. "Oh, God. That was a person. They're eating a dead man."

"Geezus."

"Shouldn't we stop?"

"What would we do? Chase off the birds and bury what's left?"

Kristi turned in her seat, looked behind her, a knot in her chest. "How can we just leave him?"

Malik reached over, took her hand. "My mission is to get

you safely back to the US. As cold as it seems just to drive by, we can't slow down. From what I saw, there's not much left anyway."

She faced forward again, breathing deep to calm her emotions.

"Do I need to stop? Are you going to be sick?"

Kristi might have laughed if the circumstances were different. "Oh, please! I'm an ER nurse, remember?"

"Right. I suppose you've seen everything."

"Now I have." She hoped never to see anything like that again.

He squeezed her fingers. "You've got such a big heart, Kristi. I love that about you. But the only person whose life and safety I can worry about right now is you."

She squeezed back. "I know—and I'm grateful. Without you..."

"Can I ask you something?"

"Of course—anything."

"How do you cope when a patient dies?"

"It can be heartbreaking, especially when it's a child. I remember so many people's faces and their last words. When we lose a patient, I try to give their family the support they need. For them, it's the worst moment of their lives. Helping them face their grief helps me get through it. But there have been lots of times when I've had to take a break and cry my eyes out."

"I can't imagine the strength it takes to do your job."

"I could say the same about you. You've lost people, too."

"Yeah—too many." He glanced down at the navigation console. "We should be coming up on the river soon. We'll pass through a village, and the river is about two klicks from there."

Kristi kept her face downturned, not wanting to be seen.

After the wildlife preserve, it felt strange to see lots of people again. A woman carrying a load of branches on her head for firewood. A young boy herding a few cattle. Two older men standing together, laughing about something. A little girl carrying a baby goat.

They drove through the town, passing through its marketplace, and then the village was behind them, the landscape becoming sandier and greener as they got closer to the river.

And then she saw it—a bend in the river giving her a glimpse of dark water off to her right. "I wonder if we'll see any crocodiles when we cross."

"There's the bridge."

She looked ahead of them and saw it. "Oh, shit."

"Yeah."

The bridge appeared to be intact, resting on concrete piles and stretching fifteen hundred feet to the other side of the Niger. But it was barely wide enough for the SUV, and it was a good hundred feet above the water.

"Are you sure this is a good idea?"

"No, but I don't see many other options, unless you want to leave the SUV, take a boat, and steal something on the other side."

Right now, that seemed like a completely reasonable alternative to Kristi.

He drew to a stop, parked. "I'll walk across, see if I think it's safe. Stay here and keep the doors locked."

"Be careful. If you fall in…"

"I won't." He grabbed the pistol, tucked it into his jeans, and was gone.

~

MALIK WALKED up to the bridge and bent down to examine the concrete piles that supported it. He couldn't see all of them, but the ones he could see looked stable and secure. Still, it was obvious that the bridge hadn't been maintained properly in a long time. Birds had built nests beneath it, and foliage had begun to grow in the concrete.

He walked out onto the structure, checking the individual ties for rot or cracks and looking for loose spikes and bolts. He wasn't afraid of heights, but walking along, the rushing water visible between each tie, made him a little dizzy. He willed himself to get over that, to focus on the ties and not the water below.

It took him ten minutes to inspect the length of it. Walking back, he noticed logs floating beneath it from somewhere upstream. Then one of the logs slashed its tail through the water, raised its head, and snapped at another.

Geezus!

Not logs. Crocodiles. Big ones.

As long as they stayed on the bridge, the crocs wouldn't be a problem. But staying on the bridge wouldn't be easy. It had been built for a relatively narrow gauge train with the rails about three and a half feet apart with the ties sticking out about a foot on either side—barely wide enough for the SUV. He would have only a few inches of wiggle room on either side before a tire went off the edge and sent them plummeting into the water below.

Great idea this was, man.

It was their only option apart from ditching the vehicle and paying someone to ferry them across. Then they'd have to walk, or he'd have to hotwire a vehicle—or risk renting one again.

No, this was their best chance of getting over unseen. All he had to do was drive in a *very* straight line.

He reached the vehicle, climbed into the driver's seat. "The bridge is in good shape. Just don't look down."

"Don't look down." Her eyes were hidden behind her sunglasses, but he could tell by her voice that she was afraid.

"If you want to climb out and walk across—"

She grabbed his hand, shook her head. "If you fall in, I'm going with you."

"No one is going to fall into the river." *Sweet Jesus, don't let us fall into the river.* "I am going to need my hand back."

"Oh. Right." She let go, clasped her hands in her lap.

He started the engine, headed toward the railroad tracks. "I'm going to try to get a tire on either side of the rails."

It was a bumpy process, but he managed it.

He climbed out to double check the tire placement, then climbed in again. "Close your eyes if you need to."

Keeping the vehicle at about five miles per hour, he nudged the SUV forward, moving down the tracks and onto the bridge. "Easy does it."

Thu-thunk thu-thunk thu-thunk.

Kristi whispered to herself. "Don't look down. Don't look down."

"I've got this, angel." He sure as fuck hoped he did.

He expected they'd survive the fall, but he wasn't sure they'd survive the river. If they didn't drown, they'd run a high risk of becoming lunch.

Fuck that.

He focused straight ahead, held the wheel steady, the tires finding a rhythm over the uneven surface of railway ties and the space between them.

Thu-thunk thu-thunk thu-thunk.

Kristi sat, absolutely silent and still, beside him.

"Breathe, Kristi." He heard her exhale, his gaze fixed on

the tracks ahead of him. "We're already a third of the way across."

"I'm keeping my eyes shut."

He couldn't blame her for that. Looking ahead, he could see they were on tracks, but if he looked out his side window, there was nothing but a sheer drop to the river.

He drove slowly forward.

Pop!

Kristi gasped as the vehicle jerked to the right.

Malik got control of it again, but he knew what had happened. "We lost our front right tire. It was probably punctured by a spike or bolt. We've got a spare in the back. We're good."

They had a spare. One spare. If they blew a second tire, they'd be in trouble. Either way, they had no option but to keep moving forward.

Thwap-thunk thwap-thunk thwap-thunk.

"We're halfway there."

The blown tire made it more difficult to steer, but he held on, fighting a constant pull to the right.

"Do you hear that?" Kristi asked.

"What?"

"It sounds like..." Kristi looked over her shoulder. "A train!"

He glanced in his rearview mirror, saw a freight train speeding toward the bridge behind them. "No fucking way!"

"I thought Ranger Tinubu said this bridge wasn't in use!"

"He said it wasn't used often. Hang on." Malik accelerated, but the faster he went, the harder it was to control the steering.

They were two-thirds of the way across now. Just another five hundred feet to go.

But the train was moving much faster.

Kristi looked over her shoulder. "It's catching up with us!"

The conductor gave them a deafening blast of his whistle, waving through his window for them to go faster, the train so close Malik could see his face.

Malik floored it, pushing hard on the gas. If they went over the side, so be it. He'd take the river and crocodiles over being flattened by a train. "Hang on!"

Kristi screamed as the train came right up behind them.

The SUV reached the other side, catching air as Malik drove it up over the rails and down the embankment, the train tearing by, missing them by mere feet.

For a moment, they sat there, Malik's heart thrumming, Kristi looking stunned.

"You okay?" Malik reached over, took her hand.

"Yeah." She gave a stiff nod, but her hands were shaking. "I'm fine."

He unbuckled his seatbelt, reached over, hugged her. "As long as we're still alive and fighting, angel, we're winning."

She leaned into him, took a deep breath, exhaled. "Well, we just won big."

He kissed her hair, laughed. "Hell, yeah, we did."

SAMUEL WALKED among the corpses at Jidda's camp, a cloth over his nose to block the stench. He wanted to see the truth of this himself, wanted to understand how one man could enter their camp in daylight, kill most of their men, and leave, alive and unhurt, with their captive.

It was as Mobo had described with most of the bodies in the center of the camp or near the river. Some had rifles in their hands—rifles they hadn't thought to use.

Idiots.

Now, flies buzzed around their rotting remains, some of the bodies torn apart by animals. Samuel had to fight not to vomit.

"Here, sir!" Kalu, a hunter who was good at tracking, shouted to Samuel from a rise about a half kilometer north of the camp.

Samuel walked over, glad to leave the reek behind. "What have you found?"

Kalu held up shell casings. "There were two men. One stayed here, concealed, providing cover for the one who ran into the camp to rescue the woman. I doubt our men caught even a glimpse of him."

"Are you certain there were two?"

"Yes, sir." Kalu pointed toward the camp with a jerk of his head. "There is a trail of these shell casings leading to the hut where Mobo says the woman was kept. But these large shell casings are only found here."

"Maybe this son of a whore had two weapons."

"Look." Kalu pointed at the ground. "One set of tracks enters the camp, but three sets of tracks return. None of those three sets of tracks matches the fourth set here. There were two men, and they left with two people. The four sets of tracks lead back to a place where they parked their vehicle, about five kilometers north of here."

Samuel bent down, looked at the tracks, followed them into the camp and back again. Kalu was right. There were four distinct sets of footprints in the dirt, two larger and two smaller. "Get Mobo."

"Yes, sir." Kalu whistled, waved to the men guarding their truck.

Samuel had brought the bastard with them in case he

needed more information—or found that Mobo had lied to him.

Mobo was escorted to him, looking so terrified it made Samuel laugh.

"Mobo, why are you afraid? Is there something you forgot to tell me?"

Mobo shook his head. "No, sir. I told you all I know, sir."

"Kalu found that there were two men—one here and the one who charged into your camp. Does that surprise you?"

"Yes, sir. I never saw two men."

"Here's another surprise. They didn't leave with just the woman. They took someone else with them. Was there a second woman in the camp?"

"No, sir." Then Mobo's eyes went wide. "The boy. They must have taken Obi."

"Who is Obi?"

"Obi is Jidda's young nephew, sir. Jidda took him in after he was orphaned. He lived with us. The woman cared for Obi's burns after Peter pushed him into the fire. Obi showed her respect after that."

Samuel could understand now why Jidda made a deal with this woman. She had saved his life and cared for his nephew. She had apparently also taken this Obi with her.

But Obi didn't belong to her. He was Jidda's blood, and that meant the boy belonged to the Sky Kings. His fate was to take up his uncle's work.

"Is there anything else I need to see, Kalu?"

The hunter shook his head. "No, sir."

"Gather the weapons. Leave the bodies." Samuel walked back to the vehicle mulling over what he'd just learned.

Who was the second man? Was he a friend of this American—a military buddy?

No, Samuel didn't think so. When the woman had been

spotted at the airport, she'd been alone with her husband. Either his accomplice traveled separately—or he was still here in Nigeria. Perhaps he was even Nigerian.

Samuel sat in the front passenger seat of the truck, waited for Mobo, Kalu, and the guards to climb into the back. Then he nodded to his driver. "Back to Kaduna."

He needed to find this second man and the boy—not a simple task when he had no idea what either of them looked like. To find them, he must first find Kristi Chang and her husband Malik Jones.

They'd almost had them in Abuja, but the two had fled in a taxi, their trail disappearing in the market. Samuel had focused on the hotels and car rental places in the city, and that had eventually led them to Gulu, where they'd found the anti-theft device. From there, the trail had gone cold.

But they were out there somewhere, and Samuel would find them. He would get the truth from them about this second man and the boy one way or another. When he did, the Sky Kings would find Samuel worthy. They would shower him with gifts and lift him up. A new house. Maybe a truck. Maybe a position in Lagos or Spain or London.

Samuel could never be one of them—he hadn't gone to their college—but he would not always be in this lowly state, working with strike groups and dealing with men like Mobo and that accursed Peter. God had better plans for him.

Of this, he was certain.

17

K risti helped Malik change the tire, then walked to the edge of the bridge and looked across at the other side while he packed up the tools, a giddy sense of relief coming over her. They'd made it this far, facing bad guys, lions, quicksand, and the river. Nothing had stopped them.

That's when she saw. "There are crocodiles down there."

He shut the vehicle's liftgate. "I saw them earlier when I crossed on foot."

"You didn't say anything." She walked back down to the vehicle. "Smart man."

He met her at the front passenger door, drew her into his arms, held her, his embrace warm and reassuring. "We've come this far. With luck, we'll be in Benin tonight."

"God, I hope so."

Malik found a road not too far away from the river. They followed it through one small village after another—Kpada, Rogun, Pategi, Regada, Bongi—sharing childhood stories, telling secrets. He liked Ludacris. She had a soft spot for the Grateful Dead and Green Day. They both liked *Star Trek*.

"What are your guilty pleasures?" Malik asked. "I know you must have some."

Kristi thought about it. "Okay, well, I like to lie in bed on my days off and watch Disney cartoons. Does that count?"

"Ah, man, that's lame. Where's the shame in that?"

"You want shame?" She thought about it for a moment. "Right before my period starts, I get a wicked craving for Ben and Jerry's Chocolate Fudge Brownie. I buy a pint and eat the whole thing myself."

"Women and chocolate. My elder sister, Jasmine, used to keep a stash of period chocolate. God help any stupid younger brother who snuck into her room and got into it."

"You stole your sister's period chocolate?"

"I didn't understand what a period was at the time. I had no idea that women and chocolate have a magic, hormonal connection. Would I do that now? Oh, hell, no."

Kristi laughed. "Now it's your turn. What's your guilty pleasure—and if you say internet porn, I'm going to be disappointed."

He seemed to think about it for a moment. "I like to sing along to Dolly Parton sometimes when I'm driving."

"Seriously? I did *not* have you pegged as a Dolly Parton fan." She took his phone, went to his music app, scrolled through it. "You have a *huge* Dolly Parton play list."

"What can I say? I respect her."

Kristi picked one of the few songs she knew—*Here You Come Again*—and the two of them sang along, belting out the lyrics.

"You have a good voice," she said when the song finished.

He threaded his fingers through hers. "So do you."

But the needle on the fuel gauge was moving steadily

toward empty, and at last Malik had no choice but to use the extra gas in the cans.

"It looks like we're coming to some bigger towns soon. Hopefully, we can fill the tank before we burn through these ten gallons. If not, we'll have to walk."

The conversation moved on after that, Kristi asking questions about Malik's time as a Ranger. "Were there ever days you wanted to quit and go home?"

"There were a couple of times when I felt lucky to get back to base alive."

He told her about a time the Rangers and an element from DEVGRU—SEAL Team Six—were sent to Afghanistan's Helmand Province with some Australian commandos in two MH-47E Chinook helicopters to catch a high-value target.

"One of the birds had just gotten its guys on the ground when we were ambushed by a much larger force of insurgents. I was in the other chopper, still in the air. The pilot of the empty helicopter put himself between us and the bad guys and got shot out of the sky by an RPG. His skill enabled us to land."

"He sacrificed his life for yours."

"No, he lived to keep fighting." Malik told her how they did their best to defend their position, using the miniguns from the second Chinook to hold off the insurgents.

"When the miniguns ran out of ammo, there was this terrible silence. I knew that was it. It was over. We had nothing but our rifles to hold off a much larger force, and our ammo was running low. Then an AC-130 Spectre—that's an airplane equipped with big guns—arrived out of nowhere like an avenging angel. God, that was a beautiful sight. They held the insurgents off until the Brits sent in some birds to retrieve us. I was glad to make it back to base that night. We all made it back."

Kristi couldn't imagine. "I don't know how you do it."

"When you're part of something, like the Rangers or even Cobra, you're fighting for your team, not just for yourself. You keep fighting until you can't fight any longer. That mission is how I ended up with Cobra. Javier Corbray, one of my bosses, was with that SEAL element. We got to know each other on that mission, and when he and Tower founded Cobra, he invited me to come onboard."

The SUV was running on fumes when they came to the village of Lade. It had restaurants, a big church, a mosque— and a gas station.

Malik refueled the SUV and refilled the two spare gas cans, and then they were off again. "We've got about nine hours of driving left to reach Parakou."

But first they would have to cross the border.

MALIK PULLED INTO A GAS STATION, a huge, illuminated sign that read Truck Transit Park lighting up the parking lot. "I know you want to get out and stretch your legs, but there are too many people here. Maybe we can stop down the road somewhere."

"Don't worry about me."

Malik quickly refueled. Then he drove behind the building, hoping to pick up the transit park's Wi-Fi. He'd lost cell service after Lade and wanted to check in with Shields. "I've got bars."

Kristi had charged her phone. "So do I."

"I'm going to see if I can get Shields." He dialed her number.

Shields answered on the second ring. "Hey, Jones. Good to hear from you. I've been tracking you two, checking on you when I can. Is everything going well?"

"We'll have to talk about that at another time." He didn't want to stay in such a populated area for too long. "We're just outside a town called Gwesaro, about an hour from the border and three hours from Parakou. Do you have any intel on the border?"

"I'm sure there must be something out there. Let me see what I can find."

"I want to avoid any roadblocks or border checkpoints. I can't be sure these bastards don't have people watching for us."

"Good call." For a moment, there was nothing but the sound of her fingers clicking on her keyboard. "Tower says you've got an infrared mini-drone."

"I *had* a drone." Malik might as well come clean now. "David demanded it as payment in exchange for helping me rescue Kristi."

"Tower isn't going to like that, but then he can't fire you because you already quit, right?" There was a teasing note in Shields' voice.

Malik grinned. "Right."

"Okay, I've pulled up a recent Agency report. Good news and bad news. You shouldn't have any problem crossing if you avoid highways. It looks like the only checkpoints are on the major thoroughfares. There are lots of bush roads out there, and the terrain is fairly level with no major obstacles."

"That's the good news. What's the bad news?"

"Because the border is so easy to cross, there's a lot of smuggling—mostly drugs and consumer goods. Both Nigeria and Benin have border patrols, but that's a lot of area to cover. If you had the drone, you'd be able to manage it easily."

"Go ahead. Rub it in." He sent Kristi's cell number to Shields. "I'm sending you Kristi's phone number just in case."

"I've already got that. I got her cell info from the State Department when she was abducted. It didn't help us because her phone was left behind."

He ought to have known. "You're always one step ahead."

"That is literally my job description."

Malik went over his plan with her. "We'll take back roads through the bush, heading toward Parakou. I'll let you know when we arrive. Then we'll get some sleep at a hotel near the airport and catch a flight out tomorrow."

"Don't buy your tickets until you reach the airport, and get the first flight out of the country that you can," Shields cautioned. "We can't be sure the Sky Kings don't have a presence in Benin. In fact, it's likely that they do. The moment your names show up in the system, they might get word. Better safe than sorry."

"Copy that."

"Also, I'm sending you an alternate credit card to use so that you don't use the same one you used to buy the tickets and pay for the rental in Abuja. They might have that information."

As usual, Shields had thought of everything.

"How are things there?"

"We're wrapping up early. The deal has gone through, and our well-heeled businessmen are ready to head back to the US."

"That's good news."

"Stay safe, Malik. Watch your six."

"You, too." Malik ended the call, started the engine,

telling Kristi what Shields had said as he drove back to the dusty dirt road that had led them here.

"She's on top of everything, isn't she?" Kristi's phone buzzed. She tapped it and held it up for Malik to see. On her screen was a selfie of Shields, waving, with text that said only, "Hi!"

Kristi took a selfie and sent it back to Shields. "I expected her to be a lot older. She's so smart and good at her job."

"Our intel team is mostly women, and they're top-notch. I think Corbray and Tower see us ex-military dudes as interchangeable, but Elizabeth, Holly, and Gabriela—they're the brains."

Kristi slid a hand up his arm, squeezed his bicep. "They might be the brains, but you're the brawn. I like brawn."

"Hold that thought for a few more hours, angel. When we get to the Parakou Hilton, I'm going to show you what brawn is for."

KRISTI SAT IN SILENCE, grateful they were safe in the vehicle, while Malik narrated what he saw through his NVGs on the road below.

"They're definitely smugglers. The one on this side of the border just handed over an envelope of cash. The other guy is counting it. Now they're walking to the rear of the truck, probably to inspect the goods."

Kristi could hear the men's voices in the distance, but she couldn't see them. A cargo door clanked open. Voices. Then the door was slammed shut.

"Now the one who paid is climbing into the driver's seat."

Kristi heard the engine start, jackals or wild dogs howling somewhere nearby.

"They're driving away. I'll wait until I'm sure they're gone, and then we'll cross."

It was after midnight now, and Kristi couldn't wait to get a shower and a night's rest. It turned out that running from killers was exhausting work.

Was today the day they'd almost been killed by a train—or was that yesterday?

No, that was today.

"When you get bars again, start looking for a hotel close to the airport. I'm not sure we'll be able to get a room. We might have to spend the night in the vehicle." There was a note of apology in his voice, as if this were somehow his fault.

"As long as I'm with you, and we're safe, I don't care."

He glanced around with the NVGs, flipped them up, and handed her his helmet. "Time to roll."

She put on the helmet, adjusted it for her smaller head, and flipped down the NVGs, watching for humans, for movement, for anything that might be a danger.

Malik drove down the embankment to the dirt road and made a left, heading west once more. They drove without music, neither of them speaking, until, at last, Malik broke the silence.

"We're over the border. We're in Benin."

Kristi exhaled. "Thank God."

But her sense of relief was fleeting and incomplete, the darkness and the vast openness of the landscape seeming to press in on her. She couldn't forget Elizabeth's warning about the Sky Kings having a possible presence in Benin. Out here, it would be so easy for those bastards to abduct them and drag them back to Nigeria.

"We're going to make it, angel." Malik reached over, took her hand, his gaze on the bushland ahead of them. "I'll find a road into Parakou, and we'll be there soon."

It took them almost three hours, thanks to meandering roads, but at last Parakou came into view, the city's lights a welcoming sight.

"There's a Hotel les Routiers that says it's open." She made a reservation using the credit card information Elizabeth had given them and the surname of her nursing supervisor in Kaduna. "It says here that French is the official language. I don't know much French. Do you?"

"I can manage Spanish. I know a little Arabic and a little Farsi, but that's it."

"We are Mr. and Mrs. Okoro, by the way."

"Good to know."

When they reached the hotel, Malik went inside to get the keys, while Kristi stayed in the car. He returned quickly. "Okay, Mrs. Okoro, let's get some sleep."

"What I want is a shower."

The room was spacious with tile floors, a ceiling fan, a table and chairs, and a large bathroom with a tub and a shower that consisted of a showerhead and a drain in the floor—no walls or curtains.

Kristi set her bags aside, checked for bedbugs, then stripped, grabbed her toiletries, and walked into the bathroom to shower. The water was nice and hot as she stepped under the spray. She was rinsing the shampoo from her hair when Malik entered.

"Mind if I join you?"

"Please."

He took the pistol out of his waistband and set it on the counter. Then he removed his clothes and walked over to her in graceful strides, the sight of his beautiful naked body like a jolt of caffeine.

He turned her to face away from him, took the conditioner from her, and worked it through her hair, massaging her scalp.

She closed her eyes. "That feels good."

His fingers lingered over the sore spot where she'd struck her head. "You've still got a little lump. How's your head?"

"Right now?" She turned to face him, rinsed the conditioner from her hair. "Fine."

He took the soap and went to work on her, washing her skin in a way that was decidedly sensual, hands sliding over soap-slick breasts, his touch arousing her.

She rinsed, took the soap from him, and washed him, hands sliding over his muscles—pecs, shoulders, biceps, abs, obliques, glutes. She caressed his erection, the soap making her hand glide easily up and down his length.

His eyes drifted shut, his brow furrowing as she went faster.

But this time she wanted to give him something more.

She stepped out of the way of the spray, let the water rinse the soap away. Then she traded places with him and got to her knees.

He gave a little groan of anticipation, his fingers sliding into her wet hair as she took him into her mouth. "Kristi."

She moved her hand and mouth in tandem up and down his length, swirling her tongue around the head of his cock. But she knew what made him come apart.

Holding the base of his cock loosely, she flicked the underside just beneath the head, focusing on his frenulum, that little ridge of nerve-dense tissue. She treated it like he treated her clit—licking, sucking, caressing it with her lips.

His body tensed, his fingers leaving her hair, his arms shooting out to support him, his palms flat against the tile wall. "*Geezus.*"

Thrilled by his response, she kept at it, wanting to give him as much pleasure as she could, wanting to show him how much he meant to her.

His breath came faster now, his abs jerking. "God, Kristi."

It turned her on to see him so turned on, a deep ache between her thighs.

Abruptly, he stopped her, drew her to her feet, and backed her up against the wall. "I promised you brawn."

Her pulse skipped.

He grabbed her ass, lifted her off her feet—and pushed himself inside her.

She wrapped her arms around his neck and her legs around his waist as he drove himself into her, his deep, quick thrusts making her come hard and fast. She cried out as bliss washed through her, Malik groaning against her neck as he let himself go.

They stayed like that until the water ran cold, then dried each other off and curled up together naked in bed.

"Nurses, man." Malik kissed her wet hair. "You know anatomy."

Kristi smiled—and was soon fast asleep.

18

Malik woke early, the sounds of the city rousing him from sleep. He checked flights on his phone and found an outgoing flight to Rabat, the capital of Morocco. It was leaving in three hours. That gave them enough time to pack up, eat breakfast, and head to the airport. He'd buy the tickets there.

He kissed Kristi awake, grateful beyond words to have her here with him—safe and alive. "Good morning, angel."

She smiled, stretched, one beautiful breast appearing from beneath the sheet, inviting him to kiss its dark nipple.

Well, he couldn't resist that, but, sadly, there wasn't time for more.

"There's a flight that leaves for Morocco in three hours. We should have some breakfast and then drive to the airport."

While Kristi dressed and packed up, Malik heated two MREs and made a pot of coffee in the tiny pot that came with the room. They ate together at the table, talking about the future for the first time.

"Where are you going to work?" Kristi asked.

"When I quit, Tower refused to accept my resignation. I might still have a job—if we can get home without a major international incident."

"If it's okay with you, I'm going to look for a nursing job in Denver." She said it casually, but there was nothing casual about it—not for Malik.

She wanted to live close to him.

The thought made his pulse pick up.

Play it cool, bruh.

"You're welcome to stay at my place for as long as you need."

Yeah, you're chill. She can see right through you.

She met his gaze over the top of her coffee cup, a smile on her lips. "I'd like that."

When they'd finished breakfast, they loaded the vehicle and set off for the airport.

Malik locked the doors and then entered their next destination into the navigation system. "Did you put the GPS tag in your shirt?"

"It's in my bra."

"Lucky GPS tag."

"How do we know if those bastards have men watching this airport, too?"

"We don't. Keep your eyes and ears open. If you see or hear anything that doesn't seem right, say something."

He pulled out into the street, where it was every driver for himself, motorbikes by the dozens threading their way through traffic, not a stop sign or traffic light to be seen. "I guess it's drive at your own risk."

"Yeah, no kidding."

They headed down the road, which seemed to be Parakou's main street, following the navigation system's directions and slowing at major intersections.

CRASH!

A collision brought the SUV to a stop, the airbag hitting Malik in the face with enough force to leave him stunned. It took him a moment to realize they'd been T-boned by a white van, their path blocked in front by a black SUV.

"Kristi, angel, are you okay?"

"Yes. They have guns, Malik."

Men with handkerchiefs over their faces piled out of the van, raised their rifles.

"Hold on!" Malik kicked the vehicle into reverse and floored it, other cars and motorbikes making room for him.

Then he yanked the wheel, turning them around.

Rat-at-at-at! Rat-at-at-at! Rat-at-at-at!

Kristi screamed.

"Get down!" Malik felt one of the tires blow and then another, the rubber shredded by AK rounds.

He drove on rims as fast as he could, turning a corner, making for an alleyway. "When I stop, jump out and run for that set of stairs. Do you see it?"

"Y-yes."

"Grab your backpack. Make sure you have your phone." Malik turned into the alleyway, parked the SUV between two buildings. "Go!"

Kristi jumped out and ran.

Malik climbed out, grabbed his duffel, and followed, catching up with her. "Run!"

Her legs weren't as long as his, and she couldn't take the stairs two at a time. They had reached the first landing when the bastards found them.

"Keep going!" Malik dropped to one knee, grabbed his rifle out of the duffel bag, checked it—and fired at the men who'd jumped out, rifles in their hands.

One down. Two. Three.

The black SUV sped into the alley from the other direction, and Malik knew it was time to move. He had no cover here.

Rifle in hand, duffel on his shoulder, he ran to the rooftop.

"Where do we go now?" Kristi's panicked expression tore at him.

She was terrified.

"Do you have your phone?"

"Y-yes." She drew it out of her jeans pocket.

"Text Shields." He opened his duffel, put on his body armor and helmet. "Tell her we're under attack. Let her know they're trying to abduct us from this location and that we're under fire. I'm going to have to shoot our way out of this."

He moved to the edge of the roof, looked down to see seven men huddled together, one pointing up at them.

"Okay. Done."

"Good." Malik watched the men in the alley below. "Go and see if there's another stairway on the other side. All of the guys are over here. They won't see you."

"Okay." She hurried off to do as he'd asked.

He could easily take them all out, but that would give them time to bring in reinforcements—or the police. He didn't want this to become an international incident, and he sure as hell didn't want to waste away behind bars here in Benin.

"Yes! There's another stairway here."

"Let's go!" He shouldered his duffel and followed her, the two of them reaching the street. "See that auto-rickshaw? That's our ride."

Malik knew he would attract unwanted attention armed like this, but he couldn't do anything about that right now.

Kristi climbed into the back of the auto-rickshaw.

Malik was right behind her. "Drive! Drivez-vouz! Go!"

Eyes wide, the driver nodded and pulled out into traffic.

Kristi looked over her shoulder. "Malik, they're coming!"

Fuck.

Malik looked back, saw the black SUV turning the corner, a man with an AK leaning out the window.

KRISTI WATCHED as the black SUV drew closer, panic turning her blood to ice, making her mouth go dry. It honked its horn and threatened to run over anyone or anything that got in its way. Then the man leaning out of the window raised his rifle.

Rat-at-at! Rat-at-at! Rat-at-at!

She screamed, ducked, her heart pounding so hard that it hurt.

The tuk-tuk driver stopped, jumped out, and ran away, leaving them stranded in the middle of the street.

"Shit!" Malik was about to jump into the driver's seat, when the white van came from the other direction, blocking them.

Men with weapons leaped out, rushed at them.

Malik dropped the rifle, raised his hands, his voice soft and calm, his eyes looking into hers. "Stay strong, Kristi. Don't panic. Your job now is to survive *no matter what*. Just survive. Do you hear me? You're tagged. Cobra *will* find us."

"O-okay." She raised her hands, too, backpack slung over her shoulder.

How was she supposed to not panic?

Three men grabbed Malik and his duffel bag, while another grabbed Kristi, rough hands digging into her arms, dragging her to the van, shoving her inside. She crawled over to sit beside Malik, huddled against him.

"Breathe, Kristi," he whispered.

She tried, but it didn't stop her heart from racing or untie the knot in her stomach.

The last man jumped in and slammed the door shut, and the van began to move.

"Take his weapons and their phones, you imbeciles! Bind them!" a man in the front passenger seat shouted.

Men moved in on Malik, took his pistols, searched him for weapons and his cell phone, then ripped Kristi's backpack from her. They found her phone and tossed it with Malik's out onto the street. Then they bound Kristi's and Malik's wrists, the ropes tight.

"To the airport." The man in the passenger seat looked over his shoulder at them. "Mr. Jones. Miss Chang. Or should I say Mr. and Mrs. Okoro? I am Samuel Kuti. I am so happy to have found you."

"I bet you are." Malik seemed more angry than afraid.

"You killed three of my men, Mr. Jones."

"I've killed *nineteen* of your men, Sammy." Malik grinned. "That's the current count, right?"

Kuti's smile tightened. "I believe you are right."

Why was Malik provoking him? Did he not know that it was considered impolite to call someone you didn't know by their first name, let alone to use a nickname?

"How did you find us?"

"The clerk at the hotel called. We sent your photos to hotels and airports all around the region."

"You're one of these Sky King assholes?"

Fury spread over Kuti's face. "I am not worthy to be one of them. You will speak of them with respect."

"Not a chance."

Kuti didn't seem to know how to take Malik's defiance. "You don't know who you're up against. By the end of this day, you will have suffered so much that you will wish you had never been born."

"By the end of this day, Sam, you'll be dead."

Malik sounded so confident, so sure of himself, but Kristi had heard Kuti. Fear for Malik made her heart constrict. What would they do to him?

Cobra will come for us.

Malik had said it, and she hoped to God it was true. If they didn't come...

Adrenaline shot through her, made it hard to breathe.

"Easy, Kristi," Malik whispered.

Wasn't he afraid? Wasn't he worried about what Kuti would do to him?

It didn't take long to reach the airport. When the van stopped, they were dragged out and marched toward a large helicopter, its rotors already spinning.

Two of the men stayed behind—one with each vehicle —while Kristi and Malik were forced to board the helicopter and strapped into their seats. The others put on earphones, but left Kristi and Malik without.

"It's going to be noisy," Malik warned her.

The helicopter lifted off, the sound deafening as it nosed its way into the wind and away from the airport, Parakou disappearing behind them and, with it, the hope that had kept Kristi going. Every mile they'd traveled, the quicksand, the railway bridge—none of it meant anything now.

Malik caught her gaze, said something she couldn't hear, but she read his lips. "It's not over."

Then she remembered the story he'd told her about the ambush in Afghanistan. They'd been attacked. They'd lost a helicopter. They'd even run out of ammunition. Then, when it had seemed that all was lost, help had come. They had survived.

Would help reach them in time?

The flight seemed to last forever, though in reality it was probably less than two hours. Her fingers had long since gone numb, the ropes on her wrists cutting off her circulation. She knew where they were when she saw the Lagos skyline and the Gulf of Guinea come into view, skyscrapers and then a vast expanse of blue.

The helicopter landed in an open field outside of town, and she and Malik were both dragged out of the helicopter and taken to a waiting van, Kristi's hearing strangely muted from the noise of the chopper.

"We didn't search her," one of the men called to Kuti.

The other men laughed, the sound tinted with lust.

"I'd like to search her."

Kuti glared at them. "I told you not to touch her. The Kings will decide her fate."

Kristi was placed far from Malik this time, the door slamming shut.

Kuti once again took the front passenger seat. "Enjoy your last moments without pain, Mr. Jones."

THEY DROVE through the streets of Lagos, Malik watching, waiting for any chance to break free and attack. He couldn't risk it now, not in such close quarters, unarmed with his wrists bound. There was too great a chance he'd sustain an injury that would make it impossible to escape later—or that Kristi would be hurt or killed in the process.

No, he would watch. He would wait for the right moment.

And what if the right moment never comes?

It would come. It always did.

Kristi said she'd gotten a message off to Shields, but Malik wasn't sure how close the team was to wrapping up operations there. Shields had said they were finishing early. That meant they should be getting ready to head home today.

Of course, they would have to file a flight plan and get permission from the Nigerian government. Add flight time to that, ground transportation, and planning the operation. That meant they'd be here, guns blazing, in twenty-four hours at best.

All you have to do is survive until they get here.

He couldn't share this with Kristi, of course. She'd been through so much already, and he could see that she was terrified. He couldn't do anything about that now. He couldn't even make eye contact with her.

Hang in there, angel.

He'd been relieved to hear that fucker Kuti tell the others to keep their hands off her. But what had he meant that the Sky Kings would decide her fate?

As for his own fate, Malik knew these next hours would put him to the test. Kuti had threatened him with torture, and Malik had no doubt the son of a bitch meant it.

They turned off the road, driving through some kind of parking lot toward what looked like a large warehouse—the kind of place where people could scream without being heard.

Fear snaked through Malik's belly.

He'd withstood exhaustion and physical pain on count-less missions. He'd been wounded more than once and had almost died in Afghanistan when he'd caught a bullet to the chest. But he'd never faced torture. Still, he wasn't helpless.

He'd made it through SERE training—Survival, Evasion, Resistance, Escape—and had all the tools that the army could give him.

What he didn't have was a reason for this.

What did Kuti stand to gain by torturing him? Was it simply revenge?

The vehicle entered large bay doors and drew to a stop. The doors opened, and their captors climbed out, dragging Kristi with them first and then Malik.

Kuti spoke in rapid Naija to his men, two of whom grabbed Kristi by the arms and led her away.

She called for him. "Malik!"

Malik broke free from the men who held him and got in Kuti's face. "Where are you taking her? Where are you taking my wife?"

"I am being merciful to you both. My men will lock her in a room where she won't be able to hear you scream—or would you rather have her watch me break you?"

Malik leaned closer, his face now an inch from Kuti's. "You and what army?"

Kuti stepped back. "You have reason to boast, Mr. Jones. You are a skilled fighter. But my expertise is the use of pain to make people talk."

"What do you want to talk about?"

"I want to know who helped you rescue your wife—and I want to know what you did with Jidda's nephew, Obi."

Fuck.

That's not what Malik had expected him to say, and it raised the stakes. Malik couldn't betray David, and he would rather die than let these fuckers get their hands on Obi again. He would have to keep his teeth together, no matter what they did to him.

"I was alone out there. Your men were distracted by

murdering one of their own. They made it easy for me to scare them with the drone and get my wife."

"Mr. Jones, our tracker found two different kinds of shell casings and four sets of footprints."

Son of a bitch.

"Your tracker is full of shit. Ask the men I *didn't* kill how many men they saw."

Kuti laughed, pointed to one corner of the room. "String him up."

Malik took the scene in. Kuti with no weapon in his hands. Four men with rifles on their shoulders moving toward him. The bar hanging from the ceiling by a rope-and-pulley system. The two men standing near the bay door, talking, rifles in hand.

He drew a breath, focused his mind, then jumped up and caught Kuti in the face with his heel, knocking him to the floor.

One of Kuti's men came at him, but Malik dropped him with a scissor kick to the jaw, the man's rifle clattering to the concrete.

Malik leapt, rolled, and came up holding the rifle. But his wrists were bound, making it impossible for him to hold it properly and sight his shot. Holding the AK like a pistol, he aimed as best he could and fired at the two men by the door, killing one of them. But before he could fire again, the rifle was knocked from his grasp, the butt of an AK striking him hard in the temple.

Pain exploded inside his cranium. He staggered back, tried to give himself room to recover, but it was over. Another blow from the AK, this time to his gut, knocking the breath from his lungs.

Two men dragged him, doubled-over, to the corner and began to bind his arms just above the elbows.

"Make it tight." Kuti got to his feet, holding a handkerchief over his bloody nose. "You are strong and clever, Mr. Jones, but what do you know about *tabay*?"

He gave a nod to his men, who pulled on the rope, hoisting Malik off his feet, leaving him to hang in mid-air.

Geezus.

He sucked in a breath at the pain, his body weight hanging entirely from his shoulders, which had been forced into an unnatural angle by the ropes that bound his elbows. He gritted his teeth, looked Kuti straight in the eyes. "Fuck you, motherfucker."

19

Kristi was shoved into a dark room, the door locked behind her. For a moment, she stood there, paralyzed by fear, the thrumming of her pulse in her ears the only sound she could hear. She took one breath, then another, trying to rein in her panic.

It wasn't working.

They were going to torture Malik. They were going to kill him. Malik was only here because of her, and now they were going to kill him.

Cobra will come for us.

He was so certain.

But what if Kristi had screwed up sending that text message? Or their work on their other mission wasn't done? Or the GPS tags had stopped working and they didn't know where to find them? Even if Shields had gotten the message and the GPS tags worked, how long would it take for Cobra to get here?

Kristi didn't know.

Until they arrived, she and Malik were alone.

You can't just stand here in the dark freaking out.

Kristi turned and walked back toward the door, a seam of light coming through the crack around it. She reached with her hands, searching the wall for a light switch.

There.

She flipped it, and fluorescent lights flickered on, revealing her prison.

An old wooden table. Two chairs. A pile of discarded cardboard boxes.

She glanced inside the boxes, found them empty. There was no phone, no water, no comforts of any kind, apart from the chairs.

She sat, despair and dread heavy in her chest.

Malik.

Unless Cobra got here in a big, fat hurry...

Oh, God.

Kristi had worked her entire adult life to alleviate suffering. She'd seen people in terrible pain for all kinds of reasons—gunshot wounds, diseases, car crashes, fires—and had done all she could to take their pain away. She couldn't bear to think of anyone deliberately inflicting suffering on another person, especially not the man she loved.

He loved her—she knew he did. She loved him, too, but she hadn't told him, not yet, not with words. She'd thought there would be time to tell him how she felt later, when they weren't on the run, maybe over a candlelight dinner in Denver.

Now, she might never get that chance.

Tears blurred her vision, fear for him overwhelming her.

An hour went by, then two. She didn't have a watch or her phone, so she couldn't be sure. Each moment was unbearable. Horrible possibilities flashed through her mind, all the terrible things they could be doing to Malik, what they might do to her.

God, help us.

Rage. It hit her hard.

No! No, Malik's life could not end in this dirty warehouse in Lagos. The man who had fought his way through dozens of battles and survived two wars could not die at the hands of criminals.

When you're part of something, like the Rangers or even Cobra, you're fighting for your team, not just for yourself. You keep fighting until you can't fight any longer.

Well, Malik was her team. She would fight for him. But how? She had no combat skills, no idea how to use a gun. She'd never even struck another person.

Restless, desperate, she stood, her hip hitting the table, making a small drawer slide out. She hadn't noticed it before, maybe because it was tucked beneath the table. But there, in the drawer, was a utility knife, the kind used to open cardboard boxes.

Men's voices, a key in the lock.

She slid the drawer shut and sat just as the door opened.

The two men who'd locked her in here stepped inside with a man in a bright blue tailored business suit. He was young and well-dressed, an expensive watch on his wrist, a thick gold chain around his neck, designer sunglasses concealing his eyes.

Kristi glared up at him, her fear becoming rage. "You must be one of those fucking Sky Kings."

He jerked as if he'd been struck.

One of Kuti's minions stepped forward, hand raised as if to strike her. "You should kneel to him!"

"Kneel?" She laughed. "Never."

The man in the blue suit stopped him with a wave of his hand. He drew off his sunglasses. "Miss Chang."

"That's Mrs. Jones to you."

He gave her a tight smile. "Mrs. Jones, then. I am Captain Jonathan Bello."

"Captain of what—sex traffickers?"

He laughed, his gaze moving over her. "I heard that you are spirited and beautiful."

He spoke English well.

"I am *angry*—and married."

"I understand you made an agreement with Jidda—your nursing care in exchange for his protection."

"I agreed to help him in exchange for my safety and *freedom*."

"Yes, I understand. Unfortunately, Jidda would never have been able to release you. I'm sorry he did not make that clear. But he did his best in offering you his protection. We are prepared to honor that agreement. We will offer you our protection in exchange for your medical skills and your company."

"You want me to be your nurse whore?"

"There is no reason to put it into such crude language. You would live in comfort, caring for me, my elderly father, and our fellow Sky Kings, and we would visit your bed as we choose."

Her answer came straight from her gut. "I would rather die. I will not live my life as a glorified sex slave."

He screwed up his face as if she'd just said something ridiculous. "Come now, Mrs. Jones. You would want for nothing. You would have children—"

"Have children—with you?" She laughed, grateful once more for her IUD. "Not a chance. Do you think it's a small thing to force a woman to have sex with men she doesn't desire and doesn't love? It's *rape*."

"You would get used to it, even learn to enjoy it."

She shook her head. "No, I would hate you even more

than I do now. I would bide my time and try to escape—or kill you in your sleep."

The shock on the minions' faces made her laugh.

"Does no one talk to him like this? Do you all bow and scrape and kiss his ass? These so-called Sky Kings make millions, while you live off the crumbs that fall from their tables and die fighting their battles. They're not kings. They're not royalty. They're nothing but a cartel, a crime ring, crooks who profit off the misery—"

One of the minions struck her—hard. "Shut your mouth!"

"I will leave you here to think about my offer, Mrs. Jones. You must decide what matters more to you—your life or your pride." He turned to the minions, and they walked out the door together. "Leave her here. She could be useful later. Mr. Kuti tells me that her husband hasn't yet given him the name of his accomplice or told him what he did with Jidda's boy."

They were torturing Malik to get him to betray David and Obi.

Hearing them speak of Malik like this... knowing they would torture him until he shattered... knowing they would kill him...

To hell with them.

She opened the drawer, grabbed the utility knife, and cut the ropes that bound her wrists.

NEVER SHALL I fail my comrades. I will always keep myself mentally alert, physically strong and morally straight, and I will shoulder more than my share of the task, whatever it may be, one-hundred-percent and then some.

Cold sweat ran down Malik's temples, trickled down his forehead, and into his eyes, the pain in his shoulders, upper back, neck, arms, and hands unbearable. He'd long since learned not to kick or struggle. It only made the pain worse.

Christ!

He gritted his teeth, reciting snippets of the Ranger Creed to keep his mind focused. He could not break. He could not betray David or his family. He could not give up Obi and turn him over to be the Sky Kings' pawn.

Stay strong. Stay strong.

Cobra knew where they were. They would come.

Kuti had walked away a few minutes ago, leaving him with a few of his grunts, who alternately threatened him and found petty ways to hurt him. They had lowered him so that his feet barely touched the floor—then raised him up again. They'd grabbed his legs and had taken turns hanging on him, their weight amplifying his pain.

One pointed his AK at Malik's crotch. When they quit laughing about that, the other flicked his lighter and moved the flame close to Malik's bare feet.

Malik saw his chance. He grabbed the bastard by the neck with his legs, and lifted him off the ground with a jerk, breaking his neck and letting him fall to the concrete.

Fuck, it hurt, but it was worth it.

Malik taunted the other one. "Come here, fucker. Bring your AK. Get closer."

The guy backed off and kept his distance.

Malik remained as he was, hanging, his arms tied together at the elbows, reciting the Creed, for another ten minutes—or had it been an hour?

Then Kuti walked in with some guy dressed in a neon blue suit.

The man with the AK lay face down on the floor to greet

him, then clambered to his feet, pointed to his dead friend, and explained what had happened, Malik catching only catch bits and pieces.

Kuti walked over to the dead man, knelt down.

Malik rubbed it in, rage giving him strength. "Twenty-one."

The bastard he'd kicked in the jaw had died, too.

Kuti glared up at Malik, but made way for the man in the peacock suit.

"Let him down. Bring us chairs."

Malik was lowered to the floor, the relief in his shoulders and upper back so intense he almost moaned, though his arms still ached from lack of circulation. "Who the hell are you?"

"I am Captain Jonathan Bello. I just spoke with your lovely and spirited wife."

"Stay the fuck away from Kristi."

"As much as it pains me that you two are in this situation, we want information from you, information you refuse to give. The man who helped you raid our camp and steal your wife back—I'm certain he's Nigerian or we would have caught him trying to escape with you."

"Maybe—or maybe not."

"And the boy Obi. Where is he? He was Jidda's nephew, and Jidda worked for me. Obi must carry on in Jidda's place. He has seen too much to leave us now."

"I don't know where Obi is." Malik tried to shrug and rotate his shoulders, but the motion sent pain shooting down his arms. "We freed him and let him go."

"That is what you keep telling Samuel. Three hours of *tabay* is almost always enough to get the truth from a man, but I think you are still holding out on us. You are too defiant, Mr. Jones, as is your wife. I offered her a life serving me in bed and out, and she chose to die."

Malik's heart hit his sternum, driving the breath from his lungs. "You ... killed her? You fucking son of—"

"Oh, she's safe for now. I'm giving her time to rethink her choice." Bello stood, motioned for Samuel to raise Malik up again.

Malik tried to prepare himself, but the pain stunned him as they hoisted him up again. He clenched his teeth, afraid that if he opened his mouth he'd scream.

"I asked Samuel not to do any permanent harm until I got here and had a chance to speak with you. I made your wife an offer, and now I'll do the same for you. Tell us what we want to know, and we'll kill you with a single shot to the head. Fast, painless. All of this will end, and you can rest."

When Malik said nothing, Bello went on.

"If you don't, Samuel can do whatever he likes with you. He enjoys lighting fires beneath people and burning them slowly. They can't help but kick and twist as they try to escape the heat, but that greatly increases their pain. In the end, they always break. You will break, Mr. Jones, and you will die horribly. Why not make it easier on yourself and your wife? If we must, we can get the information from her. I don't think Kristi would last as long as you have."

The thought of Kristi suffering torture put terror in Malik's chest. "Fuck you, Bello! Stay away from her, or you'll be the one who dies today."

Bello and Kuti laughed and walked away, speaking quietly together.

But Malik overheard them.

"We use them against each other, see? Light one of your fires. We'll bring her to watch. When she sees him burning, she'll tell us what we want to know."

Fire.

Chills slid down Malik's spine.

If he could just hold out a little longer.

Never shall I fail my comrades...

KRISTI INCHED her way along the dusty ventilation shaft, flat on her belly, trying not to sneeze, dust making her skin itch. She thought she understood where she was going now, having taken some wrong turns. If she followed the shaft along the back of the building, it ought to take her to the big garage-like room where they'd last had Malik.

She'd cut through her ropes and looked for a way out of her prison, thinking at first that she could climb into the ceiling. Fear that it wouldn't hold her made her give up that idea. Then she'd discovered the ventilation shaft in the back wall. It was barely large enough for her to pass, but it was her only way out. She'd pried the screen loose, crawled inside, and had crept her way along, looking into each room as she passed.

What if they'd moved him? What if he was too hurt to fight? What would she do if she found him?

Don't think about that now.

She inched her way along, grateful she wasn't claustrophobic, the utility knife in her pocket. Then up ahead, she saw light.

Carefully, quietly, she moved forward and looked through the screen. It was a small room, like a closet. The lights were on, but she didn't see anyone. A box of whisky. A bag of rice. Bags of dried beans. A carton of cigarettes. Matches. And there in the corner were her backpack and Malik's duffel bag, their contents dumped out.

The first aid kit. One of Malik's pistols. The knife he'd worn around his ankle.

Oh, how she would love to get her hands on those. All she would have to do is crawl out, put what she needed into her backpack, and then disappear again—before anyone walked in or spotted her.

Sure. Easy. Piece of cake.

Pulse racing, she pushed out the screen, crept out, and grabbed the first aid kit and stuck it and the knife and one of his pistols into her backpack.

Voices.

She was about to crawl back into the shaft when her gaze fell on the matches and the whisky again, and an idea came to her. If she could create a distraction...

She grabbed a bottle of whisky and the matches and tucked them into her backpack. She stuck her backpack inside the shaft, then slid in feet-first and pulled the screen back into position.

The voices came closer.

A man walked in, grabbed a pack of cigarettes, and left again.

For a moment, she lay there, heart pounding.

Pushing her backpack in front of her, she moved steadily down the shaft. A dark room. A room where two men sat cleaning guns.

There was only about twenty feet left of ventilation shaft. God, what if it didn't go all the way to that garage? What if she couldn't find him?

Keep going.

She inched along toward the end of the shaft. But as she drew nearer, she saw that it didn't end there, but turned to the left where a large screen opened into the garage.

A man's shouts. More shouts.

A groan.

Malik!

She crept forward until she reached the screen—and her blood went cold.

He hung from a rod, his elbows and wrists tied together so that his weight rested on his shoulders. It must be excruciating, like crucifixion but without nails. Kuti stood there, shouting up at him, while one of his men piled something beneath him.

Kindling. Firewood.

Oh, God!

They were going to burn him.

Some part of her wanted to punch out the screen, take out Malik's pistol, and start shooting. But with her luck she'd miss and run out of ammo—or hit Malik.

If these fuckers wanted to play with fire, she would help them out.

Do you know what you're doing? What if you blow yourself up?

She was clueless, but she had to try.

She used the bend in the shaft to turn herself around and headed back the way she'd come. When she reached the closet where she'd found their gear, she went to work. She took some gauze out of the first aid kit, opened the whisky bottle, and stuffed the gauze inside like a cork, tilting it to soak the gauze. Then she pushed out the screen, struck a match, and lit the gauze, rolling the bottle toward the box of whisky.

Not bothering to pull the screen back into place, she crawled as fast as she could back toward the garage. She needed to be there and ready when the fire drew these bastards away.

Smoke. She could smell it. Could they?

Shattering glass. A small explosion.

Smoke filled the ventilation shaft, engulfing her.

Shit!

Kristi held her breath and moved faster, pushing her backpack ahead of her.

Hang on, Malik. I'm coming.

20

M alik gritted his teeth and fought to hold on, both shoulders dislocated now. He'd suffered before—gunshot and shrapnel wounds—but he'd never endured anything like this, pain tearing him apart. But worse than the pain was knowing he had failed Kristi.

He had promised to get her home, and now...

Cobra will come.

Yes. The GPS trackers.

He latched onto her with his mind. Those beautiful eyes. Her big heart. Her silky dark hair. Her soft, brown skin.

Fight. Survive.

That's what he'd told her to do. That's what he had to do, too, no matter what they did to him.

Kuti stood a safe distance from Malik's feet, talking to one of his henchmen. "Go get his wife now. Captain Bello thinks she'll tell us what we need to know when she sees him burning and hears his screams."

Kristi.

Bello was right. She'd spent her entire life fighting to end suffering. She had such a big heart. If they roasted him, it would break her—and Malik wouldn't blame her for a moment. Hell, it might break him, too.

He closed his eyes, fought to slow his breathing, to breathe the pain away.

Smoke.

His eyes flew open, and he looked down at the pile of kindling and wood below his feet, thinking they must have lit it. But they hadn't. The kindling and firewood remained untouched.

A man ran in, shouting and gesturing. "The hallway is on fire!"

"Go get the woman! The Kings will kill us if she comes to harm. I'll find the captain and make sure he's safe."

The two men ran, leaving Malik hanging—literally.

Had they said the building was on fire?

Kristi.

They had her locked up somewhere, her wrists bound. She might be trapped and unable to get out.

Malik needed to get down. He needed to find her. But any movement at all made the pain unbearable. If he could get his leg over the bar...

He tried, almost passed out.

Smoke poured into the room from the door and from a ventilation shaft in the far wall. Then he heard coughing, and the metal screen that covered the ventilation shaft fell to the floor.

"Kristi?"

She crawled out, coughing, her face and clothes filthy with dirt and dust and smoke. She ran toward the wall where the rope that held him was tied off. "I'm so sorry, Malik! I'll get you down."

She lowered him to the floor.

His feet touched the floor, and he sank to his knees, his

legs weak. He had to tell her, to warn her. "Go. Leave me. Run."

"No!" She came up behind him and began cutting the ropes that bound his elbows, words spilling out of her in a panicked rush, punctuated by coughs. "I found a utility knife ... and cut through the ropes. There was a ventilation shaft ... and it took me a while to find my way around. I saw whisky ... and I got some of our things and then made my first Molotov cocktail."

Her words didn't make sense to him.

She'd broken free and started this fire? A Molotov cocktail?

Okay, he was hallucinating. She wasn't here at all. That's why his shoulders and arms still hurt so fucking much.

He blinked, tried to make the hallucination go away, but when he opened his eyes and turned his head, she was still there, talking and coughing.

"I saw they were going to burn you, so I had to create some kind of distraction. I think I ...." More coughing. "I think I inhaled too much ... smoke. Will you be able to walk? I've got morphine."

"No drugs." They would fuck up his mind even more, and he was clearly losing his shit. "I'm seeing things. You're not really here."

"Yes, I am." A soft hand against his cheek. "I'm here, Malik, and I love you."

The ropes slipped away from his elbows, the rush of blood through his arms bringing its own kind of pain, making him groan.

But he'd heard her. Hell, yes, he had.

She went to work on his wrists. "I think your shoulders are dislocated. God, I'm so sorry. I wish I'd gotten here sooner."

Then with another tug, his wrists were free.

He groaned through clenched teeth, his arms falling useless to his sides, the pain staggering as blood flow was restored.

She helped him to sit, the sound of her voice soothing, her touch cool. "I'm going to pop your shoulders back. It's not fun, but it will help with the pain."

"Okay." That's all he could say.

Blinding pain and then... *Snap!*

It didn't take away all of his suffering, but it was a huge relief.

She moved to his other side, took hold of his left arm.

A rush of agony and ... *Snap!*

He exhaled, relief leaving him dizzy.

"Can you walk? I grabbed one of your pistols. Are you going to be able to shoot?"

"I don't know." He fought to clear his head. "We need to get the fuck out of here. They'll be back the moment they realize you're missing."

He struggled to his feet, his arms like dead things swinging, heavy and aching, at his side, his fingers swollen and tingling. She got one of the SIGs out of her backpack, held it out for him. He reached for it, but lifting his arm was excruciating.

He managed to close his fingers around the handle, but his grip was weak and clumsy. Not good. "Let's move."

Men's voices. Angry shouts.

Running on adrenaline, Malik hurried with Kristi toward the wall near the door, hoping to take the bastards by surprise.

Bello and Kuti rushed in, maybe a dozen armed men behind them, all holding handkerchiefs over their faces and coughing. They didn't see Malik and Kristi flattened against the wall behind them.

"He's gone!" Bello shouted.

Malik ignored the pain in his arms and shoulders, raised the pistol, and squeezed out ten quick shots before he could no longer hold up his arms.

Bam! Bam! Bam! Bam! Bam! Bam! Bam!

Kuti fell dead along with one of his henchmen. Bello dropped to the floor, blood spilling from his side. Two more henchmen fell. One dropped his rifle and sank to the floor, moaning. The other shot went wild, Malik's aim off.

Malik had ten bullets left, but the element of surprise was gone. The bastards he hadn't killed turned on them, rifles raised.

Fuck.

"Kill him!" Bello shrieked. "Kill him and bring her to me!"

It happened all at once.

"No!" Kristi crying out, jumping in front of him.

Weapons firing. A blast. A blinding light.

BAM!

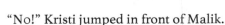

"No!" Kristi jumped in front of Malik.

Gunshots. A blinding light. An explosion.

She screamed, the sound lost in the mayhem as Malik's arm encircled her waist, dragging her to the floor beneath him, his body covering hers.

"Stay down!" he shouted.

Rat-at-at! Rat-at-at! Rat-at-at!

Shouts. Cries.

Then silence.

Smoke filled the air. A burst of static.

"Isaksen to Cobra Actual, targets eliminated."

Relief washed through Kristi, bringing tears to her eyes.

Cobra was here at last.

She and Malik were safe. They were going home.

Thor continued to speak into his radio. "We've found the package. I say again, we found the package. The place is about to go up. We're moving out."

"Cobra Actual to Isaksen, strong copy. Get the hell out of there."

"It's about damned time." Malik groaned as he rolled off Kristi, probably unable to push himself up.

Kristi got to her feet, her heart constricting at the pain on his face. She helped him to stand, Thor joining her. "God, am I glad to see you! He needs medical treatment. They dislocated both of his shoulders. Whatever you do, don't pull him by his arms. I think he's a little shocky."

"Copy that. We've got a doctor on the plane." Thor's gaze moved over Malik, probably checking for injuries. "Can you make it, brother?"

"I'm good. Let's get out of here."

Kristi put her arm around Malik's waist, steadying him as they moved together toward the exit, smoke filling the air, stinging her eyes, making her cough harder.

Thor opened the door for them, then they were out in the clean, fresh air, a helicopter landing in a field maybe fifty yards away, other Cobra operatives walking on either side of them, clearly watching for trouble.

"Where'd Tower get the helo?" Malik asked.

"Shields' buddy, David, lent it to us, along with the pilot," Thor answered.

Malik raised an eyebrow. "For how much?"

Next time she saw him, Kristi would give David a big hug.

They crossed the field, Thor helping Malik to board, then reaching down for Kristi, the others piling in behind them. They settled into their seats, Kristi buckling Malik's safety belt and putting the earphones on his head.

Malik watched her, his lips curving into a smile. "You're a pro at this."

"This *is* my third helicopter flight this week." She broke into another fit of coughing, her eyes watering.

"Kristi set the fire with some kind of Molotov cocktail," Malik told the others. "She freed herself, escaped through the ventilation system, and set the fire to create a distraction. Then she came after me. I think she inhaled a lot of smoke."

It was hard to argue when she was still coughing.

Lev gaped at her. "*You* did that? Badass."

"I couldn't let them kill him."

"Nick Andris. Thanks for saving Isaksen's life in Antarctica and for freeing Jones. That took courage."

She felt awkward accepting thanks from men who had just saved her life. "Thanks for coming after us."

Nick gave her a nod. "That's what we do."

"I'm Dylan Cruz. We've heard a lot about you these past few days. You are one tough chick."

Kristi didn't feel tough.

A big man introduced himself next, his accent unmistakably Scottish. "Quinn McManus, ma'am."

"Shields is his much better half," Malik said.

Quinn didn't seem insulted. "Aye, that she is. We're glad you're safe now."

"Is Elizabeth on the plane, too? I really want to meet her."

"Aye, and she'll be chuffed to meet you, too."

The helicopter lifted off and carried them over the city of Lagos to the Murtala Muhammed International Airport, black smoke from the fire rising into the blue sky, a reminder of the hell they had just escaped.

She found Malik watching her, a smile tugging at his lips. "What?"

"You look like a living, human dust bunny."

She laughed, but her laugh became a cough. "The ventilation shaft was filthy."

Malik frowned. "Our medic should check you out, too."

She wouldn't disagree with that. "Good idea."

It wasn't a long flight, but Malik quickly lapsed into unconsciousness.

Kristi checked his pulse at his wrists, where dark bruises had begun to form. She found the others watching her. Between coughing fits, she explained. "I'm just checking the circulation to his arms. They tied his elbows and ... wrists together behind his back and hung him up that way for hours. When I found him, he was hanging ... from dislocated shoulders, and they were getting ready to burn him."

Thor's expression hardened. "Jesus."

"Fuck. That must have hurt." Lev shook his head. "I wish we could have gotten here sooner, but we moved as quickly as we could. I don't think I've ever seen this team scramble faster than they did this morning."

Quinn removed his helmet, revealing a head of red hair. "We boarded the jet an hour after Elizabeth got your message."

Nick held up a canvas bag. "We got cell phones and a laptop. With any luck, the Nigerian government will be able to bring down the entire Sky King network."

God, Kristi hoped so.

Dylan looked angry. "If they do, I hope we can be a part of it. I'd enjoy taking these bastards out. *Hijoeputas*."

"Thank you. Thank you all."

Fifteen minutes later, the helicopter landed on a tarmac not far from a small jet.

Malik woke with a start, looked around.

Kristi took his hand. "We're at the airport."

He glanced over at the jet. "That's our flight home, angel."

She looked up and down the tarmac. "They can't get us here, can they?"

They'd been so close in Parakou, so close, and freedom had been snatched away.

Malik gave her a reassuring smile, lines of suffering on his face. "No way in hell."

The Cobra guys jumped out of the helicopter, Thor and Dylan turning back to help Kristi and Malik.

A tall man with dark blond hair descended from the airplane. "Good work, men. Jones, I'm relieved to see you in one piece."

"Thank you, sir. This is Kristi Chang. She's the reason I'm in one piece."

Kristi broke into a coughing fit when she tried to say hello.

"Derek Tower. Delighted to meet you, Miss Chang. I'm looking forward to the debriefing. Let's board and head home. Doc is waiting for you."

MALIK WALKED with Kristi back to the little medical bay in the rear of the jet, Kristi and Doc Sullivan helping him to lie down in one of two beds.

"Both of his shoulders were..." Kristi lapsed into another coughing fit, her struggle to breathe worrying Malik. "Dislocated. Edema in his hands from ... his elbows and wrists being tied. I suspect ... he's shocky. I can start an IV and..."

"You sit, Ms. Chang." Doc pointed to a chair. "I'll get his IV going, and then I'm going to check on you."

"I can wait." Malik's pain wasn't going anywhere. "Take care of her."

Doc ignored him, starting Malik's IV and insisting on giving him morphine. "You'll hate me a lot less when I examine you. Trust me on this."

Malik drifted in and out while Doc checked Kristi. "Your oxygen is ninety, and you're wheezing pretty badly. I'm going to neb you. When you're done, I want you to take a shower. I think it's the dust as much as the smoke. You need to get that off your skin. The steam will help. If your O2 is still low, I'll start an IV and give you a bolus of steroids. I'll get Elizabeth or Gabriela to help you."

"Thanks, Doctor Sullivan."

"It's just Doc."

Then it was Malik's turn.

Drowsy from the morphine, Malik did his best to answer questions, wincing as Doc checked his shoulders, back, elbows, and wrists. "For now, I'm going to stick with anti-inflammatories and ice. When we get back, I'm ordering an MRI of each shoulder, your neck, and maybe your thoracic spine. You might need surgery on your shoulders."

"Will I be able to work again?"

"I can't say. We'll have to see."

Fuck.

"Right." Malik had been focused on survival. He hadn't thought about what survival might bring—being permanently sidelined, losing his job.

Kristi loves you.

That thought was a balm to his battered body and soul, as potent as the morphine.

Whatever his future held, Kristi would be a part of it.

That mattered more to Malik than anything.

With Doc finished bothering him, Malik drifted into a drugged sleep.

KRISTI COUGHED her way through her introduction to Elizabeth Shields and Gabriela Marquez. Elizabeth showed her how to work the shower, gave her shampoo, conditioner, and a comb, while Gabriela, who was close to Kristi in size, went to get Kristi something to wear.

Kristi stepped under the hot spray, trying to breathe deeply, the albuterol from the nebulizer treatment making her shaky. The water ran dark, smoke and dirt and dust, washing down the drain.

We're safe now. We're on our way home.

It was hard for that thought to sink in, some part of her on guard, waiting for the worst to happen.

She finished her shower. It was good to be clean again, the stink of smoke gone. The steam and the nebulizer treatment together had reduced her coughing. She dried off and found panties, a T-shirt, and jeans waiting for her, folded neatly on a chair.

She dressed, combed her hair, and stepped out of the small shower room to find both Elizabeth and Gabriela waiting for her. It was the first female company she'd had since she was abducted. Maybe that's why she broke down.

She told the two of them everything from the moment she'd been abducted to the moment she'd recognized

Thor's voice, leaving out the sexy parts and her feelings for Malik. The two of them listened, both seeming to understand—how afraid she'd been, how unsure of herself she'd felt as she'd dragged herself through the ventilation shaft, how she couldn't seem to believe she was truly safe.

"Both Gabriela and I have survived abductions." Elizabeth took her hand. "I was kidnapped by a terrorist who would've slit my throat if not for Quinn. Gabriela was taken captive by a Colombian drug cartel for a week. We both know what it's like. It will take some time, but you'll get through this."

"You don't have to go through this alone." Gabriela handed her a tissue. "You're part of the Cobra family now. You saved one of ours from those *cabrones*, and Malik loves you. You can call me or Elizabeth any time you need to talk. I'm still blown away by the fact that you made a Molotov cocktail and set the warehouse on fire."

Elizabeth smiled. "Says the chick who gunned down the head of the Andes cartel and a bunch of his *sicarios*."

Kristi gaped at Gabriela. She was young and small like Kristi. "You did that?"

Gabriela nodded. "That's a story for another day. I think Doc wants to see you."

Kristi followed the two women back to the infirmary, where Doc stuck the pulse oximeter on her finger. "Ninety-six. That's better."

"How is Malik?" Kristi saw that he was sound asleep.

"I'm pretty sure he's going to need surgery. He'll be laid up for a while. I'm hoping he won't have permanent damage."

"Thanks."

"I'm told you started the fire to stop them from roasting

Jones, so thank *you*." He pointed to the other bed. "Now, rest. Doctor's orders."

Kristi went to lie down, but she couldn't sleep.

When Doc left the room, she got up and went to sit by Malik, her gaze moving over him. The exhaustion on his face. The dark purple bruises on his arms and wrists. The edema in his fingers. Overwhelmed by tenderness for him, she bent down, pressed a kiss to his forehead.

His eyes fluttered open, and he smiled. "Hey, beautiful."

She touched a palm to his cheek. "How do you feel?"

"Better."

"I think that's the morphine."

"Doc says he thinks I might need surgery on my shoulders."

"I wouldn't be surprised. Your poor shoulders sustained a lot of trauma, your arms and upper back, too. It's going to take you a while to heal."

"I've never felt pain like that. Those bastards wanted me to hand over David and Obi. I couldn't do it, Kristi. I couldn't —no matter what they did to me."

A hard lump formed in her throat. "I don't know how you did it. I don't know how you held out for so long. You're my hero, Malik. I love you."

She'd already told him, but she wasn't sure he remembered.

His lips curved in a smile. "I love you, too. I think I've been in love with you this entire time. I just didn't know how to tell you—or how to deal with the fact that we lived such different lives. Besides, we said no strings."

"Too hell with that. I want strings, Malik—all of them."

"Are you sure? What about working as a nurse on all seven continents?"

"Five out of seven isn't bad. All I wanted was adventure.

After lions, quicksand, and driving across the narrowest railway bridge in the world ahead of a freight train a hundred feet above croc-infested waters, what more is there?"

He chuckled. "I see your point."

"I think it's time for a different kind of adventure—one where we do normal stuff together."

"Yeah? Like what?"

"Watching TV. Eating real food. Sleeping in a bed made for two."

"That sounds pretty dull for a woman who slings Molotov cocktails." She could tell by the gleam in his eyes that he was teasing her.

"With you, nothing is dull." She bent down, kissed him.

21

They landed in Denver at four in the morning the next day. Malik and Kristi were taken via ambulance to University Hospital, where Cobra's concierge physician team met them and took over Malik's care.

Grateful for the morphine now, Malik slept through the MRIs—and woke to the unwelcome news that he would need surgery.

"Torn rotator cuffs," the doctor said. "With surgery and good physical therapy, you should heal well. You're relatively young and in peak fitness."

"How's my wife?" Malik had gotten so used to calling Kristi his wife that he didn't realize he'd said it, but once the words were out, he didn't take them back.

Okay, maybe that was the morphine. Or maybe it wasn't.

The doctor looked confused. "I didn't realize you two were married."

Malik cleared his throat. "It's a secret. We haven't told our parents."

"She's doing well. Her smoke inhalation was mild, and the irritation in her lungs will settle down over the next few days. I told her to wait outside because I didn't know she was family. She ought to have told me she was your spouse. I'll bring her right in."

"Please." Score.

She walked into his room, sat beside him. "The doctor says he thinks you'll make a full recovery after surgery. That's good news, isn't it?"

"Yeah." He hoped the doctor was right. "When are you leaving for San Francisco?"

Some selfish part of him wished she could stay, but he knew she wanted to see her parents, and they wanted to see her.

"I'm staying, Malik. I can't leave now, not when you're about to have surgery. We'll get through this together."

That was exactly what Malik had hoped to hear. "What about your folks?"

"They know I'm back, and they know what happened. I told them I hoped to be home for Christmas but that I would be living in Denver and taking care of you until you're back on your feet. They seemed to understand." She took his hand. "Also, I told them that I'm in love with you—and that you're Black."

Uh-oh.

"Is that going to be a problem?"

Kristi considered his question. "I've heard my grandfather say a few things I didn't like when I stayed with him in Beijing, so I was worried about how my dad would take it. My mother said you could be purple for all she cared. My father said, 'We are Americans. In our country, such things do not matter.'"

"So, you're sticking around, huh?"

"I'd stick around no matter how they felt about it. Strings, baby. You couldn't get rid of me if you tried."

Kristi stayed by his side until they took him to surgery. She was there in recovery when he woke up. She stayed with him overnight, making sure he got pain meds on time, keeping his ice bags refreshed, helping him to get out of bed, waking him when he had bad dreams, watching over him like his own personal angel.

He was discharged just before noon the next day, both arms in slings. She went with him then, too, opening the door of the Cobra limo, buckling his seat belt, carrying his medications.

"Welcome home," he said when they walked inside his condo. "I hope you like the place."

It had three bedrooms, three bathrooms, wooden floors, an ultra-modern kitchen, a gas fireplace—and a great view of the city lights.

She glanced around, walked to the window. "I love it."

It was only when she'd gotten him settled that he remembered Kristi only had the clothes on her back—and even those didn't belong to her.

Because he couldn't use his arms and had no phone, he had no choice but to ask Kristi to send an email to Isaksen, asking him and Samantha to come over and do him a favor. After that, he dictated another email to Tower, reminding him that neither he nor Kristi had passports, driver's licenses, or cell phones.

By the time Kristi had given Malik a sponge bath and settled him on the sofa with ESPN on the screen and a glass of water with a straw, Isaksen and Samantha had arrived.

"Samantha!" Kristi and Samantha hugged, their happiness at being reunited putting a smile on Malik's face.

Isaksen sat beside him. "You said you needed help, brother. What's up?"

"Samantha, can you please take Kristi out to buy

clothes? She doesn't have any ID or credit cards or even a cell phone. All of that was lost or burned in the fire. Can you do that for her? We'll pay you back."

"Of course! How awful. Thor told me what happened—or most of it. I'm so glad you're safe. Why don't you work on a list of what you need, Kristi, and we'll head out."

But Kristi wasn't happy, worry on her pretty face. "I don't want to leave you."

"He'll be fine. We'll watch some football. I'll take care of him." Isaksen paused. "But I won't hold your dick when you pee, dude. You'll have to sit."

Kristi told Isaksen when Malik was due for his next dose of Percocet, and then she and Samantha left together.

"So, you and Kristi, huh?" Isaksen went to the fridge, got himself a beer.

"Yeah. I never quit thinking about her. I should have called."

Isaksen took a drink of his brew and sat again. "Who would have thought Cobra's crazy mission to Antarctica would have such an impact on our lives?"

"That is a strange thought."

"Yeah, we both shot the parrot on that one."

Malik knew he was on Percocet, but that made no sense at all. "Is that more Viking-speak? What the hell does that even mean?"

Isaksen spoke English so well, Malik sometimes forgot it wasn't his primary language.

"You don't say that in English?"

"Nah, man, not unless you literally shot a fucking parrot."

The Viking looked surprised for a moment, then laughed. "In Danish, it's an expression that means we had good luck."

Good luck.

"Isn't that the truth?"

KRISTI HELD Malik's hand and slowly moved his bent arm thirty degrees to the outside, working on external rotation. "Don't force it. This is passive motion. Let me do the work. Your arm is just going along for the ride."

"Passive motion. Right." He glowered, clearly unfamiliar with any kind of passivity and frustrated that his recovery hadn't been instantaneous.

Kristi had taken on the job of helping with his physical therapy, the two of them heading to Cobra's gym once a day and doing the rest of the work at their place. They didn't really need the gym—not yet—but Kristi had thought it would lift his spirits to be in that familiar environment.

"Great. That was perfect. Now the other side." She repeated the exercise on his right arm—fifteen repetitions.

The past few weeks had flown by. Cobra had stepped in to get new passports for both of them, enabling Kristi to get a new driver's license, open a bank account in Denver, and have her belongings shipped from San Francisco. Samantha, Elizabeth, and Gabriela had all been there to help with groceries and meals. Malik's Cobra buddies had done their best to buoy his spirits, their camaraderie a comfort to him.

Best of all, Tower had told Malik that he still had a job.

In her free time, Kristi had filled out job applications at area hospitals. After Nigeria, she wasn't excited about going back to the corporate medical environment—top-down directives, daily pressure to expedite patient discharges, policies based on profit and not patient outcomes. With Malik's encouragement, she'd started applying for jobs at nonprofit community clinics. The money wouldn't be what it was in a hospital setting, but then she hadn't become a nurse to get rich.

"And now your favorite—the squeeze ball." She picked up the little black ball and placed it in his upturned palm.

"My favorite. Right." He squeezed, his expression going tight. "If I can't squeeze the damned ball, how will I hold a firearm?"

"It will come with time. I promise." Kristi knew he was afraid that he wouldn't be declared fit for duty and would find himself out of a job. She'd tried to reassure him that he was doing well, but he didn't seem to believe her.

She couldn't blame him. It must be discouraging for him to find himself so limited. He wasn't used to being helpless, and right now, with restrictions on how he could use his arms, there wasn't much he could do for himself. That overflowed into everything from eating to getting dressed to taking showers. It affected their sex life, too, forcing him to take the passive role—not that he seemed to mind getting lots of head.

She counted out the squeezes with him. "Great! It's getting easier. I can tell."

He nodded. "Table stretches?"

"Yep. It's almost like you don't need me."

His gaze shot to hers. "That's not true."

She guided him through the exercise, watching to make sure he didn't overdo the stretch or put any weight on his arms.

Tower walked in. "Can I see the two of you in my office when you finish here?"

Malik answered for both of them. "Yes, sir."

Kristi watched Tower walk away. "Why does he want to see me?"

"No idea."

Ten minutes later, she found herself sitting in Tower's very nice office with its flat-screen monitor, windows overlooking the city, and black leather furniture.

"A short time ago, Corbray and I got some news from the State Department. The phones and laptop we confiscated during our raid in Lagos proved to be extremely useful. Last night, the Nigeria Police Force took down the Sky Kings in cooperation with law enforcement in several countries."

The breath rushed from Kristi's lungs, tears filling her eyes. "They're gone?"

"Good fucking riddance," Malik said.

Tower nodded. "Their leaders have been killed or arrested, and their overseas operations have been shut down. Hundreds of trafficked Nigerian women are getting medical care and therapy and being repatriated."

Kristi wiped her tears away. "That's the best news."

"We're glad to hear it, sir."

"There's more. US forces participated in the operations in Nigeria. An element from DEVGRU was there, along with a company from the Seventy-Fifth Ranger Regiment. They were told they were there to avenge one of their own. They wanted to know they got the job done."

"Thank you, sir." Malik's voice sounded tight.

Kristi reached over, squeezed his fingers, barely able to imagine how that felt for him—vengeance at the hands of his brothers in arms. "It really is over."

Malik squeezed back. "It's been over since the day they abducted you. They just didn't know it."

"Jones, I'd like to speak privately with Ms. Chang for a few minutes if you can bear to be away from her for any length of time."

Kristi exchanged a glance with Malik, who clearly had no more idea what this was about than she did.

"Sure." Malik stood. "I'll be outside."

Tower waited until Jones had gone. "I'd like to offer you a job."

MALIK WALKED with Kristi to the elevator. "What was that about?"

"He offered me a job."

"He offered you a *job*?" That's *not* what Malik had expected.

Kristi punched the call button. "He says Cobra is expanding and they need more medical staff. He said he was impressed by my grit—that's what he called it—and how I handled the situation at the warehouse."

Malik had to agree with Tower there. "You kicked ass."

"He's also watched me helping you with PT. He wants to hire me."

"Wow." Malik liked the idea—as long as Kristi understood what she'd be getting herself into. "What did you say?"

"I told him that I had my heart set on working with underserved populations at one of the low-income clinics. He said working full-time for Cobra comes with lots of time off, so I could have the best of both worlds—traveling with Cobra and volunteering at one of the clinics in my free time."

"Huh." Malik fought not to roll his eyes.

Tower had known *exactly* what to say to catch Kristi.

That Green Beret bastard.

The elevator car arrived with a *ding*.

They stepped inside, and Kristi pushed the button for the parking garage.

"He said he'd give me a fifty-thousand-dollar signing bonus. Can you believe that? The salary he offered is a lot more than I'd ever make working anywhere else, though the money isn't that important to me. He said it would be a way for me to finish my goal of working on every continent."

"Did he also tell you that you'd be on call every day of the year?"

"Yes, he was clear about that. He also told me I might find myself in a situation—God forbid—where you were gravely injured or even dead and I would have other injured people to care for. He wanted to know if I'd still be able to do my job."

It was a valid question. "What did you say?"

"I told him about a time the six-year-old son of a fellow nurse, a friend, was brought in after being hit by a car. His mother was there at the hospital working. He died while I was fighting to save him, and I was the one who had to tell her."

"God. Sorry." Malik couldn't imagine. "That must have been hard."

"It *was* awful. Tower asked a few other questions, too— whether I'd thought of getting a master's in nursing, how I felt about working in a male-dominated environment."

"He turned it into a job interview." Malik couldn't help but laugh.

That was so like Tower.

She hadn't applied for a job, but Tower was grilling her anyway.

"I haven't gotten to the best part. He talked about the vacation and parental leave policies and then wanted to know if I could remain professional if you and I got divorced. I told him we'd have to get married first. He said he thought we were married already. I guess that little lie caught up with us."

Malik laughed, but he wasn't sure it was a lie. "Did you give him an answer?"

The elevator stopped, and the doors opened, cold air rushing in.

They walked toward Malik's vehicle.

"I told him I'd think about it and talk it over with you. I don't want to accept it if having me on staff would make it hard for you to do your job. I also don't want you to get tired of me too quickly."

He laughed out loud at this. "*That* isn't going to happen. Besides, we won't see each other as often as you might think."

He explained that she'd be on the medical team, not the tactical team. They wouldn't be part of the same staff meetings. Sometimes, the medical staff flew out first, so they wouldn't always be on the same flight. Whenever they operated in a country where Cobra had a compound—Uganda, Afghanistan, Iraq, Australia, and now South Korea—she would stay in the compound while the tactical team was in the field.

"Once in a while, when people are badly injured, they'll transport you to the scene by helicopter. On this last mission, Doc never left the jet. It just depends on the situation. Most of the time, there aren't serious injuries—just scrapes, sprains, grazes."

"I'll take that over broken, bleeding bodies any day." She opened the front passenger door for him, buckled his seat belt, then went around to the other side and got into the driver's seat. "What do you think?"

"I think it's your career, and you should do what interests you. If that's working at a clinic for low-income families, you should do that. If it's working in a busy urban ER, do that. I support you, whatever your decision."

"You mean that?"

"Hell, yeah, I mean it. I want you to be happy."

Even as he said those words, Malik knew she would accept Tower's offer. At her core, Kristi was as much of an adrenaline junkie as he was.

22

Five weeks later

K risti followed Malik into the condo. "What would you like for dinner?"

"No cooking tonight." He took off his coat, hung it, then reached for hers. "We're going to get dressed up and head out. I've got a reservation at the Palace Arms at seven. Tonight, we celebrate."

This was a fun surprise. "What are we celebrating?"

He drew her close, smiled down at her. "Your new job. My being free of those damned slings. Besides, you've done a hundred percent of the cooking and cleaning these past two months. If I want to treat you, I will."

He kissed her, soft and slow, the feel of his embrace precious. He hadn't been able to hold her like this for eight long weeks, and, oh, she had missed it. He stepped back, released her. "Go. I'll be right up."

She went upstairs, washed her face, and put on fresh makeup. She was searching the closet for her favorite little black dress when Malik walked in and stripped off his fatigues. Her gaze moved over him, taking in the view. "Are you sure we shouldn't just stay home and have crazy animal sex?"

He grinned. "We can do that afterward—and I finally get to be on top."

That sent a flutter through her belly. "Please."

Ten minutes later, they walked out the door, hand in hand. Malik drove, heading downtown to the Palace Hotel, where he left the car with a valet.

"Valet parking? Fancy." Kristi took his arm, walking with him into the Palace Arms, one of the city's most upscale restaurants. "Wow."

The Napoleonic decor reminded her of Paris, the scents wafting through the air making her mouth water. They left their coats in the cloakroom and then checked in with the host, who picked up two menus and led them to a candlelit table in the corner.

Malik held her seat, whispering to her, his breath hot on her nape. "You look incredible in that dress."

Was she blushing? "Thanks."

No matter where they were, he always made her feel special.

They perused the menu and placed their orders—filet mignon and a glass of Shiraz for him, chicken marsala and Chardonnay for her.

"This is lovely. Thank you." Kristi glanced around, ran her hands over her bare arms. "It feels strange to be sitting in public and not looking over my shoulder or wondering where the lions are."

She'd had a few nightmares over the past weeks, but so had Malik.

Malik reached over, took her hand, his gaze soft. "It's hard to go from fighting for your life to living in normal society. We call that 're-entry.' One minute, you're under fire, wondering if this is the end, and the next you're buying toilet paper."

The way he said it made Kristi laugh, but it wasn't funny, not really. "You must have been through this dozens of times."

He nodded, caressed her knuckles with his thumb. "It doesn't get easier, in case you're wondering. You just get used to it."

Every day, Kristi found another reason to respect and admire him. She thought about what he'd just said—and unexpectedly found herself smiling.

"What is it?"

"If it hadn't been for the bad parts, those days with you would have been the greatest adventure of my life. I want to hold onto the good memories and not let the bad stuff steal them away."

"You got it."

They laughed together while they ate, talking about quicksand and Kristi whispering when the lion walked by and the frantic drive across the railway bridge.

"Do you think that conductor has recovered?" Kristi asked.

"Oh, hell, no. He's still telling anyone who will listen about the crazy tourists he almost killed." Malik feigned a Yoruba accent. "I waved to them to go faster, but they did not. Praise the Lord, I missed them by a meter. Tourist *wahala!*"

Kristi laughed. "You should have seen your face when you saw that train."

Malik smiled, then grew serious. "What I'll never forget is the look in your eyes when you realized I had come for you."

"I was beyond all hope—and then you were there. After so long, you were there."

Malik got quiet for a moment, then stood and knelt before her, taking something from his pocket.

It was a ring made of string, a little bow tied on top.

Kristi stared, tears filling her eyes.

"You said you want strings, Kristi. I want them, too. I want all of the strings, starting with this one."

"*Malik.*" Tears ran down Kristi's face as she held out her hand and watched him slide the bit of string onto her ring finger. "Are you asking me to marry you?"

"Hold on." He reached into the pocket of his sports jacket. "I think I've got something better here."

He drew out a box, opened it.

There against the dark blue velvet sat a sparkling pear-shaped diamond, surrounded by a halo of tiny diamonds, all set in white gold.

"Kristi, will you marry me and have a lifetime of adventures with me?"

Kristi stared, astonished. "Oh, God. It's beautiful."

She looked up, the intensity in his brown eyes making her breath catch. "Yes. Yes! I would love to marry you. I love you so much."

As he slid the ring onto her finger, the restaurant broke into applause.

MALIK WALKED up the sidewalk toward his parents' front door, Kristi beside him, each of them pulling a suitcase. "If you feel like my old man is cross-examining you, don't take it personally. He's just like that. He used to do that to my friends all the time."

"Don't worry. It's going to be fine."

Malik hoped so.

They had flown to San Francisco last week to share the good news with Kristi's parents and her brother. The Changs were much more reserved than his family, but they had made him feel welcome. Her father's words of thanks to Malik had put to rest any fears he and Kristi might have had about race being an issue for him.

"Thank you for bringing my daughter home," he'd said. "Now, I will have a son who is an American military hero. I am proud."

Kristi smoothed her hands down her ochre-colored sweater and her black and white plaid ankle pants. "I hope I wore the right thing."

"Now who's nervous?" He squeezed her hand. "You're gorgeous."

Before they reached the door, it opened wide, and Malik's niece Jade and nephew Kamran ran out.

"Uncle Malik!"

"Hey!" Malik scooped them up, one at a time, and hugged them, careful not to hurt his shoulders. "Kamran, man, look how big you are! Jade, you're just as pretty as your mama. Are you two doing well in school?"

Jade nodded, her braids bobbling, her gaze fixed on Kristi. "She's pretty."

"Thank you! I think you're pretty, too, Jade. I'm Kristi. Nice to meet you, Kamran. I think you're going to be as tall as your Uncle Malik."

Malik watched, proud to be the man in Kristi's life. She had such a natural way with people, no matter how young or old they were. But before she could say another word, the door opened, and Amira, one of his two sisters, let out a loud squeal.

"Is that my baby brother?"

"Hey, Amira." Malik hugged her. "I can't believe how much your kids have grown."

"If you'd visit more often, it wouldn't come as such a shock." Amira turned to Kristi and hugged her, too. "Welcome, Kristi. Let me see that ring."

Kristi held out her hand. "Malik picked it out on his own. I just love it."

"Malik picked this? It's gorgeous!"

"Is that Malik?" That was Jasmine, the older of his two sisters. "They're here, Mama!"

Jasmine rushed out and joined everyone else on the sidewalk, her husband Dustin and their two kids, Cade and Caitlyn, watching from the open doorway. "Let your big sister get a good look at you. Are you keeping out of trouble?"

"I *am* the trouble." Malik met Kristi's gaze and found her smiling. "Jasmine, this is my fiancée, Kristi."

Jasmine hugged Kristi, too. "It's so good to meet you."

His mother rushed outside, a big smile on her face, and threw her arms around him. "Malik! Hug my neck, son."

Malik hugged her tight. "It's good to see you, Mama."

Then his mother turned to Kristi. "Welcome to our home, honey."

"Let the man come into the house!" Malik's father called from the doorway. "Give him room to breathe. Good gracious sakes!"

"Hey, Dad."

They piled back inside, everyone speaking at once. Kristi kept up with it all, answering a barrage of questions and seeming to enjoy the kids, who competed with the adults for her attention.

"We met at Amundsen-Scott Station at the South Pole

where I was the station RN. You have a hamster, Kamran? What's its name? What a pretty toy pony, Caitlyn. Yes, Antarctica. It will be two years ago in April. You want to be a ballerina, Jade? I wanted to be a ballerina, too."

Jasmine walked over to Malik. "Well, she's holding her own. In this family, that's something."

Yeah, it was.

Then it was time for dinner—roast chicken, mashed potatoes, green beans, and pecan pie. That's when Malik's father started on Kristi, asking about her education, her job experience, her faith, her family.

"Dad, give it a rest."

"I'm just getting to know her."

After dinner, Dustin took the kids outside to play so that Kristi and Malik could tell his parents and sisters the whole story—how they'd met, how much they'd missed each other, how they'd gotten together again.

Kristi held tightly to Malik's hand as she told them what she'd done to free Malik. By the time they'd finished the story, his mother and Jasmine were in tears and his father and Amira looked stunned.

His mother wiped her eyes. "You set a building on fire to save my son?"

"I had to do something. I couldn't let them kill him."

"Please tell me Cobra nailed those bastards," Jasmine said.

"Cobra took out everyone at the warehouse that I missed. Then the Nigeria Police Force, with some Navy SEALs and Rangers, brought down their organization a few weeks after we got home. I've been recovering from shoulder surgery. Kristi has taken good care of me and is helping me with physical therapy."

"I thought working for Cobra was supposed to keep you

safe." His father's face bent in a frown. "Since you went to work there, you've been shot and now tortured and almost killed."

"It's the roll of the dice, Dad. The risk goes with the job."

Then Amira smiled. "Well I don't know about you all, but I'm trying to decide what bothers me more—hearing what those guys did to you two or seeing the two of you laughing about quicksand and lions and almost getting mowed down by a train. She's as much of an adrenaline junkie as he is, Mama."

"I think you're right." His mother stood, sat beside Kristi, wrapped an arm around Kristi's shoulders. "I know I only just met you, but I love you for what you did for my son. I know he loves you, too."

"He's everything to me, Mrs. Jones."

"From now on, just call me Mama."

Later, when Kristi had gone upstairs to get ready for bed, Malik's father called him into his office and closed the door.

"What is it?" These private conversations always put Malik on edge.

What would the old man have to criticize tonight?

"You've done well for yourself. Kristi is one special woman—brave and beautiful and crazy in love with you."

He'd get no argument from Malik about that. "Yes."

"As I recall, I didn't support your decision to join the army out of high school. I had other plans for you. Well, that's how parents are. I was wrong, and I'm sorry."

Malik stared at him. He would never have expected this.

His father went on. "You have served your country in a way few people can, and you've distinguished yourself again and again. And what you did for Kristi..." His father drew him into a hug. "I want you to know that I am proud to call you my son."

Malik swallowed the lump in his throat, hugged his father back. "Thanks, Dad."

KRISTI LOOKED at her reflection in the mirror, her heart so full she could sing.

In a few minutes, she would truly be Malik's wife.

"I wish I had your cleavage." Samantha, Kristi's matron of honor, took Kristi's bouquet of red and pink peonies from Gabriela, and handed it to Kristi. "There. Perfect. You're a beautiful bride."

"You really are stunning." Gabriela came to stand beside her. "I can't wait to see how Malik reacts to your gown. Does he have any idea?"

"No. I wanted to surprise him." Kristi and Malik had chosen to have a simple Western ceremony, but she had wanted some Chinese touches.

White was the color of death and funerals in Chinese culture, while red and gold were the traditional wedding colors. So, Kristi had chosen a red satin mermaid dress with barely there off-the-shoulder lace sleeves and beading on the bodice, while Samantha, Gabriela, and Elizabeth wore gold gowns.

A knock came at the door, and Elizabeth stepped in. "Your father is coming, Kristi. They're almost ready for you."

Kristi drew in a breath, excitement mixing with nerves. "Thanks to the three of you for your help. Elizabeth, I wouldn't be standing here today if not for you."

Then the door opened and her father stepped in.

He stopped, stared, spoke to her in Mandarin, calling her by her nickname. "Oh, my beautiful daughter, my sweet Meimei. You fill your parents' hearts with joy."

Kristi answered in English. "Be careful, Daddy, or you'll make me cry."

"Before you go down the aisle, your mother and I wanted you to have this." He held out a long, narrow box.

She opened it to find a white gold chain with a pear-shaped solitaire diamond. "Oh! Thank you! I love it. It's beautiful. It matches my engagement ring."

She kissed her father's cheek.

He grinned. "For good luck."

Samantha took the necklace and put in on Kristi. "That's perfect."

Then it was time to go.

She and Malik had decided to get married outdoors at a resort in the mountains west of Denver. The wedding itself would take place in an amphitheater outside that had unparalleled views of the white-capped high peaks, while the reception would take place in the main hall of this same building afterward.

Kristi walked out of the bride's dressing room to find Jade and Caitlyn waiting for her, looking adorable in their little gold gowns. "Do you remember what to do?"

They nodded, visibly excited to be part of the ceremony.

"You look so pretty," Jade said.

"You two look like fairy princesses." Kristi gave each little girl a kiss on the cheek. "Are you ready?"

They went downstairs as a group and walked to the edge of the amphitheater, keeping out of sight until the music began—Pachelbel's Canon in D.

Little Jade and Caitlyn walked down the aisle first, tossing red flower petals willy-nilly and glancing back at Kristi.

She blew them a kiss.

Next went Gabriela, then Elizabeth, and then Samantha.

At last, Kristi's father offered her his arm. "You are marrying a good man."

"Thank you, Daddy. I was raised by a good man, too."

They stepped off and came into view of the altar.

Kristi's breath caught at the sight of Malik, standing, tall and proud, in his Army Ranger dress uniform, Dylan, Thor, and Lev beside him. God, she loved him. She loved him so much she thought her heart might burst.

Heads turned, a murmur sweeping through the crowd, people rising to their feet as she and her father headed down the aisle, but Kristi was aware only of Malik.

He took her hand from her father, raised it to his lips, the love in his eyes making her heart melt. "God, you look beautiful—and *hot*."

From there it was a blur. Somehow, she said her vows, and Malik said his. They slipped rings onto one another's fingers—rings presented with great solemnity by Kamran and Cade.

"By the power vested in me by the state of Colorado, I now pronounce you husband and wife. You may kiss... Oh, my!"

They'd beaten the minister to it, Malik drawing her against him, lifting her off his feet, kissing her deep and long and slow.

Cheers and whistles from the Cobra guys brought them back, the two of them laughing along with the minister and their guests as they made their way back up the aisle with the wedding party.

Inside the reception hall, their guests divided into three groups—their Cobra coworkers, Kristi's family, and Malik's family.

Malik chuckled. "Notice how quiet your folks are, standing politely."

She had noticed. "Yours looks like they're getting ready to cut loose. Your grandma has a glass of champagne in her hand and is talking with the DJ."

"This is going to be an interesting reception."

Kristi smiled up at him. "It's going to be an interesting life."

EPILOGUE

June 15

Dear Obi,
    Thank you so much for your latest letter. I'm always so excited to hear from you. Your English is impressive, and your penmanship is better than mine now. You have worked so hard, and it shows.

Your Uncle David wrote to tell us that your adoption went through. He sent some photos of the party you had afterwards with that lovely cake. Congratulations to you and your new family. Malik and I are so happy for all of you.

It's great to hear that you are doing very well at school in both reading and math. I really loved both of those subjects, too. Do you have a favorite book that you've read?

How fun that you're on the school's football team. David says you're very athletic. (We call football "soccer" in the United States. I have no idea why.) We are so proud of you! You look sharp in that uniform, too.

Malik doesn't play football, but he does play basketball. One day, when you come to visit us here in Colorado, he would like to teach you how to play.

You wrote that you sometimes have nightmares and that you feel bad because now and again you miss Jidda. You have no reason to feel bad about any of those things. After all the sadness of losing your parents and the scary months of living in Jidda's camp, it makes sense that you would have nightmares and feel afraid sometimes.

When people go through scary times and see bad things happen, part of how our minds deal with those memories is through dreams. I have bad dreams of being abducted, too. Even Malik has bad dreams about battles he fought in the army. Please don't be hard on yourself about that. It will get better with time. I'm sure of this.

Although Jidda wasn't a good man, he did care about you. It's okay to miss him and to feel sad because he's gone. You have a good heart, Obi. I knew that from the moment I first met you. But sometimes when you have a good heart, that heart aches. It's okay to feel sad.

One thing that helps me when I am hurting is to help someone else. You know how hard it is to lose someone you love, so you can comfort other people who are grieving. You know how bad it feels to be bullied and hurt, so you can speak up for those who are bullied. You know what it is to suffer, so you can work to stop suffering. I hope that makes sense.

We are thinking of going on safari in Tanzania for our honeymoon. If we do go on safari, we're hoping that you, your family, and your Uncle David might be able to join us for part of it. We would love so very much to see you.

Sending lots of love from the USA.

Love,

Auntie Kristi

. . .

P.S. You've gotten so tall!

KRISTI SIGNED and printed the letter, tucked in a wedding photo, and sealed the envelope. She quickly addressed it, put on the proper postage, and carried it down to Cobra's front desk.

"Can you make sure this goes out in today's mail?" Kristi wanted to get it into the mail before they took off so that Obi would receive it, no matter what happened on this mission.

"Yes, ma'am."

Kristi hurried to her locker, finished packing her gear, and put her hair up in a bun. She looked in the mirror, smiled to see herself dressed in fatigues, and ran her fingers over the name tag sewn onto her jacket.

CHANG-JONES.

After months of training, emergency drills, and completing a medic certification, she was going on her first mission.

Malik walked in, looking sexy as hell in camo. "You ready to go?"

"I'm so excited. I hope to make you proud."

"You've already done that." He took her into his arms and kissed her. "We'd better go. Tower doesn't like tardiness."

"Right. I need to make a good impression." She shouldered her duffel bag.

They rode the elevator down to the parking garage, where one of Cobra's vans waited to take them to the airport. They were on their way to Ethiopia to provide protection for a delegation of UN observers studying the conflict there. Kristi would stay at the hotel in a state of readiness in case the worst should happen.

God forbid.

"We're wheels up in less than an hour, folks." Tower called to Quinn and Elizabeth, who had just arrived. "Let's get a move on!"

Malik put Kristi's duffel in the back with his own, and the two of them climbed into the van to find most of the others waiting.

"This is your first official mission, isn't it?" Thor asked.

"Yes." Kristi couldn't keep the smile off her face. "I finally get to hang out with the cool kids."

"You were always one of the cool kids." Malik leaned over, kissed her.

"Are we going to have to put up with this all the way to Addis Ababa?" Lev rolled his eyes. "Do *not* put me in the room next to theirs. I like my sleep."

"Says the single guy," Dylan teased.

Quinn and Elizabeth loaded their gear into the back.

"Sorry we're a few minutes late." Elizabeth settled into her seat. "Traffic."

Quinn sat beside her. "Bloody feckin' bawbag on a motorbike hit a lorry."

Kristi understood part of that.

Dylan must have noticed the confusion on her face. "Don't worry. We don't understand most of what he says either."

"You're full of shite, Cruz."

Laughter.

The doors closed, and the van set off, leaving the parking garage and slipping into Denver traffic.

Malik leaned down, spoke for her ears only. "It's time for our next adventure."

Kristi threaded her fingers with his. "I can't wait."

THANK YOU

Thanks for reading *Hard Pursuit*. I hope you enjoyed this Cobra Elite story. Follow me on Facebook or on Twitter @Pamela_Clare. Join my romantic suspense reader's group on Facebook to be a part of a never-ending conversation with other Cobra fans and get inside information on the series and on life in Colorado's mountains. You can also sign up to my mailing list at my website to keep current with all my releases and to be a part of special newsletter giveaways.

ALSO BY PAMELA CLARE

Romantic Suspense:

Cobra Elite Series

Hard Target (Book 1)

Hard Asset (Book 2)

Hard Justice (Book 3)

Hard Edge (Book 4)

Hard Line (Book 5)

Hard Pursuit (Book 6)

I-Team Series

Extreme Exposure (Book 1)

Heaven Can't Wait (Book 1.5)

Hard Evidence (Book 2)

Unlawful Contact (Book 3)

Naked Edge (Book 4)

Breaking Point (Book 5)

Skin Deep: An I-Team After Hours Novella (Book 5.5)

First Strike: The Prequel to Striking Distance (Book 5.9)

Striking Distance (Book 6)

Soul Deep: An I-Team After Hours Novella (Book 6.5)

Seduction Game (Book 7)

Dead by Midnight: An I-Team Christmas (Book 7.5)

Deadly Intent (Book 8)

Contemporary Romance:

Colorado High Country Series

Barely Breathing (Book 1)

Slow Burn (Book 2)

Falling Hard (Book 3)

Tempting Fate (Book 4)

Close to Heaven (Book 5)

Holding On (Book 6)

Chasing Fire (Book 7)

Historical Romance:

Kenleigh-Blakewell Family Saga

Sweet Release (Book 1)

Carnal Gift (Book 2)

Ride the Fire (Book 3)

MacKinnon's Rangers series

Surrender (Book I)

Untamed (Book 2)

Defiant (Book 3)

Upon A Winter's Night: A MacKinnon's Rangers Christmas (Book 3.5)

ABOUT THE AUTHOR

USA Today best-selling author Pamela Clare began her writing career as a columnist and investigative reporter and eventually became the first woman editor-in-chief of two different newspapers. Along the way, she and her team won numerous state and national honors, including the National Journalism Award for Public Service. In 2011, Clare was awarded the Keeper of the Flame Lifetime Achievement Award for her body of work. A single mother with two sons, she writes historical romance and contemporary romantic suspense at the foot of the beautiful Rocky Mountains. Visit her website and join her mailing list to never miss a new release!

www.pamelaclare.com

facebook.com/PamelaClareFans

twitter.com/Pamela_Clare

CPSIA information can be obtained
at www.ICGtesting.com
Printed in the USA
BVHW072259150421
605033BV00003B/133

9 781735 293943